LOVE IN HIDING

DIANE HOLIDAY

This book is a work of fiction. Names, characters, places, and incidents either are products of the author's imagination or are used fictitiously. Any resemblance to actual events or locales or persons, living or dead, is entirely coincidental and not intended by the author.

LOVE IN HIDING
Love Beyond Danger, Book 1

CITY OWL PRESS
www.cityowlpress.com

All Rights reserved. Except as permitted under the U.S. Copyright Act of 1976, no part of this publication may be reproduced, distributed, or transmitted in any form or by any means, or stored in a database or retrieval system, without the prior consent and permission of the publisher.

Copyright © 2017 by Diane Holiday.

Cover Design by Tina Moss. All stock photos licensed appropriately.

Edited by Mary Cain.

For information on subsidiary rights, please contact the publisher at info@cityowlpress.com.

Print Edition ISBN: 978-1-944728-49-6

Digital Edition ISBN: 978-1-944728-50-2

Printed in the United States of America

PRAISE FOR DIANE HOLIDAY

FIRST PLACE in 2015 Pages of the Heart Contest.

Golden Heart® Finalist 2016 for romantic suspense.

* * *

"Diane Holiday's debut, LOVE IN HIDING, kept me hooked from the first page to the last."
- *Historical Romance Author, Renee Ann Miller*

"A strong heroine, sexy hero and downright scream-worthy villains—a page-turner with spunky dialogue and suspense that kept me up way past my bedtime because I just couldn't put it down."
- *Contemporary Romance Author and Golden Heart Award Finalist, Christina Hovland*

"LOVE IN HIDING combines the laid-back atmosphere of country life with the suspense angle of a crazed stalker beautifully. Great characterization, perfect pacing and witty dialogue top off this exceptional read."
- *Contemporary Romance Author, Jessie Gussman*

"Solid storytelling featuring a classic hero and a daring heroine."
- *YA Author and Golden Heart Award Finalist, C.R. Grissom*

For Steve,
My husband, best friend, and biggest supporter

CHAPTER 1

IF SHE HOPED TO LIVE, Sarah Cooper needed to pull off the most convincing performance of her life.

A disappearing act.

The GPS's robo-voice announced she'd arrived at her destination. A white wooden sign that read *Oak Ridge Farms* with a bucking black stallion marked the entrance. She glanced in the rearview mirror one last time to make sure no one had followed her. Tension eased from her stiff neck. She'd white-knuckled the drive on the freeway out of San Diego almost a week ago. At least the quiet country lanes in rural Maryland had prevented anyone from sneaking up on her.

She turned onto a tree-lined, dirt driveway, and her heart rate kicked up a notch.

This ranch was her last hope and the only job left that included room and board. No more sleeping cramped in her car.

She eyed the low-fuel light. The gas tank was as empty as her stomach. Nerves jitterbugged up her spine. She knew nothing about horses or farms. From the time she could walk, her life had been dance, dance, dance. Her slim build, perfect for ballet, wasn't an asset when interviewing for jobs requiring manual labor. None of the other jobs had panned out. She clenched her molars.

This interview would be different. It had to be.

Rocks and dirt crunched under the tires of the dinged-up Honda she'd bought. At some point, she'd owe a boatload of money to a parking garage in California where she'd abandoned her almost-new Toyota.

It didn't matter. A dead woman had no use for a nice car.

She pulled up to a maroon and white-trimmed barn. In the distance, a sprawling, tan house sat atop a grassy hill. Horses grazed in spacious fields enclosed by brown, split-rail fences between the stables and woods. Open meadows stretched for miles.

Peace and freedom. What she wouldn't give to have those again.

She took a deep breath, snatched the help-wanted ad from the seat beside her, and stepped out to find the owner. On her way toward the stables, she zipped her baggy jacket. Early May weather didn't call for a coat, but with luck, her slight frame would look bigger, and Debbie wouldn't worry about hiring someone too small to do the work.

A gust of wind blew the newspaper clipping out of her hand. The scrap skittered along the dirt, and she lunged to grab it. Her fingers touched the edge but another gust set the paper back in flight. She scrambled, rounding the corner of the barn, and smacked headfirst into a pair of booted legs. The impact threw her back, and she landed on her butt. Her fight-or-flight instinct kicked in before logic, and she tensed.

Her gaze climbed and climbed before reaching a man's face shadowed by the brim of a navy ball cap with a Wounded Warrior emblem. Electric blue eyes stared down at her with such intensity her breath caught.

"Are you okay?" He offered a hand.

God no, but she couldn't tell him that. "Yes."

Her first lie of the day.

One flex of his strong forearm and she found herself on her feet again. She'd never had one of her dance partners lift her up with such ease. Or grace. But something told her if she called this guy graceful, he wouldn't take it as a compliment.

He stepped back and crossed his arms. "Can I help you?"

She glanced up at his still-shadowed face, from his chiseled chin to the jagged scar at the edge of his right cheekbone. Thick, corded muscles lined his neck, and broad shoulders stretched his camouflage T-shirt. No doubt, physical work shaped his body, not a weight room.

His guarded eyes seemed to see right through her.

She forced herself not to squirm.

The breeze blew the clean fragrance of soap and leather toward her. She inhaled the pure, masculine scent, getting a little lightheaded.

He cleared his throat.

She jumped and mentally slapped herself, kicking her libido to the backseat. With her life in danger, she needed to stay focused.

"I'm looking for Debbie. I called about the ad in the paper, and she told me to come out." Sarah squared her shoulders and ignored the warmth rising to her cheeks.

He hitched an eyebrow. "You're here to apply for the farmhand job?"

"Yes." She nodded. Best to keep the conversation short. The doubt on his face only meant more questions and possible trouble. "Can you tell me where I might find Debbie?"

"She's probably at the house for lunch." He waved up the hill at a large rancher with a white wraparound porch. "And you are?"

"Sarah." At least she'd kept her first name the same. Less chance of slipping up.

He held out his hand. "Bruce."

When her palm pressed against his calloused one, a ripple of awareness passed through her.

Wheels crunched on the gravel behind them. She whipped her head around and froze, straining to make out the person behind the wheel. A woman emerged from the car, and Sarah heaved a big sigh.

A frown tugged at the corner of Bruce's mouth. "That's some grip you have."

She jerked her hand away and bit her cheek. Not five minutes on the premises and she'd panicked. She couldn't blow this chance. The small horse farm, located on the opposite coast from California, would make her hard to find. Sure, she'd have to learn about horses, but the job didn't call for any experience.

"Should I wait here for Debbie to come back?"

He adjusted his cap. "I was just headed up. I'll take you to find her."

"Thanks. I appreciate that." Although, she'd rather not spend any more time with the man.

She turned to follow him and stepped into a rut. He whipped an arm out and steadied her before she fell. Damn. Another wave of heat burned a path to her face. She'd have to watch her footing and calm her nerves around this guy or he'd think her a total klutz. The furthest thing from the truth.

He drew his hand back and glanced at her mud-caked tennis shoes but said nothing. She'd need boots if she got the job, which might be a stretch given her rocky start.

"Why do you want to work here? You don't look like a typical farmhand," Bruce asked as they trekked across the field.

"I need a job, and this one includes room and board. My lease is up." Only a half lie because she did need the work. She'd better change the subject. "Do you keep a horse here?"

He nodded. "Yes. But I also run a therapy program at the farm."

Sweat trickled down the side of her neck. She glanced over her shoulder. Every step farther from her car tightened the knot in her stomach. At least she had her gun in her purse. Not that she'd learned to shoot it yet.

Bruce climbed the steps leading to the porch. A couple of wooden rockers and a wicker table with two chairs sat under the shade of the roof. An orange tabby cat, rolled into a lazy ball, slept in the far corner.

"Deb, you there?" Bruce called through the screen door.

"Come on in," yelled a woman with a gruff, husky voice. "I got plenty of soup. You hungry?"

He shot a glance at Sarah and opened the door, holding it wide for her. "No, thanks."

Sarah entered the house. The scent of biscuits wafted through the room, and her stomach grumbled. She hadn't eaten since last night. Her body ran on nothing but adrenaline now.

Sun streamed through a bay window in the airy, open kitchen. Hanging plants dangled over clay containers of fresh herbs on the ledge. A large pot simmered on the stove. Homey. She missed the feeling. Homey had ended for her at age fourteen when she'd left for the dance academy in New York.

Her gaze went to the windows. Neither the bay one nor the two over the sink had curtains. Anyone could see right in. She pressed a hand to her throat.

A woman with short brown hair, wearing jeans and a red flannel shirt, stood by the stove, stirring soup. She glanced over her shoulder at them and placed a lid on the pot. Probably in her mid-fifties, though hard to tell with her deeply tanned skin, she had several inches and a good thirty pounds on Sarah.

"This is Sarah. She wants to apply for the job you listed," Bruce said.

Sarah stood as tall as possible while Debbie looked her up and down.

"You a friend of Bruce's?" Debbie crossed the room to them.

"No. I kinda bumped into him." At least the first words out of her mouth to Debbie weren't a lie.

Debbie scratched her head, as if she didn't know what to make of Sarah, and faced Bruce. "Since when do you turn down my chicken soup?"

Bruce's gaze darted from Sarah to the door. "No time. I have to get the horse ready for Charlie."

Debbie checked her watch and frowned. "But it's only—"

"Gotta go."

He left without a backward glance and let the screen door slam behind him.

Sarah blinked at his abrupt departure. His relationship with Debbie must be solid for him to feel free to act so rudely.

* * *

Bruce hiked away from the house at a brisk clip, not sure what to make of Sarah. The tiny woman wearing a jacket two sizes too big didn't belong doing a job that required hard physical labor.

No mistaking that look of fright on her face earlier. He'd seen it enough to last a lifetime. He set his jaw and scanned the perimeter. Tall grass swayed in the empty fields, and the surrounding woods were quiet. Nothing out of place. Yet something or someone had this woman spooked.

Despite her small frame, she carried herself in a way that made her seem taller, and he hadn't missed the spark in her eyes when he'd questioned her about working at the farm. But the dark half-moons under them and the tightness in her face were textbook signs of stress and lack of sleep.

With large emerald eyes, fair skin, and wavy, dark hair, her striking features could turn any man's head. Yet, something had stirred inside him when her cheeks turned pink.

He tamped it down.

Didn't want it.

Didn't need it.

Most of the women he'd worked with in the Navy were tough from the job and didn't blush. Not much different at the farm, for that matter. Sarah had a softness about her, a vulnerability, but also spunk to think she could hold her own.

He frowned and continued on his way.

"Whoa."

Someone tapped his elbow, and he swung around to find himself face to face with his uncle Joe.

Crap.

Of all people.

"Where's the fire?" Wrinkles formed on the sides of his brown eyes as he squinted against the sun.

A vein pulsed in Bruce's temple. He never flew under Joe's radar. All the years Bruce had spent in the Navy, no one could read him. It's what had made him one of their best operatives. But Joe? It was like he was hardwired to Bruce's brain. The man didn't miss a damn thing.

"I'm headed to the stables." Bruce glanced at Joe's hand still on his arm.

Joe let go but didn't move to leave. "Why do you look like you saw a ghost?"

Bruce would rather break in new boots with a blister than discuss his feelings. Yeah, he had a ghost, and he wasn't about to betray her. "Everyone's full of questions today. I'll never get to the barn at this rate."

"Uh-huh." Joe's eyes narrowed. "I just left there. The place is still standing."

"Well, I have stuff to do before Charlie shows up." He needed to get away before Joe dug any deeper. Turning his back, Bruce called over his shoulder, "See you later."

He strode toward the barn. When he entered, the sweet scent of hay filled his nostrils. Horses snorted in their cool, dark stalls. He worked his way down the aisle, stopping to stroke their heads as they poked them over the half doors.

As usual, when he came to Misty's stall, the old mare neighed and nudged his hand. His heart squeezed. She might not be around much longer. The last of his father's horses, and what a trooper. Misty had turned out to be a perfect therapy horse. She'd been gentle and sweet from day one. His father had chosen well when he'd bought her for Bruce's early lessons. Maybe his dad would have been proud of what Bruce had done with Misty and the program. He needed to stay focused. The veterans depended on him.

He pulled a sugar cube out of his pocket and held out his open palm. Her warm, fat lips swiped the treat away to crunch.

Through his work, he'd found a way to cope with the losses in his life. He didn't need complications like Sarah stirring up unwanted feelings.

Debbie wouldn't hire her. Hell, the twelve-year-olds who helped after school in exchange for riding time were bigger. She'd have to find someplace else to work. They didn't need whatever trouble might follow her to the ranch. This farm, his patients, and the people he worked with were his family. He'd protect them at all costs.

Any minute now, Sarah would get back in her car and leave.

A kitten Debbie had taken in rubbed against his leg, and a knot formed in the pit of his stomach.

Shit.

Debbie had a soft spot for strays. He'd have to make sure Sarah wasn't her next one.

CHAPTER 2

SARAH FORCED herself not to look away from Debbie's intense gaze. Between the hard lines of her face and her direct approach, the woman had a roughness about her, like she didn't take BS from anyone.

"You have experience with horses?" Debbie asked.

"I used to ride." If one time on a pony, and a few occasions with a friend counted. She had to sell herself, or Debbie would probably kick her butt out for wasting her time.

"How long ago?"

"It's been a while, but I know I can do the job, and I'm a decent cook. Whatever you need, I'll do."

Debbie rubbed her jaw.

A door slammed.

Sarah's nerves jumped. She fumbled for the pepper spray she kept close at all times.

A man entered from the other side of the kitchen.

Debbie's eyes narrowed as her gaze trailed down to Sarah's hand in her jacket pocket.

The man meandered over to the pot of soup without a glance in their direction and opened the lid. "Smells good. What's up with Bruce? I ran into him and…"

He turned. His sharp, dark eyes fixed on Sarah.

His resemblance to Bruce had to make him a relative. Gray hair and a weathered face placed him probably in his sixties. His lack of paunch suggested he kept in shape.

"Joe, meet Sarah. She's here about the job I posted," Debbie said.

"You don't say." He nodded and waved at the pot. "This ready?"

"Yup. Help yourself."

Well, at least *he* hadn't looked at her like she was a mouse auditioning for a tiger act in the circus. He whistled off-key as he dished out a bowl of soup.

Debbie returned her gaze to Sarah and sighed. "I'm going be honest with you. The cooking and cleaning I'm sure you can handle, but I don't know if you're strong enough for the outside tasks. It's a lot of physical labor. Hauling buckets, tossing hay bales, mucking stalls."

"I'm tougher than I look. I can do it." She'd trained every day at the dance studio and taken self-defense classes. Maybe the jacket wasn't helping. She slid the coat off, curled her arm, and tapped a well-formed biceps. "See? I'm in shape."

Joe glanced at her, and the corners of his mouth twitched. He took his bowl and sat at the table.

Sarah sensed Debbie's hesitation and pushed. "Please. I really need this job. Give me a chance. I'll work the first day free. If you're not happy, you can fire me."

As Joe stuffed a biscuit in his mouth, Debbie's gaze flicked to him. Sarah could swear he gave an almost imperceptible nod, but then again, he might have just been chewing.

Debbie turned back to Sarah. "Why do you need this job so bad?"

"I don't have a place to live, and your ad said room and board were part of the deal." Another truth. Hey, she was on a roll.

Debbie stared her down.

Sarah's insides twisted, but she didn't flinch.

"What the hell, I'll give you a chance." Debbie shrugged.

"Thanks so much." Sarah let out the breath she'd been holding. "You won't be sorry."

"If you work out, you'll get paid weekly on Fridays."

Sarah cleared her throat. "Could it be in cash?"

Debbie rubbed her chin and squinted. "You running from someone you owe money to?"

"No." Another truth.

"How about the law? You wanted for something?"

"No." Not until someone figured out the tags on her car were stolen or that she possessed an illegal gun.

Again, Debbie held her gaze and then must have been satisfied because she nodded. "Cash it is. Come on. I'll show you the place. The in-law suite is below."

She opened a door off the kitchen and led the way down a flight of stairs. A plaid sofa with a folded afghan draped over the back sat behind a wooden coffee table and a small television on a TV tray. A mustard-yellow refrigerator lined up with a matching stove and sink in the kitchen. The clean scent of bleach hung in the air.

Debbie pointed to a door at the end of the room. "That leads out back."

The muscles in Sarah's shoulders tensed. While it meant another escape route if she needed one, it also provided a second access to the suite. She'd have to check out the lock. The windows in both rooms only had valances. Most people enjoyed the sun peeking in. She had more to worry about than the sun.

"The bedroom is back here." Debbie led her to the chamber with an oak dresser, nightstand, and a double bed covered with a pastel-floral comforter. Only one window. At least it had a full curtain. A door opened to an attached bathroom with a shower.

"Nothing fancy, but everything works," Debbie said.

Sarah nodded. "It's fine. Thank you."

"Besides cooking and cleaning, I'll also need you to do chores in the stables until summer when I have more help. Right now, only a couple of girls come after school. You may need to tack up a horse from time to time for a boarder."

She'd have to learn how first. "Okay. When can I start?"

"How about now?"

Sarah let out a deep breath. She wouldn't have to spend another night in her car. A real bed and people around for a little security. "Sounds good."

"Get yourself settled. I'll go over more with you later." Debbie headed to the stairs. "There's not much in the way of restaurants around here. Plenty of soup in the kitchen. Help yourself. I gotta get back to the barn." She climbed the steps and disappeared into the upstairs kitchen.

Sarah hurried over to the windows. Simple pocket rods held the valances. She could get longer curtains, but it wouldn't take much of a push to pop off the rusty locks. Next, she checked the door leading outside. No deadbolt. Her pulse quickened. She opened the door and examined the knob. The two small screws attaching it would be easy to remove.

A shadow crossed the door, and she jerked her head up to find Joe peering down at her. She straightened. Crud. Nothing came to mind to say, and silence stretched between them for a moment.

He pointed to a dirt drive beside the house. "You can park your car up here. Seeing's you don't know the place yet, that path winds through the woods back to the main road."

More than one way in and out could mean trouble. "Thanks."

"Yup." He moseyed off toward the barn, whistling.

Sarah frowned at the woods across a short field close to the house. Anyone could hide in the trees and watch the suite. She went back inside to the bedroom and dug through her purse for her throwaway phone. Her wallet fell out, and she opened it to a picture of her two older sisters, standing with her by a fountain in San Diego. Anne, wearing glasses, stood in the middle, her short blond hair clipped and neat. On her right, Maddie gave a thumbs-up sign, her red curls wild from the wind. Sarah's eyes misted. Bright, happy smiles lit all three faces. So much had changed in the two years since they'd posed for the picture.

She grabbed the phone from her purse and dialed Anne's number.

Her sister's strained voice came across the line. "Sarah? Thank God. Are you okay?"

"Yeah, for now."

"Is there any sign he knows where you are?"

"No. I did everything the private investigator told me. Like Alec said to, I drove through Seattle and looked at an apartment. They ran a credit check. I put in an order for phone service there." She ran a hand through her hair. "I paid cash everywhere. What's going on with my credit card? Is your friend using it?"

"Yes. She's been traveling all over the place. Purchases should come up in several states."

"Good. I don't know if the bastard can access my accounts, but maybe it will keep him busy if he does." She pinched the bridge of her nose. "I cut and dyed my hair."

"That had to be hard."

"I stole license plates. Twice. In different states." She waited for the admonition. Anne followed rules and always colored inside the lines. As a teacher, she had a strict moral code.

"Good idea. They called me from the studio. I told them I didn't know where you were."

A knife twisted in Sarah's chest. Even if she could return to the ballet company, she doubted they would take her back. She'd left without notice, and plenty of dancers waited in the wings eager to take the place of the principal. "I'm sorry you have to deal with all this."

"Don't worry about me. All I want to do is help."

Sarah rubbed the back of her neck. "I appreciate it. I need to go now."

"I'm so scared for you. I don't know what else we can do."

"Me either. Just pray he doesn't find me."

"Be careful. Love you," Anne said.

"Love you too. I'll be in touch when I can."

Sarah hung up. She sank to the floor and rested her head on her knees. Rocking back and forth, she let the tears she'd held in for the past week flow. It might be a long time before she saw her family again.

She took a deep breath and wiped her eyes on her sleeve. Thanks to Alec, she had a new last name and ID. With any luck, all the diversions he'd told her to set up would work. If not, she had a backup plan.

She grabbed her purse and dug in the bottom to pull out a small gun she'd purchased at a pawnshop. Alec had told her about a place where money talked and the owner didn't. The shady part of town had made her nervous, but she'd walked away with a silver .380 pistol not much bigger than her hand. If her life depended on it, she'd be ready.

After slipping the gun back into her bag, she stood. She needed to find some boots and move the car. Fewer people would see the stolen license plates with it parked at the house.

She hiked across the lawn toward her Honda. As she passed a window in the stables, Bruce's voice sounded from within.

"She doesn't look strong enough to—"

"I'm giving her a shot. Someone gave me a chance once when I was in a load of trouble, and I made sure they never regretted it. And since when do you get into my business?" Debbie asked.

Sarah stopped under the window. Bruce might be sabotaging her chance at the job. Her ears burned. He had no idea how tough she could be.

Debbie continued, "Tell you what. I need someone to show Sarah how to tack up a horse. Let her help you get Misty ready for your patients tomorrow and take her for a ride. See how she handles everything, and then tell me what you think about her."

"I'll pass."

"Really? Because you're the one questioning her. We all have to work together. At the end of the day, if you don't think she has what it takes, I won't hire her."

Sarah stomped to her car. Fine. He didn't think she could cut it.

She'd prove him wrong.

CHAPTER 3

Bleep. Bleep. Bleep.

Sarah sprang out of bed.

Dance. She had to go to the studio.

She smacked a hand at the glowing red light of the clock radio on the nightstand until the noise ceased.

Submerged in darkness, she stood still and waited for her eyes to adjust. The sound of crickets brought reality crashing back, and a heaviness settled in her chest. She wasn't in her city apartment. No warm-ups, no dancing, no performances. Her old life didn't exist anymore, but for a fleeting moment, she'd had her dream back.

She dragged on pants and a T-shirt, brushed her teeth, and opened the bedroom door. The soft glow of an outside light cast shadows around the room. The stalker shouldn't be anywhere near, but she wasn't taking any chances. She shuffled across the floor to avoid tripping and went upstairs to the kitchen.

"Coffee's ready if you want to bring a cup to the barn." Debbie, dressed in jeans and a flannel shirt like yesterday, poured the steaming brew into a large mug.

"Thanks, but I'm good." Caffeine. Her body craved it, but her stomach fluttered from nerves, and coffee would make it worse.

"Suit yourself."

Debbie opened a bag of bagels and handed one to Sarah. "You're gonna need energy."

Despite not being hungry, if she didn't eat, she'd have no stamina. She couldn't afford to appear weak, so she took the bagel. "Thanks."

"Let's go."

Sarah followed Debbie to the mudroom off the front of the house and slipped on a pair of flat, rubber-soled boots. She'd picked them up at a thrift store in town yesterday with her last five bucks. They really weren't suited for farm work, but until she could afford something else, they would have to do.

A beat-up, blue Chevy truck pulled in as they approached the barn.

"Well, hell's bells, Greg actually showed up on time today. Wonders never cease." Debbie nodded. "This'll make life easier."

A wiry guy wearing a ball cap loped toward them, stopping once to yawn and rub his eyes.

"Wake up, Greg. This is Sarah." Debbie turned to her. "Greg's been here for a year. He works weekdays and takes classes at the community college at night."

Sarah smiled and held out a hand.

He shook hers hard. His Adam's apple bobbed. "Nice t-to meet you."

Debbie waved to the stables. "I'll turn out the horses. Sarah can help you with the barn chores."

"Sure." Greg straightened and stood taller.

The morning went fast, and Sarah busted her butt working. She mucked stalls and swept away cobwebs. Spiders. Ugh. Her dad had almost died from a bite. She hated the hairy nightmares. But not as much as threats from a delusional psycho.

Somewhere around eight o'clock, they had the barn cleaned. The buckets to fill the troughs had taken a while to lug back and forth. She never realized how heavy water could be. Stress and a fast-food diet had sucked the energy out of her. That would teach her for eating crappy meals on the run. Hot, sweaty, and thirsty, she grabbed the hose and sprayed water on the back of her neck before taking a long drink.

Boots scuffled through the dirt behind her.

She whirled around.

Bruce stopped across the aisle from her.

If he'd accepted Debbie's proposal, he probably couldn't wait to find reasons to get Sarah fired. So far, she'd done everything asked of her, and Greg said the stables had never looked better. Bruce would have to search hard for grounds to dismiss her.

His gaze dropped to the hose still gushing water, now making a muddy puddle.

She let go of it and cranked the knob to Off. When she turned back around, he had come closer. His soap-and-leather scent wafted across the barn, distracting her the same as it had yesterday. A crisp denim shirt highlighted his clear blue eyes. Her gaze lingered on an open button where a curl of dark chest hair peeked out.

"Working hard?" he asked.

She glanced up. An answer didn't come right away as she focused on the jagged scar by his cheek. Maybe he'd been in a fight. Or with his short haircut and that Wounded Warrior hat he'd worn yesterday, he could have been in the military.

The puckered line ran from his ear to his jaw, hooking under his chin. Such an imperfection should have made him less attractive. It didn't.

The dancers in the company—both men and women—went to great lengths to take care of their bodies. A scar like that would have been limiting, perhaps even career-ending. Not that Bruce didn't take care of his body. No one could argue that he didn't take *very* good care of it. From head to booted toe, he was perfection. Solid, Herculean biceps. A lean stomach that would probably break every bone in her fist if she punched it. The man oozed raw masculinity.

Her nipples, which had grown painfully taut, could attest to that.

"Sarah?" He waved his hand in front of her face.

"Huh?"

A deep crease appeared between his eyebrows. "I asked if you were working hard."

"You did?" Shit. Focus. "I'm up to it."

He stared at her for a long second, and then brushed past her. "We'll see."

Mr. Aloof sure didn't waste words. She hadn't done a damn thing to merit his disdain. He'd better not give a bad report on her. She picked up a broom and swept the aisle. Hard.

A few minutes later, Debbie and Bruce came out from the tack room and headed in her direction. Debbie dipped her head into the stalls along her way.

Sarah's stomach knotted. Her work better pass the test.

"How you doing?" Debbie cocked her head and gave Sarah the once-over.

"I'm great." Sarah thrust her shoulders back and thumped the broom on the ground.

Debbie shot Bruce a look. "Bruce is going to show you how to tack up a horse in a bit."

He scowled like someone who picked the short straw and got bathroom clean-up duty.

"When you're done with that, I'll give you a list of stuff to get from town. Add whatever you need for making meals. I've got dinner tonight, but starting tomorrow, assuming things work out, it's your job."

Sarah nodded. Bruce didn't look happy about having to teach her to tack up. Debbie must have made a deal with him. He probably figured he could get rid of Sarah if he had the last word.

She glanced at Greg across the stables. Time to make a good impression. "Would Greg show up earlier in the morning for a hot breakfast?"

Debbie scratched her temple. "Dunno. Never offered."

"I could make one and invite him."

"It's not part of the job, but I'm all for anything that gets him here on time."

"Sounds good. It can't hurt to try."

"Your call." She pointed outside the barn to an old red pickup in the parking lot. "You can take that when you go to town. We use it to run errands."

Tension eased from Sarah's back. Perfect. The less she drove her uninsured car with stolen plates, the better. "Great. Thanks so much."

Debbie's mouth set, and she muttered something as she stepped past Sarah.

Uh-oh. She must have sounded too excited to have access to the rusty truck.

Sarah faced Bruce, who wore a slight frown. The man missed nothing. If she didn't keep her emotions in check, everyone would become suspicious. Like it or not, she had to make a good impression, or she'd be on the run again. She tugged her lower lip with her teeth. "We seem to have gotten off on the wrong foot. Is it something I'm doing?"

His gaze dropped to her mouth. When he raised his eyes, their icy blue had turned to fire.

"Yes."

Her thighs tightened. No man had ever looked at her with such raw heat. Sure, she'd had her share of fans, but none who made her melt. She blinked and focused back on the issue at hand. Whatever his problem was, he needed to give her more than one-word answers. "We've spent less than fifteen minutes together since I got here. What could I possibly have done?"

"I'll be back in about an hour." He strode away without answering.

What bullshit. He had no right to leave her hanging. She bit back a caustic reply and squeezed her hands into fists. She'd need mind-reading classes if she continued to work around him. Where she came from men had manners and didn't act like arrogant barbarians.

Greg rounded the corner of the stable wall and stopped. "You okay? Your face is really red."

No doubt. She blew out a breath. "Yeah. What do we need to do next?"

"Bring the grain in." He took her out to the side of the barn and pointed to the stacks.

A young woman led a white colt with black spots on his rump past them to the arena. She mounted as Greg and Sarah dragged the bags toward the stable entrance.

"She's new here." Greg cocked his head. "I've never met her because she usually comes at night, but Joe said she's training that Appaloosa. He seemed surprised since she told him she hasn't been riding long."

"I guess she must think she can handle it." Sarah mopped her brow and gazed at the open fields where Bruce and the chestnut stallion he rode flew across the grassy slopes. Graceful and beautiful, the scene could be on a postcard. "He sure looks like he knows how to ride. That horse is fast."

"One of the fastest here. Bruce is working him for the owner." Greg waved a hand at the stables. "You should see him ride Batal. He's an ex-race horse Bruce trained."

"He trains?"

Greg shook his head. "Not anymore. He grew up on a horse farm, though."

"Really?" She squinted into the sun as Bruce and the stallion tore across another open field.

"Yeah. He's been around them his whole life."

"Huh. I guess that's why he rides so well."

Greg's eyes lit up. He leaned closer and kept his voice low. "Bruce's family's horse farm caught fire, and he ran into the burning barn and got every horse out. He was only fifteen, and the story made the papers and news. Between that and some of the wild stallions he trained, people called him the young horse whisperer."

"Does he talk to horses?" Because he sure as hell didn't converse with people.

Greg's gaze went to the field. He clamped his mouth shut. "I think we better get back to work." He frowned and pointed to the arena where the woman rode the spotted horse. "She left the gate open again."

"I'll get it." Sarah jogged toward the rink.

A strong gust of wind blew over a black trash can next to the fence. The colt leaped in the air and took off running.

"Runaway!" Joe shouted.

Sarah gasped and sprinted to the opening. The horse closed the distance fast, leaving her no time to shut the gate. She stood in the entrance making herself as big as possible and waved her arms wide. The steed reared. She gazed up at the powerful legs churning above her.

Her adrenaline spiked.

In one swift move, she kicked the gate shut, pirouetted, and whirled to the right. The horse's hooves came down inches from her shoulder as she ducked behind the end post.

The colt bolted, and the rider's eyes bulged as she gripped the reins. With the gate now closed, the horse raced inside the arena.

Bruce came galloping in from the field, sprang from his horse, and jumped over the fence. He called out instructions to the rider, who bounced and bobbed in the saddle.

Joe, Debbie, and Greg appeared beside Sarah. Bruce spoke in a calm, low tone, walking in circles inside the middle of the rink until the horse slowed to a trot. The rider pulled on the reins, and the colt halted. The woman dismounted and bent over, holding a hand to her chest. Bruce patted her on the back, leaned down, and spoke to her.

"Holy shit, Sarah. You could have been killed," Greg said.

Her pulse still cantered. "I had to do something."

"That was ballsy. Coulda ended up ugly," Debbie said.

Greg sucked in a breath. "You'd think she's the one who'd been a Navy SEAL."

"Why don't you see if you can help with the runaway?" Debbie frowned at him.

"Oh, right." He jogged into the arena.

A Navy SEAL. So she'd been right about Bruce and the military. It might explain why she couldn't read him. Maybe they'd trained him to conceal his emotions. If so, he must have aced that class.

Greg took the reins of the runaway horse. The woman shuffled out with him and stopped to sit on a bench in front of the barn. She removed her helmet and rested her head against the wall. Her pale face glowed in the sun. The poor thing was still shaking. Sarah fished out a water bottle from one of the coolers. "Here, maybe this will help."

The woman placed a hand on Sarah's arm. "Thank you. I can't believe what you did. You probably saved my life. If he'd gotten into the open fields, I'm not sure I could have stayed on."

Sarah shrugged. "Everything happened so fast. I didn't have time to think."

"Well, I can't thank you enough." She took the bottle, her hands still trembling.

"Let me help you." Sarah twisted the cap open. She glanced up to find Bruce standing beside her.

"You okay now?" he asked the woman.

"Yes. I don't know what I would've done without the two of you."

"Glad you didn't get hurt. Be careful with that colt. He's young and skittish."

She nodded, her eyes wide. "I will. Thanks."

"No problem." Bruce gave Sarah a long, unreadable look before he headed back to his abandoned horse, grazing in the field beside the arena.

Sarah sighed. Whatever Bruce thought of her actions, he clearly didn't intend to discuss it with her. Not exactly a news flash, him keeping her in the dark.

* * *

Bruce mounted the horse he'd been working and rode him back to the fields. Away from Sarah. He could wring her neck for that stunt she'd pulled, regardless of the guts it took. His heart had false-started at the sight of her under the rearing, wild horse. The only thing that had saved her life was the crazy, gymnast-like move she'd made to get out of the way at the last second.

With no helmet, one good kick to her head and she'd have been toast. In mere seconds, a person could be gone.

God, he missed Emily. The early morning rides they'd shared when the dew-covered grass glittered under the rising sun. Her challenging smile as she nudged her horse faster, ever the competitor. His chest constricted.

Four years since she'd died in the car accident. With no other choice, he'd learned to cope. The days weren't so bad now. He kept busy with the therapy program. But dreams of his wife haunted him at night. In the morning, he'd wake to her empty side of the bed. The scab would rip off again, leaving his wound fresh and raw. The same painful pattern, for years.

Until last night.

His hands tightened on the reins as he spotted Sarah near the barn with Greg. She had snuck into his dreams where Emily belonged. Sarah roused emotions he didn't want to relive with another woman. The hole in his heart would never heal. Best to keep Sarah far from it.

Urging the stallion faster, he focused on his connection with the horse. As always, a calmness soothed him as they sped across the meadow together.

After a long ride, Bruce brushed the stallion and shot a glance at Sarah when she entered the stables. Despite his resolve to keep his emotional distance, every cell in his body tuned in to her presence.

He blew out a breath. The oversized jacket she'd shown up in had done a good job of hiding her body. Muscles, sleek and toned, lined her arms and legs. Tight jeans accentuated her pear-shaped bottom. He forced his attention back to his horse. Two brushstrokes later, he glanced again at Sarah. She'd stopped sweeping and stood with the broom handle pressed against her cheek, staring in his direction. Only her gaze wasn't on his face.

For chrissakes, were they back in middle school? He cleared his throat and she jumped, dropping the broom.

Enough of this. He had work to do. "When I'm done here, a word?"

Her face turned crimson. She nodded and snatched up the broom. "Of course."

His gaze followed the graceful way she moved as she glided down the aisle. He tried not to focus on her sweet ass. And failed. Muscles bunched at the back of his neck. Best to get it over with. He'd teach Sarah how to tack up a horse, give her a ride, and be done.

He untied the stallion, led him back to his stall, and approached Sarah. She probably wouldn't last the day. Images of the close call with the runaway rushed back, and his ears burned. She could be dead instead of standing in front of him with those pink, pouty lips and eyes that mirrored the grassy slopes. "Are you ready?"

"Yes." She set the broom aside and brushed her hands together.

"Follow me."

He led her down the corridor between the stalls. With each step he took, the recklessness of her behavior and the danger she'd put herself in sank deeper. No matter she'd risked her life for someone; she had no business being on the farm if she knew nothing about horses. And whatever had driven her to take such a job had to mean trouble. This wasn't the place for her, and the sooner she realized it, the better.

When they reached the tack room, he crossed his arms and faced her. "Do you have a death wish or something?"

"What?"

"What you did out there earlier? You could have been killed."

Her brows drew together, and her nose wrinkled. "I didn't have time to think about it. I just reacted."

"Never step in front of a wild horse. You're damn lucky he stopped. If they're spooked, they'll run right into a person, a tree"—he tapped the wall with his hand—"even a building."

She planted her hands on her hips. "Well, he didn't, and no one got hurt."

Damn her stubbornness. He shook his head. "You have a lot to learn."

"I'm more than willing."

He rubbed a hand down his face, picked up a saddle, and pointed to Misty's name above a set of pegs where her gear hung. "Could you grab a bridle and girth from there?"

Sarah's gaze flitted to the wall. She bit her lower lip.

He tensed and forced his gaze away from her mouth. "Is there a problem?"

"I...uh..." She tugged again at her lower lip.

Christ, she needed to stop doing that. He huffed and shoved the saddle back on its stand. "What?"

Her eyes flashed. "I don't know what a bridle and girth is. I didn't grow up on a horse farm like you."

He bristled. "How do you know that?"

"Greg mentioned it."

Bruce never discussed his past with anyone.

A coldness settled in his breast. He'd been away at college when Joe had shown up at his door and broken the news that Bruce's mom and dad had died of carbon monoxide poisoning. If he'd stayed and taken over the horse farm like his father expected, they might still be alive. Instead, he'd gone off to college and let his family die with the house closed up one winter night.

He shut his eyes for a second and opened them to find Sarah staring at the eagle tattoo high on his upper arm with his team number. The brothers who became his new family. So much blood and pain. His gut churned. He'd returned in one piece. Others weren't so lucky. He couldn't give the amputees back their limbs, but he sure as hell could help them adapt and recover.

"So you do some sort of therapy here?" Sarah asked.

He nodded, relieved to derail the trip down misery lane. "It's called hippotherapy, and it's working with horses to help patients with their mobility and balance." He crossed to the wall, grabbed Misty's gear, and handed it to Sarah. "My clients are veteran amputees."

Sarah's eyes softened. "That's really special. When you mentioned therapy yesterday, I thought you meant psychotherapy or—"

"Most people don't know about it." He held out a carryall filled with various grooming tools. "Can you bring these?"

"Sure."

He picked up a saddle, placed a pad on top, and carried them out of the tack room.

Greg led Misty down the aisle toward them. His gaze never strayed from Sarah. When he stopped, his face flushed pink.

Bruce frowned. He'd laugh, but she had the same effect on him, only he was thirty-two—and didn't blush.

Greg handed Misty's lead line to Bruce. "Need anything else?"

"No, thanks."

"Hey, Greg. What do you do for breakfast in the morning?" Sarah asked.

"What do you mean?"

"Debbie said you eat here sometimes. You ever come for breakfast?"

Greg shrugged. "No."

Sarah gave a curt nod. "You show up at six, and I'll dish up a mean meal."

"Sounds awesome." A big smile formed on Greg's face.

"Shouldn't you wait to see if you get this job before you invite him?" Bruce raised an eyebrow at Sarah.

The corners of Greg's mouth fell. "She will. Least I hope so. I'll check before I come. If there's anything I can say to—"

"Don't worry, Greg. I intend to be here." Determination rang in Sarah's voice.

Bruce kept his gaze on her. She was full of surprises. Plenty of confidence, and she might even get the kid to work on time. But just because she could make pancakes didn't mean she'd cut it as a farmhand.

"I'll see you later." Greg patted Misty and then headed toward the barn entrance.

The horse nuzzled Bruce and gave a little nicker. He might as well get things over with. One way or another, Debbie needed a report by the end of the day.

"This is Misty." He ran a hand along the white streak on her nose.

Sarah reached out to pet her. Inches from Bruce, the sweet strawberry scent of her hair floated up. Made it hard to concentrate. He took a step back. "You want to brush her?"

"Sure."

He showed her how to groom the horse and look her over for any possible problems.

"Am I doing this right?" Sarah asked over her shoulder as she brushed.

"Yes." His gaze followed her body, stretching and flexing with every move. Blood blazed a hot path to below his belt.

"There." She stepped back, whirled about, and almost knocked into him.

They stood inches apart, her pink lips slightly parted as she looked up at him with a glow of pride on her face. Her soft breath puffed against his neck and floated up to his mouth. He could all but taste her. Wanted to.

She swallowed, and his gaze fell to the elegant line of her throat. No doubt, her skin, so white and pure, would feel like velvet under his lips.

Misty neighed and pawed a hoof into the ground.

He shook his head to clear it. Sarah made him lose his mind. In a harsh voice, he said, "The horse is getting restless."

Sarah held her hands up. "Just tell me what to do, then."

Damn, she brought out the worst in him. Her eagerness to learn and take on any task spoke of her work ethic. And she didn't mind getting dirty or wearing muddy boots. Still, no one should smell as good as she did in a barn, and those soft hands of hers would soon callus from hauling hay and turn rough from scrubbing buckets. That bothered him, which gave him pause. A hardness settled in his stomach.

Business. Keep it to business.

He showed Sarah how to put the saddle on and feed the bit into the mare's mouth before buckling the bridle. "I told Debbie I'd give you a ride. Grab a helmet from the tack room."

"Are you sure you—"

"Yes." God forbid she missed a chance to argue with him about anything.

"Never mind." She hastened down the aisle, and he led Misty to the arena and tied her to a fence post.

Sarah sauntered out of the stables carrying a helmet. She stopped in front of Bruce. "I think this is the right size. There were a couple to pick from."

"Sorry. I should have checked them out. This looks okay."

A car roared into the lot.

Sarah jumped and spun around.

CHAPTER 4

WHERE HAD his beautiful ballerina gone? He clutched the autographed picture of Sarah he kept on the kitchen table so they could have meals together. By now, he should have heard something from his source. He paid him good money to keep tabs on her. No news in a week since she'd left. Inexcusable.

He checked his watch and stood. Eighty-five seconds until eight o'clock. If he followed his rituals and kept to the routines, everything would be okay. The teakettle whistled on the hour, and he went to the counter to pour a cup. After he dipped his tea bag in the hot water exactly five times, he set the mug aside to steep and popped two slices of whole wheat bread into the toaster oven. He'd never own a toaster. Crumbs collected in the bottom of them. This had a tray he could pull out and scrub clean after each use.

When the timer bell rang, he placed the toast on a plate large enough for both pieces to fit without hanging over the edge and peeled back the foil of an individual butter serving. Every Sunday, when he ate at the diner, he snuck them into a plastic bag in his pocket. Six each time, to last the week. Toast buttered, tea steeped, he sat in the one chair at the round kitchen table. He took small bites, wiping his mouth after each one with the folded napkin.

The muscles in his neck tensed. Nothing would be right until he found her, and he'd never stop until he did. She belonged with him.

Over a year ago, he'd gone to the ballet and discovered her. His soul mate. One night, after her performance, he'd given her a bouquet he'd arranged with perfect symmetry. The big smile on her face told him she recognized the difference in his flowers. A few weeks later, he waited in line for her to autograph a picture, and she brushed his hand as she gave the photo back, a sign she loved him.

She shouldn't have left town. He'd warned her to stop listening to the police and her family. They'd probably told her not to take his calls and to fight him if he ever showed up. He fisted his hands and winced. A week since she'd stabbed him with a glass shard, and he still suffered.

When she came back, he'd have to punish her for hurting him and leaving. She'd pushed him to the point of losing control. The way he'd left her apartment in total chaos and disorder still haunted him. A film of cold sweat formed on his arms, drawing goose bumps.

His Sarah would never want to harm him. After he got her away from the people who influenced her, she'd be able to show him her love. Their life together would be magical. He'd work on the computer during the day, and she'd dance for him at night. Oh, how they would look forward to the weekends when they had tea and muffins together and talked about his job.

Unlike the kids who had bullied him growing up, Sarah appreciated his intelligence. That's why she'd let the police set up the cameras. With his technical expertise, she knew he'd find a way around them. Stupid cops. He took a sip of tea and placed the mug back in the precise center of the coaster.

Even his own parents hadn't understood him. When he'd hacked into the school's system, instead of praising his talents, they'd punished him and taken away his laptop for weeks. As if that would stop him. He'd simply gone to the library and used the public computers. In short order, he'd compromised dear Dad's work database. His father's boss had reamed the old man out for losing "sensitive" client files. Sweet revenge.

After finishing the rest of his toast, Leonard took the empty plate to the sink. Rinse, wash, rinse. Dry, dry, dry. He placed the dish back in the cabinet. Even though he didn't use the dishwasher, he ran the machine on high heat once a week and left the door cracked open to keep mold from growing.

Sarah would be impressed with his clean, organized living space. She deserved nothing but the best. Unlike Audrey. His mouth twisted. If only he'd found Sarah first. Audrey hadn't been worthy of him. She'd left him no choice but to end her life when she'd soiled herself with another man. That wouldn't happen with Sarah. His beautiful ballerina loved him and only him.

He crossed through the living room to his office where pictures of Sarah covered every inch of the walls. Pausing in front of one, he stroked a finger down her face. "Where did you go?"

He sat at his desk and clicked on a video of her dancing. Every day he watched it at the same time. He'd memorized the performance. Each movement precise, graceful, and impeccably timed. One-two-three, lift two-three, down two-three. Yet another thing that bound them together, both being perfectionists.

Upon her return, she'd dance only for him. He clenched his teeth. No partners lifting or touching her. No other men in her life.

He slid aside the closet door, opened his safe, and pulled out a picture. Audrey's lifeless eyes stared at him from what was left of her face. She'd taken the first shot in the mouth, for kissing another man. What a mess. He'd been unprepared for so much blood and had to burn all the clothes he'd worn.

After tucking the photo back into the vault, he picked up his pistol. The cold, metal weapon weighed heavily in his hand. He'd only use the gun to get Sarah's attention and force her to come back with him. Hard to tell how much influence her family still had on her. He wouldn't need the gun once they were alone long enough for outsiders to stop interfering. Then, she'd admit her love for him. After she announced it to the world, people would accept that she wanted to be with him.

From the back of the safe, he pulled out a set of pointe shoe ribbons. Soft, silky, and tied in perfect slipknots, one to restrain each delicate wrist.

He'd never need to use them. Sarah loved him and would choose a life together.

His phone beeped, signaling a new email from his source, and his pulse skipped. He put the gun away, locked the safe, and returned to the computer.

At last, some news.

CHAPTER 5

A RED JAGUAR convertible with the top down whipped into a parking spot by the arena. Sarah blew out a breath at the sight of a woman behind the wheel and turned to find Bruce staring at her.

Shit. She had to stop thinking every person who pulled into the lot was the stalker. She hadn't told anyone where she was, so he shouldn't be able to find her. But he was resourceful. If only she knew what he looked like, she wouldn't panic every time she ran into a man.

"Is there a problem?" Bruce asked.

"No." She shut down the thoughts, put the helmet on, and snapped the buckle with shaking fingers.

He reached a hand out and wiggled the top of the helmet. "Too loose."

She fumbled with the chin straps to pull them tighter. He leaned down, bringing his face close to hers, and adjusted the band, brushing her skin. His breath tickled her cheeks, and the sensitive flesh of her neck tingled under his touch. The muscles in his arms firmed, and he yanked his hand away.

"Thank you," she said.

"Just doing what I promised Debbie."

Of course, it wasn't like he wanted to help her. He must practice in the mirror at being so damn abrasive.

A car door slammed, and Sarah glanced at the lot, her nerves still on edge. A striking blonde wearing skinny jeans and a pink shirt that clung to her ample curves leaned against the side of the red Jag. Phone to her ear, she faced the arena. Her hand tapped her outer thigh. Because of the distance, Sarah couldn't read the woman's expression, but her body language spoke angry. The small hairs on the back of Sarah's neck prickled. She frowned. Growing up, she'd learned to trust her instincts, and right now they were sending a bad vibe.

"Who's that?"

"Morgan."

Sarah rolled her eyes. So much information. She'd never process it all. "I meant who is she, not what's her name."

Bruce picked up something that resembled steps from near the fence and dragged them next to Misty. He pointed to a white mansion on a hill at the edge of the woods past the open fields. "She lives next door and boards here."

Morgan had to be stinking rich.

"Climb up this mounting block so you can get on the horse easier." Bruce held out a stirrup. "Put your foot in this and swing your other leg over."

Sarah straddled the mare.

Misty pawed the ground and swiveled her ears.

"Hey, hey. What's up, girl?" Bruce ran a hand down the side of Misty's face, leaning closer. He rubbed her temples.

"What's wrong?" Sarah asked.

He stroked Misty and spoke in soothing tones to her until she somewhat settled. "She's nervous, and this is the calmest horse you'll ever find. She can sense when a rider is anxious."

Great. Sarah couldn't even hide her emotions from a horse. Yeah, she was always on edge, and cars screaming into the lot didn't help. She had to get a grip. "I'm sorry. I haven't ridden in a long time. I guess I'm a little tense."

Bruce glanced up at her, still stroking Misty's flank. "She's used to novice riders. It's more than that."

Silence stretched between them. He held her gaze as if challenging her to deny it. Clearly, he hadn't wanted her at the farm before, and now she'd made it worse by upsetting his horse. She took a deep breath, closed her eyes, and willed her body to calm down. Just like before a performance. She could do this.

Bruce placed a hand on her thigh. "Try to keep your bottom half relaxed and move with the horse."

Heat spread up her leg from his contact. If she wanted to gain any respect at the farm, she had to ignore what his touch did to her and focus on learning the ropes. She nodded. "I'm ready."

Bruce tugged on the line, and Misty walked. After a lap, Sarah relaxed a little. Her hips moved in rhythm with the horse. "It feels like I'm walking, but I don't have legs."

"Good. Keep it up."

They rounded a turn and passed close to Morgan, who stood by her car, still talking on the phone. Her eyes narrowed to slits.

Sarah tensed, and Misty jerked forward.

"Whoa." Bruce pulled on the lead. "Walk, girl." He tapped Sarah's thigh. "Relax your legs. You're giving her the command to trot."

"What?" Sarah dragged her gaze from the blonde.

"When you squeeze your legs, the horse thinks you want to go faster." He rubbed his hand over Sarah's knee. "Relax."

She took a breath and forced her legs to soften. Not so easy with him touching her. She glanced down at him, and hot blood rose to her face.

He snatched his hand off and frowned. "Why are you here? You don't know anything about horses."

The truth stung. "The ad was for someone to cook, clean, and do barn chores."

"This *is* a horse farm."

"I'm a fast learner." She sat taller in the saddle.

He shot a sidelong look at her. "We'll see. I need to get ready for my patient now." He stopped Misty near the gate and tied her to the post. "I'll help you off."

"I can do it." Sarah swung her leg over the back of the horse but stumbled with a foot still caught in the stirrup. Shit. The straps had seemed lower when she'd mounted from the block. She seldom lost her balance, but did this time.

Bruce's arms came around from behind, preventing her from falling. She yanked her foot out of the stirrup and fell back against his chest.

"Goddamn, you're stubborn." He spun her to face him.

Out of habit from ballet, she grasped his shoulders. Only they weren't dancing, and she'd never been held by anyone like him. Rugged and hard with no soft spots. His muscles flexed under her fingers, sending a shiver through her. She craned her neck to gaze up at him, her breath shallow.

He swallowed and let go of her abruptly, all but pushing her away. "You could've gotten hurt. That's twice today. You have to do what people tell you around the horses."

Misty snorted and pawed at the ground. Bruce turned to her and once again spoke softly, stroking her side.

Sarah would never keep her job if she spooked the horses. And Bruce had a point. It wouldn't look good for either of them if she broke a leg because she didn't listen to him.

She touched his arm. "I'm sorry. You're right. And thank you for the ride and lesson."

He gave a terse nod and continued stroking the horse. Sarah glanced across the rink to find Morgan glaring at her, a hand on her hip, off the phone at last. Maybe she was his girlfriend. That would explain the evil looks. Sarah raised her chin and stared back.

"I think she's all right now. I need some gear from the stables. Follow me. We're done here." Bruce led Sarah back into the barn.

Greg met them at the entrance and gave Sarah a big smile. "I can't wait for breakfast tomorrow."

"You won't be disappointed. I'm going to make banana pancakes and killer hash browns." She kept her voice light. Maybe she would sound less stressed.

He licked his lips. "Sounds great."

She grinned. Guys and their food. "If I can get some sausage, I'll—"

"I know how much you two enjoy talking, but I need to get ready for Charlie." Bruce faced Greg. "Can you take Misty to the trough for a drink? She's tied up by the arena."

Greg bobbed his head. "Sure. Sorry. I, uh—"

"Thanks." Bruce nodded and proceeded down the aisle.

Greg scratched the side of his face. "Huh."

"What's wrong?" Sarah asked.

"Beats me. I've never seen Bruce act like this."

"What do you mean?"

"Like he's in a bad mood or something." Greg shot another look at him.

Sarah frowned. Probably her fault. If she didn't need the job and a place to hide, she'd leave. But she had no other options, so they'd have to find a way to work around each other. She picked up a broom and sighed.

A tall, lean woman with long auburn hair tied back in a ponytail entered the barn, passing Greg on his way out. She approached Sarah with a warm smile. "Are you the new person Debbie hired?"

"Yes. I'm Sarah. It's my first day. Do you board here?"

"No. I work with Bruce. I handle the horses for his therapy program. I'm Lynn." She extended a hand.

When Sarah shook it, she caught her breath, and her gaze went to the cool, prosthetic hand she held.

Lynn gave her an apologetic smile. "Sorry. I sometimes forget to warn people."

"Oh, no problem." Sarah rushed to cover her surprise.

"Lucky for me, I'm still able to work. I came here as a veteran patient and ended up with a job."

"Wow. That's fantastic."

"Yeah, it works out really well since Bruce's clients are amputees like me, so I can relate. In fact, one of the vets, Charlie, will be here pretty soon." Lynn shifted to peer over Sarah's shoulder.

Sarah followed her gaze. Debbie had entered the barn with a man. Average height, with brown hair, and a face that glowed white.

Lynn shrugged. "I guess Debbie has someone new interested in boarding here. Looks like she's showing him around the place."

"You don't know him?"

"No. She only has room for a dozen horses, so she doesn't get many new people. She has one open stall, though."

Sarah's pulse quickened. With his pasty coloring, he couldn't spend much time outside. Neither did hackers. She glanced out the barn entrance to the parking lot, where a shiny black Corvette gleamed under the sun. His sports car, along with the Gucci logo on his shirt and designer pants, meant he had money. Maybe rich people didn't always go to big ranches. Morgan seemed to be loaded, and she boarded here.

As they came closer, Debbie talked to him until they stopped in front of the empty stall. She entered, but the man paused and gawked at Sarah and Lynn. No, not Lynn.

Her.

Sarah's lungs deflated. She had to think and not jump to paranoid conclusions. With all the people around, he wouldn't do anything.

"Nice to meet you, Sarah. I have to work with Bruce and Charlie now." Lynn gave a quick wave and left.

Debbie continued to talk to the man, but when she glanced down at her clipboard, once again, he leered at Sarah.

She gripped the broom and fought to breathe.

He tapped his cheek with a gloved hand. "I think this will work out fine for me. Do you have anyone to help tack up and groom my horse? I prefer not to perform the menial tasks that tend to be messy. I'll pay for the service, of course."

Sarah glanced at his feet. His boots were either brand-new or polished.

"You'd have to come at certain times, but yes," Debbie said.

"Not a problem. Can I bring my horse later this week?"

"Sure, I'll write up the paperwork."

"I'll wait around to sign. I'm not in any rush."

Sarah leaned the broom against the stall and stepped outside. The stalker had told her he had eyes everywhere. Maybe he'd hired this guy to watch her. Sucking in deep breaths, she counted and waited for her heart rate to slow. The bright sunshine and the sight of Lynn and Bruce helped. She wasn't alone.

Bruce glanced over at her and frowned. Of course, he would see her upset. The last thing she needed was to scare the horses again. She wiped her damp palms on her jeans and headed to the trash cans that needed emptying.

Her gaze darted to the parking lot. Morgan hadn't left, talking again on her phone by the Jag. It didn't make much sense to come to the farm and spend the day on the phone. Maybe she was hanging around to be with Bruce.

A car pulled in. A man and a pregnant woman got out. They approached the rink, the man with an uneven gate. Bruce met them by the fence. He shook hands with the man, clapping one on his shoulder as he nodded to him. Next, he greeted the woman with a big smile. She laughed at something he said. He led her to a bench, dropped to his knee, and put a hand on her arm. To whatever question he asked, she shook her head and adjusted her swollen belly.

Sarah stared. When Bruce smiled, his entire face transformed.

He and the man made their way toward Misty. Bruce dragged the mounting block next to the mare and stood back. Lynn emerged from the stables carrying a helmet. She shook hands with the vet and positioned herself on the other side of the horse. The man mounted on his own, but Sarah knew how fast Bruce could leap into action to help if necessary.

As Lynn led Misty around the rink, Bruce kept pace alongside and gave instructions to the vet. The man held his hands out to his sides as he rode a lap. After that, he took the reins and maneuvered the horse between some obstacles. Sarah headed to the end of the arena to dump a trash can but stopped along the way.

"Pretty amazing, huh?" The pregnant woman shifted on the bench.

Sarah glanced down at her. "I've never seen anything like this."

The lady labored to stand, holding a hand under her stomach. "Are you new here?"

"Yes. I'm Sarah."

The woman smiled and introduced herself as Hannah. She pointed to the man on the horse. "That's my husband, Charlie. He lost his leg in Afghanistan. Bruce saved his life." She rested her arm on the fence. "Twice, actually."

"Really?"

Hannah nodded. "Bruce led the mission to rescue these guys from enemy hands. It was a setup. They all should have died, but he somehow managed to get them out, despite being shot."

"Shot?" Holy shit.

"They all came home. Everyone injured, but none lost."

"Wow." Sarah followed the action in the arena.

Bruce jogged beside the horse calling out instructions.

"How did he save Charlie's life twice?"

Hannah waved her hand at the rink. "This program. It's done wonders. He went through a hard time and was depressed for a while, but this has given him confidence. He's excited about life again." She smiled and rubbed her belly. "Says he's going to ride with our child one day."

Sarah's gaze drifted to Charlie. He sat tall in the saddle and appeared to be in complete control. "He looks so comfortable riding."

"Yeah. He loves it. We come twice a week." Hannah shook her head. "We could never afford to do this if not for Bruce. The government provides some funds, but Bruce doesn't charge us for his time. He uses the money to pay the handler and horse expenses."

Generous and caring, he sure had a different side to him than the one around her. She shaded her eyes with a hand and gazed at him. "That's pretty amazing."

"Wait until you see the others. Four of them bus from the VA hospital. Bruce set up a pilot program, and the results are all positive. He's documenting everything and hoping to get some exposure so other farms might start their own programs."

Sarah glanced back at the arena. She'd have to keep a low profile if they ran a story and news cameras or reporters showed up.

Bruce gave Charlie a high five and smiled at Hannah from across the rink. Sarah's heart skipped. So far, he'd only scowled or frowned around her. God help her if he grinned like that at her.

The afternoon sun blazed, and beads of sweat formed on Hannah's forehead. Sarah touched her arm. "Would you like some water? It's really hot."

Hannah nodded. "I left mine on the counter at home. Would you mind?"

"Of course not. Be right back." Sarah fetched a bottle from the cooler in the stables. She glanced up to find the new boarder leaning against the outside wall of the empty stall, his eyes intent on her. He didn't look away or even pretend not to be staring. Her nerves jittered. She shut the cooler and hurried back to the arena and the safety of people. She'd have to keep her guard up around the guy.

In front of the rink, Lynn held Misty's reins as she talked to Charlie. Bruce and Hannah chatted on the side by the bench. Bruce glanced at Sarah when she held the bottle out to Hannah.

"Here you go."

"Thanks so much." Hannah twisted the top off and took a deep drink.

Sarah stole a glance at Bruce, whose focus shifted from Hannah back to her. Something flickered in his eyes. As usual, she had no clue what.

Behind Bruce, Morgan approached from the parking lot. She stopped and looked Sarah up and down in a way that would get a guy slapped. Wearing skintight clothes, Morgan had a body that could rival Marilyn Monroe's. Sarah met her gaze. Cold hazel eyes with the beginnings of crow's feet at the corners glowered back at her.

Sarah guessed Morgan to be in her late thirties. Overly tight cheeks hinted at cosmetic surgery, and her perfectly applied makeup made Sarah aware of her own bare face. The only thing on hers was the sun and probably some dirt. No mistaking the hostility from the Ice Queen, who looked familiar for some reason.

Morgan cleared her throat and Bruce turned. Her bitter expression changed into a beaming smile as she said hello to Hannah and then glanced at Sarah.

Bruce introduced Sarah to Morgan.

"Is she a new patient?" Morgan asked.

She spoke as if Sarah wasn't there. Stalked, tired, stressed out, and ignored, she'd had enough. "No, I work here."

"Really?" Morgan tipped her head and raised a perfectly painted eyebrow.

Sarah planted her hands on her hips. Bring it on.

Morgan shrugged and rested her palm on Bruce's shoulder. "I stopped by to drop off my check to Debbie and see if you wanted to ride with me later?"

The way she touched him implied a familiarity. Maybe they were sleeping together. Sarah's chest filled and tightened. She refused to think about why.

Bruce checked his watch. "I have patients until four."

"Perfect. I'll come back then." Morgan patted his arm.

"Okay. Batal could use the workout."

Morgan sauntered toward the barn.

"I better get to work. Nice meeting you, Hannah." Sarah headed to the can by the fence.

After dumping the trash, she returned to the stables. No sign of the ghost gawker, but his Vette was still in the lot. She'd picked up a rake to muck out the last stall when a huge spider dropped from the rafters onto her shoulder. She gasped and flung it off.

The creature from hell skittered across the floor to the corner. She shuddered and pictured her father in the hospital, deathly ill from a bite, with tubes and IV's hooked up. Her insides shook as she smacked at the spider with the rake, giving chase as it scurried along the sidewall. The last swing was a direct hit. Goo spewed from the hairy carcass, but she continued to hack away at it. "Die already, you bastard."

Someone scoffed and she whirled around.

Bruce stood in the aisle.

"What's so funny? That thing landed on me."

He waved a hand around the stall. "You're pummeling a one-inch bug with a five-foot rake."

Make fun of her. Great. He wasn't the one who'd sat next to a hospital bed for two weeks while none of the antibiotics worked on her father's infection. She blew at her bangs.

Bruce leaned against the stall and shook his head. "You do realize there are rats and bugs in a barn, right?"

Heat scorched a path to her ears. She threw the rake aside, stomped over to him, and thrust her chin up. "Yeah, I'm pretty sure I've seen a *big* rat."

For a split second, his eyes flared wider. He hitched a brow and pushed off the wall. "Really?"

Uh-oh.

Angry blood coursed through her veins. She had to crane her neck to meet his gaze, but she didn't back down. His sheer size, all muscles and man, smelling of musk and shooting daggers with his eyes, made her mouth go dry and other parts wet. Traitorous hormones.

None of it mattered. This gig was over. She'd called him a rat to his face. Surely, he'd tell Debbie not to hire her.

"Glad I could provide some entertainment." She grabbed the rake and swiped the prongs across the hay to clean off the dead spider goo. "I've done everything asked of me today. You could eat off the floor of this place, and all you can do is make fun of me." She flipped the rake and dug the other side into the hay. "To think I actually was going to apologize to you."

"For what?"

When she glanced up, for once those deep, blue eyes of his weren't mocking her.

Images of the day flashed through her mind. Bruce in the arena with Charlie, bent down on a knee talking to Hannah, calming the rider and the runaway horse. She glanced at the tattoo on his arm, a tribute to the military. He might annoy the ever-living hell out of her, but he put himself on the line for everyone else. Besides, he couldn't know her history with spiders.

The pulse throbbing in her neck slowed, and a long sigh escaped, taking with it all her pent-up fury. "I'm sorry. I misjudged you. Hannah told me all about your work and how you rescued those men in Afghanistan."

He crossed his arms and glowered. "First Greg, now Hannah. What is it about you that makes people so chatty?"

She shrugged. "Doesn't matter, I saw how much Charlie enjoyed riding." She shifted the rake in her hand. "I just wanted to tell you I think what you're doing is pretty amazing. Hannah says you're their hero."

"No." He held his hands up. "I came back in one piece. Those guys are the heroes. Don't ever mistake that," he said in a firm voice.

Huh. Now it all made sense. The survivor's guilt he must carry. A person didn't have to lose a limb to be a hero. She opened her mouth to say something but stopped at the sight of his tortured face. Raw pain radiated from his eyes. His mask had dropped.

"You need something, Morgan?" Debbie's voice came from the other side of the wall.

Morgan stood outside the stall near the opening, her gaze on Bruce. She smiled and faced Debbie. "Yes. I was looking for you."

"Well, I'm not in there." Debbie stepped up to Morgan and frowned.

"Just wanted to pay for this month." Morgan handed Debbie a check.

"I need to talk to you," Debbie said to Bruce.

Sarah's stomach balled. Decision time. Guess she'd be sleeping in the car again. She shoved a strand of hair back and met his gaze. "Go ahead and say what you want. I've done my best today."

"Out there." Debbie motioned to the entrance.

Bruce grumbled something, and their footsteps trailed off.

Morgan made a sound like a stifled giggle.

Fed up with people laughing at her, Sarah smacked the end of the rake against the ground and glared at Morgan. "Do you have some kind of problem?"

"Me?" Morgan brought a manicured hand to her chest. "No, hon. But it looks like you do." She smirked and strutted around the corner.

Sarah frowned. She'd already checked out all the help-wanted ads, and the fumes in her gas tank wouldn't get her far. Maybe she should have been nicer to Bruce, but the man pushed her buttons. And now her fate rested in his hands.

* * *

Bruce followed Debbie outside and around the corner of the barn.

"So what's the verdict?" Debbie cocked her head.

Much as he hated to admit it, the barn was spit-shine clean. Aside from her attitude with him, Sarah had gone out of her way to be courteous and helpful to everyone else. He only had one card to play. "I think she can handle the chores. I don't know what or who she's running from, though."

"Someone has her skittish as a scarecrow at a bonfire. I'd bet an ex-boyfriend. Probably an abusive one." Debbie rubbed her elbow as her mouth pulled into a tight line.

Shit. That's why she'd hired Sarah. Hard-as-nails Debbie had been through her own round of misery. Not that she'd ever speak of it. A tight ball of fire burned in his gut. Nothing worse than a man who raised his hand to a woman.

Debbie cleared her throat and planted her feet wide. "So what's the deal? I have work to do."

The last thing Debbie would want was sympathy. Whatever had happened had to be too far in the past for him to do anything about, but he hated that someone had hurt her.

Bruce kept his voice neutral. "You worried about Sarah bringing any danger to the farm?"

"Well, it's not fair of me to say, as it isn't your job, but not with you around. And I own a shotgun."

She'd nailed that one. If some bastard showed up, he would take care of him. And both Joe and Debbie knew how to shoot. Maybe she'd learned so she could defend herself against whoever had abused her.

Debbie scratched her head. "I gotta say, Sarah has spunk. Risked her life for someone she didn't even know."

"It was a stupid thing to do."

"Won't argue, but it tells me something about her." Debbie held her hands up. "Look, I told you this was your call. From what I can tell, she pulled her weight today, and then some, but obviously something's eating at you, so I'll let her go."

Yeah, something was eating at him that he didn't want to address. But he couldn't let her get fired because of him. He'd deal. Shut the thing down and treat her like any other employee at the ranch. Maybe if he stopped being so short with her, they could get along. Hell, he had nowhere to go but up from being considered a member of the rodent family. From now on, he'd act the same to her as he would anyone else on the farm. "No. Keep her on."

"You sure?" Debbie eyed him.

"Yeah. I'm sure."

He had this.

CHAPTER 6

WITH THE STALL FINISHED, Sarah turned to leave and found Debbie standing in the way.

"You did a good job today," she said.

"Thanks."

"I'm heading back to the house to make a list for the store. Come up to get the truck keys and some money."

"Oh?"

"Make sure you pick up whatever you need for breakfast tomorrow. Last thing I want to see at six in the morning is Greg crying on my doorstep."

"Tomorrow? I'm hired?" Relief flooded her body, turning her knees to rubber. Thank God she had a place to sleep and a job.

"Yeah. Trial's over." Debbie nodded and strode past her.

For whatever reason, Bruce must have told Debbie not to fire her. Maybe he realized how hard Sarah had worked after all. She glanced around the stables. Nothing but horses and hidden spiders. Just as well, because it would probably kill Bruce to accept her thanks.

She put the rake away and went to the tack room to get her backpack. After slinging her arms into the straps, she took a step and froze. The creepy new boarder blocked the exit. He didn't even attempt to hide his head-to-toe perusal of her. Her belly twisted at the lewd look in his almost-black eyes.

"Do you work here?" The man's gaze stalled at Sarah's breasts.

"Yes." She should have kept her gun in the backpack, not the purse in her room. With all the people around, she hadn't expected any danger in the stables. Now she appeared to be alone.

Up close, the man skeeved her out even more. His dark eyes contrasted with his pale face and light brown hair. Maybe in his mid to late thirties, he stood a good ten inches over her.

"I thought so. I saw you sweeping earlier."

Sweat trickled down her neck. "Is there something I can help you with? I'm on my way out."

"I'm waiting to sign some papers. Going to be boarding here. Maybe you can fill me in a little more about the farm." He stepped into the room.

She glanced behind him at the empty barn. "This is my first day, so you might want to ask Debbie."

"First day, huh? That's a coincidence, me showing up as you start. Might be a lucky sign. I just moved here yesterday." A predatory grin turned up the corners of his mouth.

She couldn't tell if he was flirting or playing cat and mouse. A wave of nausea rolled around in her belly.

"I was watching you earlier. You move so gracefully. Are you a gymnast or maybe a dancer?"

"No. Look, I really need to get going, so—"

"Have you ridden a long time?" He took another step closer, blocking her way out.

"No. I actually don't ride. I—"

"You work here, but you don't ride? How odd." He rubbed his chin. "I bought a horse this week but haven't ridden long myself. We seem to have a lot in common." He held out a hand. "By the way, I'm Todd."

God, she didn't want to touch him, but he blocked her path. Short of knocking him over, she couldn't get around him. She shook his hand, glad he wore gloves. "Sarah."

He didn't let go. "I expect we'll be seeing a lot of each other. I wasn't sure if this place would be up to my standards, but it's close to my new home. I'm convinced now I've chosen the right farm."

Sarah tugged her hand out of his grasp, her ears hot. "I work here. That's it. I'm going to be late, so if you don't mind…" She tried to push past him, but he didn't budge. The overpowering scent of his thick cologne gagged her. The odor clung to him like skunk spray on a Bearded Collie.

He looked down his nose at her. "No need to be rude." He stepped aside and waved a hand in a mock bow. "I'm boarding my horse next week. I'll keep an eye out for you, Sarah."

The way he said her name sent chills up her spine. She hurried past him and headed back to the house, sure if she turned around she'd find his gaze on her ass.

She could only pray it was a coincidence he'd shown up at the same time she did. Her heart pounded as she took long strides across the field. She stopped for a second and glanced back at the barn. His car remained in the lot, but no sign of him. She hoped the man was only a womanizer, a strange thought under normal circumstances, which hers weren't. Still, she couldn't run from everyone. For now, she'd keep an eye on him and see if he did anything suspicious aside from ogle her.

When she reached the house, she squinted at the shiny gold lock on the in-law suite door. Someone had installed a deadbolt. A huge weight dropped from her shoulders. She entered the studio to find a new set of keys on the coffee table. Perfect.

She needed time to stop at the library to check her email. She'd set up another account only Anne and Maddie knew, given them her password to the old one, and asked them to copy and paste any new email message the stalker sent.

Grabbing her purse, she headed to the bedroom. She dug inside for her wallet, fingered her fake license, and slid the real one out from behind. The original was her only link to her old life and proof of her identity, but she shouldn't keep it on her. She pulled open the top drawer and tucked the license in the back beneath her underwear. No one would snoop around in there.

After taking a deep breath, she climbed the stairs and entered the main kitchen. Debbie sat at the table writing on a notepad.

"Thanks for the new lock," Sarah said.

Debbie looked up, a blank expression on her face.

"On my door?"

She snorted. "So that's what he's been up to."

"Who?"

Debbie waved a hand and went back to writing. "Joe. I didn't know anything about it, and he's been MIA since early this morning." She stood and handed Sarah some keys, the list, and an envelope. "There's plenty of money to buy groceries for the week."

Sarah would have to come up with some meal plans. At best, she could do basic dinners. She glanced at the large corner cabinet. Cookbooks lined the shelves. Maybe she'd find some simple recipes. "I'll be up early and have breakfast ready by six."

"This should be interesting." Debbie's lips curved with the hint of a smile.

"I'll cook in my suite and bring it up when I'm done." That way she wouldn't be an easy target, lit-up in the bright kitchen.

"Suit yourself. That's not part of the job, but if you want to, I'm sure as hell not gonna stop ya. I'll tell Joe, since he usually shows up around then."

If Joe didn't live with Debbie, maybe they weren't a couple. Sarah would have to ferret out all the relationships.

Debbie told her the truck should be down by the arena. As Sarah trekked across the yard, she planned the rest of the week. She'd have no problem making breakfasts. Dinners would be simple until she had a chance to find new recipes. As a dancer, she hadn't spent much time in the kitchen.

Her chest squeezed. Both of her parents had to be worried sick. They lived in Florida, and she'd told them little about the stalker. With her father's heart issues, she didn't want to upset him. She'd saddled Anne with the task of keeping them posted. Poor Anne. She worked hard and didn't need the extra stress. A heaviness pushed against her breastbone. It could be a long time before she saw any of them again.

She reached the stables and glanced at the parking area. No truck in sight, but Todd's car was gone.

Bruce came around the corner and stopped short. "Hey."

She blinked a few times to clear her tear-filled eyes.

"What's wrong?" He frowned.

For someone so detached from her, he sure homed in on her emotions fast enough. "Nothing. I'm looking for the pickup."

He didn't say anything right away, studying her face. At last, he blew out a breath. "I think it's behind the barn. Let's check."

"I can find it. I know you're busy."

"I'm between patients."

They walked around the side of the stables and found the truck.

"Joe leaves it here sometimes," Bruce said.

The sun shined down from the bright, blue sky that matched his eyes.

Her face heated, but not from the rays. She twisted a lock of hair around a finger. He seemed to be in a half-decent mood. Maybe they could start fresh. "Hey, I, umm…wanted to thank you for whatever you said to Debbie to keep me on."

He raised an eyebrow. "How do you know what—"

"It doesn't matter. I just wanted to let you know I appreciated it."

"You earned the job."

At last, some validation from him.

The edges of his mouth twitched. "And you proved you had the killer instinct to do whatever it took to stay."

Her shoulders tensed. "The spider? Are you still making fun of me?"

His smile widened. Mischief sparkled in his eyes, and something fluttered under her rib cage.

Now that she'd seen the softer side of him, his size and rough-around-the-edges direct approach didn't intimidate her as much. She'd never been scared of him, but the alpha energy he exuded took some getting used to.

"You know how to drive a stick?"

"Umm…" She peered into the truck window, pressing her forehead against the glass. A manual four-speed. She could handle that.

Bruce's breath warmed the back of her neck when he spoke. "What are you looking at?"

The deep timbre of his voice close to her ear vibrated against her skin, causing goose bumps to pop up. He placed a hand on the side of the truck window and glanced inside as well, bringing his head down next to hers. Her stomach fluttered.

When she turned around, he inched back but kept his hand on the window. She stared at his five-o'clock shadow. Trapped with her back against the truck, she dug her nails into her palms, fighting the urge to run a hand along the sexy stubble. She moistened her lips and raised her gaze.

His eyes darkened, and he leaned a hair closer.

Her breath caught. He'd be sure to see her erratic pulse thudding in her neck if his gaze wasn't fixed on her mouth.

"There you are," Joe said as he rounded the corner of the barn.

Bruce yanked his hand away from the window and took a big step back.

She pushed off the truck and smoothed her hands down the bottom of her shirt. Holy hell. So the attraction went both ways.

Joe chewed on a toothpick and looked long at Bruce before addressing Sarah. "Debbie said you needed the truck. I was coming to get it for you."

"We found it." More heat rose to her face.

Joe nodded.

Awkward silence filled the space.

"Thank you for the new lock," Sarah said.

Bruce's gaze shot to Joe. A slow, smug smile formed. "No wonder you weren't around this morning."

Joe shrugged and waved a hand. "Been on my list for a while. Finally got around to it." He took the toothpick out and gestured to the house. "Didn't do the windows yet. Let me know when a good time is for that, Sarah."

"Well, I'll be gone for a couple of hours, but whatever works for you."

He cleared his throat. "Okay. I didn't want to invade your privacy."

"Thanks. I appreciate it."

"I didn't know if she could drive a four-speed," Bruce said.

"So that's what you were doing?" Joe faced him. "Making sure she could drive a stick?" He raised an eyebrow.

Bruce crossed his arms. "Yeah. While you were installing new locks."

The two men stared each other down.

Sarah hid a smile as their testosterone levels spiked off the charts. "It's been a while, but yes, I can."

Both men turned to her.

"What?" Bruce asked.

"Drive a stick. And I better get going, or there won't be any dinner." She hit the Unlock button. "Do you two eat here?"

"Sometimes." They answered in unison, grimaced, and shot a disgusted look at each other.

Guys hated when that happened. Sarah bit her cheek to stifle a laugh. "Well then, I guess I'll make enough for a crowd each night, and leftovers can be for lunch."

She opened the door and hopped into the truck. The engine ground to life and she put it in first gear and waved. She managed to pull out like a pro without bucking or stalling. Mental high five.

When she glanced in the rearview mirror, Bruce and Joe each had a hand on a hip, heads cocked, facing the truck. This time she did laugh. That would have pissed them off, too, if they could see themselves. Twins.

Bruce worked hard at it, but his armor chipped away the more she discovered about him. And apparently, the crazy attraction between them wasn't one-sided, but no matter. Her situation didn't allow for relationships.

Mark had taught her that hard lesson.

She'd wasted two years of her life dating Mark, the big stage producer who had to be seen in the right social circles. He couldn't handle when she didn't want to go out anymore, preferring to stay home out of sight. At first, he didn't even believe the stalker existed until the notes appeared, and then he blamed her and said she must have encouraged the man.

Mark had dumped her when things got personal. The stalker threatened to hack into his production company's accounts and deplete the funds. The next day, Sarah had gone to Mark's apartment to talk to him about moving. She arrived to find everything she'd had at his place boxed up on the porch. He hadn't even let her inside. Told her he wouldn't leave his job and couldn't risk being with her anymore.

She hadn't been enough. Not worth the effort. She never would be for anyone. Even before Mark, the people she'd dated couldn't put up with her demanding schedule. They bailed as well. Her throat constricted. Destined to be alone, always looking over her shoulder and planning where to hide next. Some life. No one would ever come along with her on this ride.

Hell, she didn't want it for herself.

She shook her head to clear the memories. What mattered now was survival. A tendril of worry wrapped around her lungs. In a few short minutes, she'd find out if her escape plan had worked.

CHAPTER 7

Sarah left the grocery store and parked at the library, planning to stay only long enough to check her email. She took a seat at a computer and opened the first of two messages from Anne.

Sarah,
I know this email I forwarded from the stalker is going to upset you. It scared the crap out of me. He's sick. Truly sick. But we already knew that.
Don't worry about me. I'm keeping a close eye on everything, and he hasn't tried to communicate with Maddie or me. We both have alarm systems. Tell me a time when you can get to a computer, and I'll go to the library. We can chat through the public ones. Or call me on the throwaway phone if you'd rather. I hope you are safe wherever you are.

A cloak of dread suffocated Sarah's lungs. Her hand shook as she brought up the stalker's message.

Dear Sarah,

It's been over a week since you left. I'm disappointed that you continue to listen to other people and follow their advice. All of them underestimate my resources and what lengths I will go to for us to be together. Nothing is more important.

The red herring that led to Seattle cost me considerable money to chase down, but it doesn't matter. I have plenty. The credit card charges showing up all over the country might have fooled someone less savvy. My source informed me about your abandoned car as well. None of these tricks will work. You are wasting our precious time letting others influence you. I know that all you want is to be with me.

You must learn there are consequences for following other people's advice. Your sisters might need a lesson for meddling in our relationship.

You're the one. The true one. And you need to come back. As I told you at your apartment, I have eyes everywhere. I'm watching to see what you will do. If you don't declare our love and return on your own, I will bring you back. Time away from those who seek to keep us apart is all you need.

Come back.

Blood rushed through her body, and a small moan escaped. The librarian looked at Sarah. She placed a hand on the side of her head to hide her face. The sick bastard would never stop, and now Maddie and Anne could be in danger. Alec had warned her some stalkers used all their resources and refused to give up. But she'd hoped and prayed hers would be the type to get frustrated and move on. Guess not.

She glanced around the room. He could be watching her right now. No, that wasn't logical. He'd never know if or when she'd show up at the library.

A sharp pain throbbed in her forehead. She'd never had headaches until now.

Maybe she should stop conversing with her sisters. The crazed maniac blamed them for her leaving. He'd sent pictures of Anne and Maddie, which meant he at least watched them. And they might have alarm systems, but he'd found a way past hers.

The security system that never went off...the surveillance cameras destroyed...She squeezed her eyes shut tight and failed to stop the memory of the time he'd attacked her.

She had been in the shower when a noise had come from the bedroom. She'd slammed her palm against the valve and shut off the water.

The floorboards in the bedroom squeaked. He'd found a way in, even with all her precautions. Her heart beat triple time. She ripped the shower curtain across the track, raced to the door, and turned the lock on the knob.

The new alarm system should have gone off. With no window, she couldn't escape or yell for help, and she'd left her phone in the bedroom. Her legs shook. She steeled her nerves and scanned the room for anything to use as a weapon. Nothing but a pink disposable razor and a hand mirror.

A shadow appeared under the door.

She gripped the knob tightly with both hands.

"Sarah?" A muffled, male voice spoke from the other side over the noise of the fan. "What are you doing here? I don't like surprises. My records show you should be at the dance studio until nine tonight. Nine, nine, nine."

He punctuated the words with three hard knocks.

She flinched at each rap.

It made no sense to talk to him. The man was insane. Alec had said not to communicate with the stalker.

His voice, frayed with madness, sounded through the door. "This is not what I had planned. I came to leave proof of my devotion, but you made me hurry. Now I'm not sure it's done perfectly."

What was he talking about?

"I wish you'd take my phone calls. You know we're meant to be together."

When she didn't answer, his footsteps moved away from the door. She snatched her robe from the hook, shoved her arms through the sleeves, and cinched the belt.

A smash came from the bedroom followed by heavy bangs. She cringed and bit her lip. Her pulse pounded under her jaw.

His voice came close again. "These mini-cams won't work anymore."

A piece of plastic shot under the door and ricocheted off her foot. She jumped and stifled a scream. He'd found the surveillance cameras. Damn. Now she'd never see what he looked like.

"You may not know a lot about technology, but I do, and these are as cheap as they come. Another lame attempt from the incompetent cops, I assume."

Her head ached. Maybe she could fake him out. She pretended to dial 911. "I'm calling the police."

"Finally. You're talking to me. I've waited so long to hear your voice again—"

"Hello? I need help. A man broke into my apartment, and he's threatening me." She prayed he'd believe the act.

"Why are you calling the cops? You know I'm much smarter than they are. I can hack into any system. In less than five seconds, I flushed out their pitiful attempt to lure me to that fake meeting with you last month. And the alarm here? A joke. I'm the only one who can keep you safe."

His shadow under the door disappeared. More sounds of destruction came from the other room.

As a dancer, she had strength and agility on her side. But small in stature, she'd have a tough time overpowering a grown man, even with what she'd learned from her self-defense classes. She needed a weapon.

She yanked open the top drawer of the vanity and rifled through the contents. A hairbrush, scrunchies, and a pack of bobby pins. Her gaze traveled to the hand mirror on the counter. She seized the handle and smashed the face against the sink. Glass shot through the air and landed around her bare feet.

Shit.

She grabbed a towel to pick up a jagged piece.

The man returned and spoke in a calmer voice. "No one understands me but you. I'm the one you love. Only me. Remember that. You don't want to end up like Audrey."

Sarah's mouth went dry. Whatever had happened to Audrey, whoever she was, didn't sound good. Sarah had to scare him into leaving. "The cops are on their way."

"I'm disappointed that you called them. I'm going, but don't forget, I have eyes everywhere. Someone is always watching you."

Bile rose in her throat and she gagged. Had he found other people to spy on her too?

"This is my last warning. Accept our love, or you'll face the consequences. If I can't have you, no one will."

Her knees buckled. The lunatic meant to kill her. He'd taken his obsession to a whole new level.

The bedroom fell quiet. Maybe he'd left. She waited several agonizing minutes. Sweat poured down her forehead into her eyes. She took a deep breath, held the shard up, and eased the door open a few inches.

The man's hand snaked in and grabbed the edge of the door.

She had gasped and thrown her shoulder against it to trap his forearm, slashing him with the piece of broken mirror from his wrist to his index finger. Her stomach had roiled as she pressed deep and hit bone.

Someone touched her shoulder. "Are you okay?"

Sarah opened her eyes and blinked at the blurry bookshelves in front of her. When they came back into focus, she glanced around at the people staring at her from their tables. Her chest ached and sweat chilled her numb body. She had to get out of the public library before she made more of a scene and drew attention. Someone might remember her.

"You look confused. Do you need assistance?" The librarian gently patted Sarah's shoulder.

"N-no. I'm okay."

"Are you sure?"

God, she couldn't breathe, let alone talk. With a nod, she shoved to her feet, grabbed her purse, and hurried to the exit. As soon as she was outside, she stumbled to the truck. She climbed in and put a hand on her ribs.

Her lungs screamed for air.

White spots appeared before her eyes.

Until her vision cleared, she couldn't drive anywhere. She forced herself to take a deep breath and blow it out slowly. The pins of light faded. She repeated it three times, and the crazy pounding in her chest subsided. Leaning her head back against the rest, she swallowed and waited for her body to settle down.

She started the engine and drove back to the farm, praying she wouldn't run into anyone right away. Her nightmare hadn't ended with her disappearance. Now that he hunted her, she had to figure out a way to stay alive.

CHAPTER 8

SARAH STIRRED a sizzling skillet of onions and ground turkey. Her second batch after burning the first. Two hours had done nothing to calm her fried nerves. She needed to get the meal ready and go back to her suite to think.

"Something smells good," Joe said as he entered with Debbie.

Sarah glanced up. She fought to make her voice sound normal. "It's tacos tonight. I'll make something fancier when I have more time to plan a menu."

Debbie moved to the sink, turned the water on, then squirted soap into her hands. "You won't hear us complaining."

"I put your change there." Sarah pointed the spatula across the room to the cabinet with the recipe books. She tossed a hot pad onto the counter for the skillet. "Everything's ready. I'll come back in a bit to clean up."

"Aren't you gonna eat?" Debbie frowned.

"Not yet." With her stomach in a tight ball, if she ate, she'd throw up. She hurried to her suite and closed the door behind her. Taking a deep breath, she picked up a bag from the coffee table and pulled out a pair of blackout curtains. The thrift store owner had let her trade a pair of sunglasses for them. Sarah never expected to have to barter her personal belongings. But she'd do what she needed.

She stood on the couch to take down the rod. Bright gold locks shined in the sun. Joe must have replaced them while she was gone. God bless him. She put up the new drapes. They should keep peeping Todd's out.

She stepped to the wall and flicked on the lights. At least now, she wouldn't have to trip through the room in the dark. Funny how the smallest things took on new meaning. Stuff normal people never thought twice about.

Satisfied, she sat on the couch and shut her eyes. When she opened them, an hour had passed. The kitchen still needed cleaning, and that was her job. She jumped up, raced to the steps, and flung the door open to find Bruce seated at the table eating a taco. Next to him, Joe held a steaming mug. Both men looked over.

"I didn't think to make coffee. I'm sorry," she said.

Bruce's gaze darted to Joe, who gave a slight nod, like an I-told-you-so look, and took a sip before standing. "Dinner was good. We can brew our own. Always have. See you tomorrow."

He shrugged on a light jacket and went out the front door.

Left alone with Bruce, but still freaked out from the crazy email, for once her hormones weren't raging over him. "Did everyone get to eat? Morgan, the girls?"

She scanned the fields outside the window as she grabbed a dirty bowl. The quicker she cleaned up, the sooner she could return to her suite. Away from all eyes. Her body ached, her mind had turned to mush, and she needed to wake up early to make breakfast. With the new lock on her bedroom window, maybe she would sleep better.

"Morgan?" Bruce's eyebrows raised.

"Yes. Doesn't she eat here?" Sarah faced him. Couples ate together.

"No." He stood. "Why would she?"

"I don't know. Debbie said she never knows who's showing up for dinner." Sarah picked up some clear wrap and ripped off a piece.

Bruce crossed the kitchen. "I'm not done eating, and Debbie said you didn't have dinner. You're going to need food to keep up the pace."

So she'd become the topic of conversation. While that was annoying, at the same time, they were looking out for her. People must be more trusting in the country. She could have run off with all Debbie's money and the truck. Sarah glanced at the taco fixings, and her stomach rumbled, but she wouldn't be able to handle the grease.

Bruce went to the refrigerator and pulled out a container. He seemed to know his way around the kitchen.

"Try this leftover chicken soup." He placed it on the counter and returned to the table.

She glanced at the plastic tub. This was exactly what she needed. After heating the soup, she sat across from him. She blew on a spoon before putting it in her mouth. Eat. Sleep. Wake up, and survive another day. That's what she had to do right now.

Bruce took a bite of his taco. "These are good."

"Nothing special."

He shrugged. "Debbie has one thing she can make. Chicken soup and biscuits from a can. Trust me, anything else is fancy."

"Really?"

He nodded. "She runs a horse farm. No time for cooking. Whatever you make will be better."

Sarah couldn't focus on small talk with the stalker's email replaying in her mind. He'd mentioned his source, so multiple people were searching for her. She tried to spoon up more broth, but her hand shook.

"What happened in town today?" Bruce asked in a low voice.

She glanced up. He wore a frown and stared pointedly at her shaking spoon. Crap. She shouldn't have sat with him. He observed too much. Although, to be fair, she probably looked like hell, and she sucked at hiding her emotions.

"I got groceries." She stirred the soup and waited for him to say something, but he didn't. The silence put her more on edge. Maybe she could change the subject. "So what's the story with Debbie and Joe? Are they together? I don't want to say the wrong thing."

"Yes, but they keep separate places and stay at each other's once in a while."

"I see." She pushed the bowl aside and tried to stand, but he shot a hand across the table and pulled her arm down.

"Are you going to answer my question?"

His gaze bored into hers, demanding a response.

"I did. Please, let it go." She bit her lower lip and held her breath, certain he'd press the issue from the determined look on his face.

Instead, he gave her arm a gentle squeeze. "Breathe."

She took a deep breath and let it out slowly, like she had before in the truck. The skin on her arm tingled under the warmth of his hand.

"Take another one."

As she did, a calmness settled in, but it didn't last. Bruce touching her. That spelled trouble. She had no room for the feelings he evoked in her.

"I better get this kitchen cleaned up." She stood.

Bruce grabbed his plate and rose. She picked up a serving platter from the counter, avoiding eye contact. He'd seen through her enough for one night. He carried his plate to the sink, rinsed, and put it in the dishwasher.

"Sarah."

She swung around.

"You're a terrible liar," he said.

She shifted from one foot to the other. So she'd been told. He stood planted in front of her.

"I can't force you to tell me what's going on, but you're not fooling anyone."

A weight dragged down her lungs. If only she could.

"When you're ready"—he took a step back—"talk to me."

She picked at the hem of her shirt as he headed to the door. Maybe it would be better if someone else did know. He could keep an eye out. But she'd have to trust him not to tell anyone else.

As Bruce pushed open the door, Sarah called, "Wait."

CHAPTER 9

HER EYES GAVE AWAY the inner battle. Bruce's training in body language came in handy. The quick blinks and the way she tugged on her shirt indicated uncertainty and nervousness. She opened her mouth, only to shut it again.

"What?" he asked.

"I'm…not sure what time you get here in the morning, but breakfast will be ready at six." She crossed her arms and rubbed them.

Shit.

He'd been sure she was about to open up, but she'd chickened out just as fast. His spirits fell. He couldn't help her if she wouldn't tell him what was going on. Then again, he hadn't exactly made himself approachable. Whatever scared her had to be major because the fiercely independent woman he'd worked around all day had gone down the rabbit hole.

"That's not what you were going to say, and we both know it." He shook his head. Couldn't force her to talk. "I don't get here that early. See you later."

He made his way to his truck, resisting the urge to go back and try again. As he drove, he couldn't erase the haunting image of Sarah's face when she'd burst into the kitchen. Something must have terrified her in town. She'd even walked differently after she returned. Her graceful movements had turned stiff and tense.

Could be an ex-boyfriend. Anger at whoever caused her to live in fear made his blood stew. She complicated his life by making the horses skittish and possibly bringing a threat to the farm, yet he wanted to dig deeper and find out more about her. The exact opposite of what he should do if he intended to keep everyone at the ranch safe. She had grit and guts, and she cared for people, but she didn't belong there.

Growing up, he'd been the one that people always turned to for help. He'd spent five years of his life fighting for people's freedom. But no war or tactical plan could keep everyone safe. And he had no idea what had spooked her. He couldn't help unless she opened up.

He slowed to allow a car to pass him. Scared as she was, she would no doubt run away soon. If he let her get too close, he'd be left with another gaping hole in his heart. No way. Not again. He'd do what he could to keep an eye out for her while at the farm. Beyond that, his hands were tied. He stopped for a red light and set his jaw.

Better to keep his distance.

* * *

Sarah yawned, flipped on the lights, and threw on some clothes. She'd made sure all the ingredients for the morning meal were in her suite refrigerator and the proper cookware on the counter. Today's breakfast consisted of banana pancakes, scrambled eggs, and a cheesy hash brown bake. True to her word, at six o'clock she had the food on the counter, plates and utensils out, and coffee brewed. Hard as it was, she had to act like nothing worried her and put on a happy face. She couldn't let her nerves show. She'd failed horribly at it yesterday. Today had to go better.

Debbie strode into the kitchen and stopped short. "Oh, I forgot about this."

A second later, Joe and Greg came in from the mudroom. Warmth spread through Sarah. They'd shown up. "Help yourselves. It's all ready."

Greg's eyes widened, and he licked his lips.

"Leave some for us," Joe said, making his way to the coffee machine.

Greg dragged his gaze from the food to Sarah, his face flushing.

The front door opened, and Bruce marched in. He must have changed his mind about coming. As usual, a shiver ran through her body at the sight of him. Damp hair, shirt snug against his pecs, she couldn't help but stare. Her stomach flip-flopped.

He raked a hand through his hair and turned to Joe, who stood by the coffee maker. "Your text was pretty cryptic. What did you need me for this morning?"

Joe handed Debbie a filled mug and dumped some sugar in his own. "Help with the trailer."

"Now what's wrong with it?"

"Need to replace some rusted springs." Joe took a sip of coffee.

"Are you serious? This couldn't wait?" Bruce frowned. "And since when do you need my help?"

Joe sauntered to the counter, where Greg stood piling up his plate. "I want to use it this afternoon, and two of us will fix it faster."

Huh, maybe she wasn't the only one who got under Bruce's skin. She smiled as Greg poured so much syrup his eggs floated and then took a seat at the table.

"Might as well eat since I am. We can't start until I'm finished." Joe grabbed a plate.

"I'm not done with this conversation."

"Then talk while I'm eating." Joe brought his food to the table and sat. He took a bite of the hash browns. "Mmm. These are great." He waved his empty fork at Sarah. "You put cheese in them?"

"Yup. Cheddar."

Greg swirled his eggs in the syrup. "Sure don't get food like this in the morning at home."

"You put onions in here?" Joe inspected the potatoes on his plate.

"Yes. You like them?" Sarah snuck a look at Bruce, who stood stiff and stoic. *Grouchy* didn't begin to describe his demeanor.

Bruce's gaze went back and forth from her to Joe. "I can't believe this."

Joe glanced at him and finished chewing. "What's got your skivvies in a wad?"

"Really?" Bruce glowered. "I got up at five thirty, took a shower, rushed over here to help you, and you're sitting here swapping recipes."

"Well, that's just stupid." Joe took a sip of coffee and dished up some eggs. "Taking a shower before coming to work at the farm."

Greg choked on his drink, spitting out juice.

Sarah bit back a grin at Joe's not-the-least-bit-intimidated attitude.

Bruce scowled across the room at Joe, who continued cutting up his pancakes. After a beat, Bruce snatched the newspaper from the counter and stomped through the door.

This could be trouble. Sarah stepped to the screen and peeked out at him as he smacked the paper down on the wicker table.

"He's gonna be a pain in the ass to work with if he doesn't get some food," Joe said. "You mind fixing him a plate, Sarah?"

"Throwing me to the wolves?"

"You can handle him."

Debbie brought her coffee to the table and took a seat next to Joe. "I figured I'd wait to eat until all the commotion was over."

With Bruce's current mood, it might not be over. Sarah loaded two plates and took them out to the porch. Bruce had opened the paper, but he gazed at the fields.

"You didn't have to bring me that." He stood.

Sarah scanned the area. The morning sun reflected off something shiny near the tree line. She squinted. Nothing natural in the woods should reflect light. Her shoulder blades pinched together.

Bruce crossed the deck and stopped in front of her, blocking her view. He took one of the plates. "Come, sit down."

She wanted to go inside, but he might ask questions if she refused. No one would mess with her while Bruce sat inches away. She nodded and followed him to the table, sneaking a glance back at the woods. The reflection was gone. A smidge of tension eased.

He put his plate down and pulled out a chair for her. "Joe pisses me off sometimes."

"He does seem to push your buttons."

"I don't know what the hell he was thinking. This isn't an emergency."

"No idea." Sarah shrugged and took a bite of hash browns. She'd stay out of it.

Bruce dove into his plate. "The potatoes are good."

"That's because there's cheddar and onions in them."

"Smart-ass." He forked some eggs, but the side of his mouth twitched. "You realize you just made things worse with Greg, right?"

"What do you mean?"

"The kid has a major crush on you. And now you're not only pretty, but you can cook."

Bruce thought she was pretty? Heat flushed through her body. "Well, I'm glad my trick to get him here early worked."

"Judging by the way he enjoyed the food, he'll be back tomorrow."

"And judging by how annoyed you are today at getting up early, I imagine you won't." She popped a piece of pancake in her mouth and licked the syrup from the fork. She glanced at Bruce, whose gaze fell to her lips.

He muttered under his breath.

"What?"

"Nothing." He stabbed at his eggs.

For some reason, she brought out the grumpy in him. He sure didn't pull any punches asking her questions. Maybe she should ask him some. He still owed her an explanation from when he'd walked out without answering her question in the barn. "You never told me what I do that annoys you. I'd like to know."

He paused, fork halfway to his mouth, and syrup dripped onto his shirt. "What?"

"Hold on." That would leave a stain. She dipped the edge of her napkin into her water and leaned over to dab at the spot. Resting a hand on his thigh for balance, she rubbed the napkin against his shirt but lost focus as his firm leg muscles contracted. She glanced down at her fingers on his inner thigh, way too close to other parts of his anatomy she dared not touch, and her mouth went dry.

He shifted in the seat, and God help her, her hand slid farther down his thigh. She pressed the napkin against his chest for balance to avoid slipping closer to…well…that…and raised her head.

Heat radiated from his body, and his rib cage rose as he drew in a breath, bringing her face to within a whisper of touching his. Afraid to move, and lost in the sensations, she clung to the space separating them like a life ring and gazed at him.

He stared back with pure, unmasked desire. When he lowered his head a fraction closer, his breath drifted across her lips.

The front screen door slammed.

With a start, she pushed herself off Bruce and settled back in her chair.

"Best breakfast I ever had. Thanks." Greg rubbed his belly and strode toward them.

"Good." She inwardly cringed at the high pitch of her voice. "Come back tomorrow." She shot a glance at Bruce, who wiped a napkin across his mouth and dropped it in his lap. "Bruce probably won't make it, and I hate to waste food."

"More for me if he doesn't. I don't like to share you." Greg's eyes widened, and he clamped his hands over his mouth. His face turned redder than ripe raspberries. "Food! I meant I don't like to share food."

She couldn't help but smile despite his embarrassment. Poor kid.

"I gotta get to work. Bye." He stumbled down the steps.

Silence followed, which brought her right back to the still-charged energy in the air, and the larger-than-life man beside her. Bruce drove her crazy. She could swear he'd been about to kiss her. And she'd wanted him to. However, the moment had passed, and he had his mannequin-like mask back on, neutral with no expression.

She avoided eye contact, stood, and picked up her plate. "I better take these inside and clean up."

Bruce grabbed his dish, and his footsteps sounded behind her as she headed to the door. A breeze blew the soap-fresh scent of his recent shower across the porch.

She stopped and inhaled. Her lungs shouldn't crave the unique, masculine smell of him, but they did. And her body shouldn't long to experience what it would be like to kiss a man with such passion for her in his eyes, but it did. With her entire life in chaos, it might be nice to feel something besides fear and panic. The strong need overcame common sense. "You know, Joe was wrong about one thing."

"What's that?"

Her heart rapped in a staccato. Keeping her back to him, she spoke before she lost her nerve. "You taking a shower? Not stupid. You smell amazing."

She pushed through the door to the kitchen.

Thump.

She turned.

Bruce grabbed the edge of the door, his mouth slightly agape. He regained his balance, squared his shoulders, and followed her to the sink.

She bent over and dumped her plate in with the other dirty ones. He came up beside her, and she held her breath. Her brain really needed to take more control of what came out of her mouth. If her face got any hotter, she'd combust. She kept her head down as she reached for his plate. "Thanks."

When he didn't let go, she glanced up. He hitched an eyebrow and held her gaze for a long moment before he finally released the dish.

Oh God. She had no clue what to make of that look. It could be a challenge, a question, or amusement.

"Ready to work on the trailer?" Joe scraped his chair against the floor as he stood.

"I've been ready. Thanks for breakfast, Sarah."

She nodded and rinsed the plates. When everyone left, she let out a big sigh. Sooner or later, she'd have to face him alone, and then she'd find out if she'd made a complete fool of herself.

CHAPTER 10

MORGAN GRABBED the fat-free hazelnut creamer from her fridge and added some to her coffee. With the phone cradled between her face and shoulder, she talked to Bruce about the arrangements to see another stupid horse together. She'd come up with a fucking brilliant plan to spend time alone with him. Her offer to donate a therapy horse to his program meant they had to travel around to check out the candidates. So far, he hadn't shown the least bit of interest in her romantically, but that would change. No man had ever resisted her. She'd swear he was gay if he hadn't been married before.

"When's a good day for you?" She twirled a lock of hair around her finger.

"I'm booked up all week. How about next Friday afternoon?"

"I'll check with the owner and get back to you."

She hung up and smiled. Perfect. The mare wouldn't work out. Morgan had already seen the horse, as usual. This one had the wrong gait for therapy according to her research. She'd never let him see a horse that could be a good match. That would end the need for them to take trips together.

She'd spend the entire afternoon with Bruce and make sure the twit at the farm knew. Time to douse some water on the sparks between

Bruce and Sarah. He lost all focus whenever she came within ten feet of him. Morgan's hand tightened on the mug. Damned if she'd let that bitch mess up her plans. Sarah could have her sloppy seconds when Morgan was good and done. And she might take her time with him. She'd earned it after suffering through two torturous years of marriage to Larry, a man older than her grandfather. At least he hadn't lasted a month after she switched his cardiac medication with a placebo.

Her phone rang. A California area code. She frowned at the screen. When she answered, the voice on the other end brought a sour taste to her mouth.

"Morgan? It's Robert. How are you?"

He had some nerve calling her after nine years. "What the hell do you want?"

"Nice way to say hi to an old friend."

"You aren't a friend. Answer my question." She slammed her coffee mug on the counter.

"Calm down. I have a business proposition."

"Like what?"

"A job for you. We want to run a new storyline in the soap with you coming back as a ghost. The writers think they can make use of a bitter older woman, you know, run a spin on—"

"Are you fucking serious?" She dug her manicured nails into her palms. "You kill me off on the show, replace me with a teenage bimbo, and think I'm going to come back and play the part of a shriveled old bitch? Kiss my ass."

"I know you, Morgan. Don't tell me that little shampoo commercial gig is supporting your extravagant lifestyle."

"Guess what? I might have fucked you to get a spot on the show, but you're not going to fuck me. I don't need you or your sappy, grade-B hack show. Don't call here again." She hung up and paced the room. Nothing could get her to play an old woman. Screw them. She had enough money to buy the rights to the whole damn show and fire everyone, including Robert, that dick. She shook her head and huffed out a breath. Right now, she had bigger fish to fry.

She drummed her fingers on the counter. Sarah stood in her way. Every guy at the farm had a fucking hard-on for the bitch. Greg kept trying to impress her, and Bruce couldn't keep his eyes off her. Time to find out more about Sarah and use it against her. The girl spooked easier than the Arabian horses. Oh, she had secrets all right. But Morgan had her own secrets. She'd plotted too long and worked too hard. She wouldn't let Sarah get in her way.

No one would derail her plans to seduce Bruce.

CHAPTER 11

LEANING against the arena fence by the parking lot, Bruce glanced at Sarah when she came out of the barn. She had dodged him all week. Every time he came near, she found a task to pull her away. He hadn't wanted to make her more uncomfortable, so he'd given her space. Figured she probably had blurted out the comment about him smelling good and regretted it. No sense putting her on the spot.

And for that matter, he'd just as soon forget about having to toss a napkin in his lap to hide his hard-on after he'd come within an inch of kissing her. One second they'd been talking about Joe, and the next her hands were on his leg and chest. With maple syrup on her breath, and her sensual lips so close, he'd lost it. Almost took a taste. Thank God Greg had come out and broken up the party.

Sarah had interrupted a long string of Navy-worthy curses running through his head when she'd shot that remark over her shoulder. It came out of nowhere, and with Debbie and Joe in the kitchen, Bruce couldn't talk to her. Not that he'd needed to. Her bright pink cheeks and still-dilated pupils said it all. The question was what to do about it.

Sarah stopped short and shielded her eyes. Must have seen him. She pivoted, took a step back toward the stables, and stopped again. Her shoulders squared, and she swung back around. She tucked a strand of hair back and strode toward him.

Might be best to clear the air since they had to work around each other. Her dance of avoidance had gone on long enough. He should apologize, but technically, he hadn't done anything, and it might make her even more uncomfortable.

Damn the way her hips swayed and her pink T-shirt hugged her breasts.

She stopped a couple of feet in front of him and cleared her throat. "Hi. I...uh...haven't had a chance to talk to you much this week."

He nodded. "Seems like you've been pretty busy."

"Yeah, well, you know. There's a lot to do, and I'm still learning the ropes." She shifted her feet and glanced down.

A blush colored her cheeks. The scent of her fruity shampoo caught in the breeze, and his jeans grew tighter. Christ, he had to stop this shit. They both had work to do, and he wasn't some eighteen-year-old with a puppy-love crush on her like Greg. "Look, I think we need—"

"I wanted to—"

Bruce held up a hand. "Sorry. You go first."

"Oh, that's okay." She touched his arm and then drew her hand back like it burned. "What did you want to say?"

Not a chance in hell. She had something on her mind and he'd find out what. "Ladies first."

She caught her lower lip between her teeth.

Heat shot to his groin. He forced his gaze from her mouth to her eyes.

"About the other—"

Morgan's convertible raced into the lot, top down.

Shit. Bad timing. Sarah would never talk in front of Morgan. Those two mixed like gunpowder and matches.

Morgan hopped out of the driver's seat and tossed the keys across the car to him. He caught them one-handed. She gave Sarah a cursory nod as she sauntered to the passenger side, lifted a picnic basket off the seat, and set it in the back.

"Ready?" Morgan flashed him a smile and placed a hand on his shoulder.

"Just a second." He stepped away from her toward Sarah. He had to at least try to find out. "What were you about to say?"

Sarah's gaze flitted to the picnic basket. She rubbed the back of her neck. "Nothing. It doesn't matter. Don't let me hold you up."

Morgan opened the passenger door and slid in. "We should go if we want to be on time."

Bruce frowned.

A truck with a horse trailer pulled into the lot. Todd sat behind the wheel. He slowed and stared at Sarah as he passed.

She swallowed hard but didn't look away from him.

Bruce itched to yank the asshole from his truck and tell him a thing or two about gawking at women. "We might need to reschedule, Morgan."

"Why?"

Debbie came out of the stables with Greg. They headed to Todd's trailer.

Morgan shifted in the seat. "I know another person is interested in this horse. I'd hate to miss the chance to see her."

Damn it to hell. Morgan had set this all up, and he owed it to her and the horse owner to follow through. He glanced at Greg and Debbie as they helped unload Todd's horse. Sarah should be safe with them around.

"I need to get back to work. See you later." Sarah spun on her heel and strode toward the stables.

"So we're good to go?" Morgan asked.

Bruce kept his gaze on Sarah until she disappeared into the barn. He lowered himself into the driver's seat. "Yeah."

As he drove, he couldn't get past Todd leering at Sarah. He showed up at the farm dressed like a model for an equestrian outfitters magazine and acted like everyone should wait on him. Bruce knew guys like him. Rich brats who did what they wanted and paid their way out of trouble. He fought the urge to turn the car around.

"Is something wrong?" Morgan asked.

"What?" Bruce glanced in her direction.

"Nothing." She waved a hand. "Princess nearly beat Batal the last time we were out."

"Yeah. She really gave him a run for the money."

"They're beautiful together, don't you think?"

"Uh-huh." Bruce ground his teeth. He'd seen a flicker of fear in Sarah's eyes before she'd covered it up. Todd clearly unnerved her.

"I think these ex-racehorses miss the competition. As soon as they get next to each other, their instincts click in. Sometimes it's like that with people too. You know?"

Despite Morgan trying to have a conversation, Bruce couldn't get the farm out of his head. He hadn't seen Joe around. Greg would try to help if Sarah got into trouble, but the gangly guy didn't pose much of a threat.

Morgan rattled off something else and then tapped his arm.

"Sorry, what?" Bruce blinked.

"I didn't want you to miss the entrance. Right up there." She pointed.

He pulled into the farm and parked. "Give me a second. I need to make a call."

"Okay. I'll go talk to the seller." Morgan opened the door and got out.

Bruce dialed Joe.

"What's up, Bruce?"

"Are you at the farm?"

"Yeah, why?"

The tension in his neck eased. "Just checking. Everything okay there?"

"Yeah, why wouldn't it be?"

"No reason. I gotta go. Thanks." He hung up and shook his head. Sarah made him act like an overprotective idiot. Joe had to wonder why he'd called. But knowing Joe, he wouldn't press the issue.

Bruce found Morgan and the man selling the horse, who introduced himself and showed them the mare. She had the right temperament for therapy but not the right gait. Too bad she wouldn't work out. Bruce thanked the seller for his time and explained why she wasn't a good fit.

On the way back to her car, Morgan hung her head. "I'm so sorry. I thought this might be the one."

"No problem. It's hard to know exactly what type works for therapy. I'm sorry you wasted your day."

She lifted her head and waved her hands. "Hey. It's gorgeous. We had a nice drive and saw a horse. What's better than that?"

"All true." He opened the car door for her.

"Oh, I almost forgot. I packed some snacks in case we wanted to stop by the lake. Do you have time?"

He needed to talk to Sarah and clear the air. "I'm sorry, but I have to get back."

"Okay. Maybe another time." She flipped on the radio.

When Bruce pulled into the arena lot, Morgan glanced around. "Where's your pickup?"

"At the house." He drove up and parked next to Sarah's Honda on the side. No sign of the farm truck. Maybe she had taken it into town.

"Hey, there's something I wanted to ask you." Morgan shifted in her seat.

"What?" He shut off the engine.

"Well, Sunday's gonna kind of be a tough day for me." She fingered the hem of her shirt. "It's the anniversary of my husband's death."

Never easy to get through those. "I'm sorry."

She sniffled and nodded. "I was wondering if maybe we could ride. It takes my mind off things."

He had a packed week, but he'd find time. Connecting with a horse sometimes chased the grief away for a short while, as he could attest. He pulled out his phone and checked his calendar. "Does noon work?"

"Sure." She gave him a sad smile. "Thanks."

"No problem."

Bruce got out and went up the steps to the house. When he entered, the scent of chicken filled the kitchen, and his mouth watered. A large crockpot sat on the counter with a note posted in front of it. *Went shopping. Help yourself. There's bread in the basket.* A hand-drawn arrow pointed to it right next to the pot. He snorted.

Sarah had made sure dinner would be ready. Plates, utensils, and napkins were stacked in a neat pile next to the note. He glanced at the table. A vase filled with cut flowers sat in the center.

He ran a hand down his face and sighed. Damn if she hadn't turned the farmhouse into a home. All Greg could talk about were the breakfasts, and Joe, a man of few words, even raved about them. Somehow, she had managed to bring everyone together.

Growing up as an only child meant meals at Bruce's house had been quiet, but it didn't matter because he'd been with family. His heart twisted. What he wouldn't give to have even one more of them. The image of Sarah sitting with him at the wicker table on the porch flashed in his head.

He paced the kitchen. Somehow, she had found a way past his defenses. When he opened his eyes in the morning, he pictured Sarah's face. Her smile, the way she cared for the horses, the little things she did behind the scenes, like leaving homemade brownies and lemonade on the bus for the vets after their lesson. He didn't miss anything, because despite himself, he couldn't stop watching her. She'd kept her distance all week and still had taken over his dreams. He shook his head.

She didn't belong there.

Emily did.

He glanced at the door to Sarah's suite. She may not stay long before she bolted from whatever had her so freaked. Maybe it would be for the best. If she weren't around, he wouldn't be plagued by the guilt that accompanied the feelings she stirred. Yet, his protective talons clawed his ribs at the idea of her on the run, panicked, and alone. No, he wouldn't allow it.

He'd watch for her while he worked in the stables. When she came back, they'd have a talk. Time to find out what she'd wanted to tell him earlier, and what had scared her enough to go into hiding.

CHAPTER 12

THE NERVES that played hopscotch under her skin every time she left her safety zone kept Sarah alert as she drove to the library. She adjusted the ball cap she wore to help hide her face. All morning she'd caught Todd leering at her, but she had made sure they were never alone. She turned into the parking lot and dialed the number Anne had given her for Maddie's throwaway phone. Maddie had been off the grid at an archaeology dig since Sarah had left, so they hadn't talked.

As soon as Maddie answered, she peppered Sarah with questions about the stalker. Sarah leaned back on the headrest. The lack of sleep and stress of talking about him wore her out.

"Anne and I are worried sick about you. I want to see you. I have a symposium coming up at Penn State. Is that anywhere near you?"

Sarah picked at her cuticle. Her stomach did a flip at the possibility of seeing her sister. But she didn't want to put her in danger. "It's not real far, but I don't think it's a good idea. Too risky."

"Bullshit. This gherkin-sized-pickle-prick isn't going to keep me from you. I need to see with my own eyes that you're okay."

A van parked beside Sarah's truck. She had selected a space well away from the building so she'd have extra room and not hit anyone if she had trouble with the stick. All the empty spots, and this person chose one right next to her. Her gut tightened.

A lanky man got out and glanced at her. He whipped a pair of sunglasses from his pocket and slid them on, hiding his eyes. She hit the Lock button and dipped her head as if searching for something on the floor or passenger seat. "Hold on, Maddie."

"What's wrong?"

Seconds passed as she held her breath, straining to hear if his footsteps approached.

"Are you okay? You're scaring me." Maddie's voice pitched higher.

"Wait." Sarah raised her head. Under the brim of her hat, she glanced in the rearview mirror.

The man entered the library.

She swallowed and sat up straighter. He'd definitely checked her out.

"Sarah? What the hell's going on? Talk to me."

"Sorry. I'm moving the truck. This guy in the parking lot gave me a weird look, and I don't want to be near his van when he comes out."

She started the engine, drove around to the other side of the building, and found a spot where she could see the front. If she didn't need to check her email, she'd leave. She kept her gaze trained on the library entrance. "Look, I don't know about you coming to see me. What if the stalker follows you? I mean, assuming he's not already here, which I can't be sure."

"I'm not even flying out of California. The week before the symposium, I'll be in Arizona and leave from there. I'll switch around taking busses and cabs so he can't follow me to you from Pennsylvania."

"When is the symposium?"

"In two weeks. It runs for five days, but I could stay a couple extra and see you before I fly back. I ran it by Anne, and even as careful as she is, she thought it would work out. Please, say yes."

Sarah sighed, allowing room for hope to creep in. "I mean, I guess if you—"

"Yes. Gimme your address."

"Do you think it's safe over the phone?"

"We're both using throwaways. He can't possibly have these numbers or track these calls."

"All right." Sarah rattled off the address and then frowned. "On second thought, I think it would be better if I pick you up outside of town."

"Okay. If that makes you more comfortable."

Nothing would make her comfortable, least of all having her whereabouts on paper. "Did you write my address down?"

"Yeah."

"Tear it up. I can't take any chances. Better yet, burn it." Her gaze flitted to the white van on the other side of the lot.

"Seriously? Sarah it's—"

"I mean it. Burn it now. I shouldn't have told it to you. And this is a bad idea. I changed my mind. You can't come." She glanced around as if she expected the man to teleport from inside the library and appear beside her truck.

"Calm down. I'm getting some matches."

A scraping sound followed by the pop and hiss of a flame carried over the line.

"Burning as we speak."

"I'm sorry. It's just too risky." Sarah forced a deep breath.

"Please, rethink this. I know you're nervous and have a right to be, but it sounds like you're being a bit paranoid."

"I can't help it." The library door opened, and she squinted.

The guy who'd parked beside her emerged from the entrance holding the hand of a little girl with bright blond pigtails. An armful of books pressed to her chest, she skipped along beside him.

Sarah puffed her cheeks out and exhaled. Through her eyes, everyday normal events took on sinister shades.

She unlocked the truck. "Maybe you're right."

"I know I am. Nothing will happen. I'll be super careful."

"Okay." After all, if she'd gotten the stamp of approval from Anne, it had to be a solid plan.

"I promise. I'll cheer you up. I have so much to tell you. This guy flew in from Greece for the dig, and holy shit was he hot. You know I don't sleep around, but with him I couldn't even—"

"Whoa, Maddie. Spare me the details."

"Fine, I'll save it to tell in person."

"All right. I need to go now."

"I'll be in touch. Love ya."

"You too."

Sarah hung up and climbed out of the truck. She entered the library and logged on to a computer. Sweat formed on her brow. One new message from Anne. As she read it, love for her sister welled up. Only two years older, with Maddie between them, Anne had taken the role of the big sis seriously. Both Sarah and Maddie looked up to her. She always had their backs. Sarah smiled at the newsy update about their parents and Anne's third grade students. Those kids kept her on her toes. She ended with a promise to keep working with Alec, a wish that Sarah stay safe, and signed it with love.

Before Sarah could log out, a new email from Anne came in. Sarah opened the message and froze.

I tried to call but you aren't answering. A message just came in from the stalker. I copied and pasted it below. I'd hoped he'd given up. CALL ME ASAP!

She'd left her phone in the truck. Trembling, she scrolled down to read the message.

Dear Sarah,

I warned you this should not go on long. It's been sixteen days now. You haven't returned, and I'm losing patience. No matter what other people in your life tell you, you know we are meant to be together. Only I can provide the life you deserve. Nothing is too good for you, and no one can take care of you the way I can.

You'll see when we live together. Everything will be perfect. Just the way you like it. I've had it all set up for quite a while. My source emailed me pictures of your apartment all cleaned up after our *incident*. I call it that because I know you weren't acting like yourself. You would never hurt me on purpose and must be very sorry about it. My hand is finally healed, but I've had to wear gloves for weeks since I don't like the sight of blood or bandages.

And since you will live with me, you don't have to worry about your soiled old apartment. It isn't fit for you. They didn't even put in new carpets. No amount of cleaning can remove the stain and scent of blood. I've tried in the past.

To make you feel at home, I even made a special purchase for you. I know how much you liked your fish, so I bought a beautiful, artificial lighted tank. This way no mildew or mold will grow. It's still in the box because I didn't want to set it out until I would be home every day to clean the glass. When you come back, we can shop together online to pick out the fake fish you like.

I also plan to buy you a new car. Perhaps a Lexus. I think it's important for you to have a nice vehicle with a five-star highway safety rating. Of course, you will only be allowed to drive it to certain places. We'll be together most of the time, and I will drive. But I'll let you pick the color. Anything but black, which shows dirt.

You must understand that as much as we love each other, you belong with me. Think of the fun we'll have. You'll dance for me, but just me. You're my ballerina. I won't share you with anyone.

This is very important. Audrey made that fatal mistake and needed to be punished for it, but I know you won't.

This is your last chance to come back on your own. That would mean so much to me. But if you don't, I'm done waiting.

A wave of nausea choked Sarah. She rushed out of the library, got into the truck, and shot out of the lot, checking the rearview mirror every couple of seconds. Images of the *incident* flashed in her mind. She turned onto a side street and parked the truck against the curb. She needed a minute to calm down. The fish tank...the blood...

She pressed a hand to her forehead and squeezed her eyes shut but couldn't keep the image out. It all flooded back.

Trapped in the bathroom, thinking the stalker had left, she'd opened the door.

The man's hand snaked in and grabbed the edge of the door. Sarah gasped and threw her shoulder against it to trap his forearm. With the glass shard, she slashed from his wrist to his index finger. Blood spurted.

He cursed and let go, yanking his hand back. She slammed the door shut and turned the lock. Her heart battered so hard she couldn't breathe.

"How could you do this?" He banged on the door. "You love me."

The guy was crazy. Delusional beyond belief.

"I'm bleeding. Making a mess." His voice cracked and raised to a new level of madness. "Now you have to be punished." He pounded harder. "Punished, punished, punished. This can't happen again."

She pressed her full weight against the door.

Glass shattered in the bedroom. The wall shook as something crashed against it. She couldn't make out the words, but he ranted and raved as he moved around in an obvious frenzy. If he found her phone in her purse, he'd know she hadn't called the cops. Her breath came in shallow bursts.

"Look what you've made me do. Everything is out of order."

Sirens sounded in the distance, and she clutched a hand to her chest. Thank God. A neighbor must have heard the noise and called.

"The cops won't stop me, Sarah. Nothing will."

The back door banged. A minute later, the sirens screamed past her apartment.

They weren't coming for her. Her stomach dropped. No one had called. She had to get out of her apartment before he came back.

But he might be tricking her again and hadn't actually left. She took a deep breath and opened the door, bloody shard of mirror raised.

She dropped her jaw as she gazed around the empty bedroom. Complete devastation. The mini-cam pieces scattered among toppled lamps, busted snow globes, and broken picture frames. Water ran down the front of her dresser from her smashed aquarium. Broken glass littered its top and the floor beneath. Blood stained the carpet and bureau. He'd trashed her home and violated her privacy. She dug her nails into her palms.

At least she'd fought back.

Fish flopped on the rug. She grabbed a vase from the shelf over the toilet, yanked out the silk flowers, and filled it with water. With shaking hands, she scooped the fish into the vase.

She must have lost her mind. He could return at any second. She needed to call the police.

Her gaze darted to her purse on the floor beside the dresser. She reached for the bag, pulled her phone out, and hurried down the stairs to the kitchen where she received better reception.

As she passed the counter, she stopped cold. Photos covered the entire surface. He'd laid out pictures of her, evenly spaced in neat rows. Several from performances, a bunch of close-ups taken in public places, and the last few, asleep in her own bed.

Sarah opened her eyes in the truck and blinked at the blurry side street. A choking sensation closed her throat. Air rasped through the narrow passage, and sweat drenched her shirt as she struggled to breathe. Her body shook so hard her teeth clattered.

With trembling hands, she yanked on the truck door and shoved it open. A car horn blared. She gasped and jerked the handle back. Little moans escaped as she shook even harder. She snatched her purse off the passenger seat, opened it, and pulled out a folded brown lunch bag. After her last anxiety attack, she'd tucked one inside. Just in case.

She brought the paper sack to her mouth and breathed into it. In and out until her lungs stopped burning and her throat remained open. Her pulse still raced, but her brain kicked back in gear.

The stalker's email mentioned keeping the aquarium in a box until he was there to clean it, which must mean he wasn't home, but not necessarily that he'd found her. She couldn't even process the fact he'd bought a fake aquarium and had researched which car to buy for her.

Someone apparently watched her empty apartment and kept detailed track of what they'd done to clean up after the attack. She grabbed a tissue from the glove box and wiped the sweat from her forehead. She'd told the police everything the stalker had said when he'd attacked her. Maybe they could figure out who Audrey was and what he'd done to her.

Sarah took another shaky breath and started the engine.

The stalker had talked about wearing gloves. She closed her eyes and pictured Todd. Every time she'd seen him, he'd had them on. Still, if every person who wore gloves became a suspect, she'd have a lot of people to fear. But Todd also was also a neat freak. His car shined like it went through the wash daily. He never wore soiled clothes and didn't even groom his own horse.

She couldn't take the chance with Todd.

The stalker said she was out of time.

She had to run again.

CHAPTER 13

Morgan waited until Bruce went into the house. She glared at the door. He was probably looking for Sarah. Damn that little bitch. Bruce hadn't paid any attention to Morgan the entire trip to see the therapy horse. She'd bet her boob job whatever he'd been so preoccupied with had something to do with the tramp. That girl had to go.

Morgan glanced around. With no one in sight, she pulled out her phone and hurried to the Honda. She snapped a picture of the VIN through the windshield and then one of the license plate.

She drove back to her house, stormed through the front door, and tossed the still-full picnic basket on the table. Tapping her phone contacts, she looked up the number for Pete, the private investigator she'd hired years ago to keep tabs on her sister.

Stupid bitch. After adopting and raising her for seven years, Morgan's parents forgot all about her the second their own baby popped out. The child they never thought they could conceive. Bad enough the little brat sucked up all the attention of her parents and everyone around her, but she bled the family dry with expenses causing Morgan's life to change for the worse.

She poured vodka over ice, added a splash of tonic, and sat at the kitchen table. Adoption agencies should never give babies to loser parents. Hers couldn't make ends meet with one child on their waitress and mechanic salaries. Forget about two. Belts tightened and sacrifices were made, at Morgan's expense. She wore ugly secondhand clothes and never went to movies or the mall like the other girls. Every penny went to the princess for horseback riding lessons, show fees, and travel expenses. Nothing was too good for her.

Morgan gulped down the rest of her drink, shoved the chair out from the table, and stood. As she punched Pete's number into her phone, she paced the kitchen.

"Morgan? Didn't expect to ever hear from you again. What's it been, five years?"

"You answered your phone, so I assume you're still in business. I have a new job for you."

"As always, right to the point. What is it?"

She could picture him, leaning forward, oversized belly against the worn desk as he grabbed his notebook.

"I have a car VIN and some plates for you to run. I want to know who they're registered to."

"Easy enough. That's it?"

"For now. How long will it take?"

"Not long. I'll call you back. By the way, my rates have gone up since we last did business."

Greedy bastard. Like he had rates. "Same as last time. You deliver. I'll pay."

She gave him the information and hung up. An hour later, he called her back.

"Those plates are reported stolen, and the car is registered to a James Lawson. Lives in California."

No shit. Sarah, if that was her real name, must be on the run, hiding from the law or an abusive boyfriend. If not, maybe someone had filed a missing person report.

"You there?" Pete asked.

"Yes. I have another job for you."

"What?"

"If I send you pictures of a woman, can you find out who she is and if she's reported as a missing person?" Morgan rubbed a finger under her chin.

"Possibly."

"Start the search in California since that's where the car was registered."

"Okay."

"Get me all the information you can on her. If she so much as farted in public, I want to know. Call me when you have something." Morgan hung up.

She tapped her phone, and pictures of Sarah walking a horse to the stables appeared. As always, Morgan was one step ahead. She'd taken those shots on a hunch. And now they would come in handy. She forwarded the photos to Pete. Soon enough, she'd have the goods on the meddling little bitch.

CHAPTER 14

DIRT AND DUST kicked up as Sarah drove along the path to the house and parked the truck. She stuffed her hat into her purse and eyed Joe, hammering on a fence post near her back door. Praying no one would be in the kitchen, she slipped through the front.

Her unsettled stomach lurched at the scent of chicken and onions cooking. She ran to the sink and gripped the cool, metal tub.

Apparently, the worst of her anxiety wasn't over yet. With a twist of the knob, she turned on the cold water and splashed a handful on her face. She had to get her emotions under control and figure out her next move. It wouldn't take long to pack, but she had nowhere to go.

The screen door squeaked, and steps sounded behind her. Heavy steps. Another punch to her gut.

"Sarah?" Bruce's voice echoed through the kitchen.

Shit. He couldn't see her like this. She grabbed a paper towel and dried her face.

"We need to talk," he said.

With her back to him, she concentrated on breathing. She didn't trust her voice to speak, so she just stood there with the water running.

"Sarah?"

"What?" She managed to squeak out the word. To avoid looking at him, she shut off the spigot, snagged a sponge, and wiped surfaces that didn't need cleaning.

"I came to ask you about earlier."

He probably meant when she'd approached him at the farm before Morgan showed up. She had intended to apologize for the stupid comment she'd made about him smelling amazing. That had moved way down on the list of her priorities. She'd be gone by morning, and it wouldn't take long before Bruce forgot about her altogether.

His boots entered her line of vision. She kept her head down and continued wiping the counter.

"You're shaking. What's wrong?"

Of course, he'd notice. She snatched her keys from the counter and stepped past him to the suite, where she fumbled to unlock the door. "Dinner's ready. Help yourself."

Bruce's hand covered hers on the knob.

She stilled. So much for escaping.

He tightened his fingers, pressing her clammy palm against the handle. His breath brushed across the damp skin of her temple. "Let. Me. In."

A quiet demand.

What she wouldn't give to have a strong partner to catch her if she fell. Only, this dance had to be a solo, or someone might pay the consequences. *You're my ballerina. I won't share you with anybody.*

Her heart ticked a countdown. She needed to get away before it was too late. "I'm sorry, but I can't talk to you right now."

"Too bad, this has gone on long enough," he said in a not-open-for-debate tone. He slid her hand from the knob and swung open the door.

The front screen slammed, and Joe entered.

Great. Another person to scrutinize her. But he might distract Bruce from his mission to make her talk.

"I have some bad news about your car, Sarah." Joe wiped a hand on his jeans. "Hmm...something smells awfully good. Is that chicken?"

Alarm zipped through her system. "What do you mean about my car?"

Joe wandered over to the crockpot and peeked through the glass lid. "I was fixing to go home and make a sandwich, but this looks a helluva lot better. I keep forgetting that you make good food. Now, Debbie—"

"What's wrong with Sarah's car?" Bruce asked.

Joe squinted at the glass lid. "Are there carrots in there? I can't see too well with the steam all—"

"Enough with the food. What about the car?" Bruce waved his hands in the air.

"Cripes, take it down a notch. You're wound tighter than a clock spring." Joe tapped the lid of the pot and continued his inspection. "It has a hole rusted through the gas tank. Gonna need a new one."

Sarah's heart climbed her ribs to her tonsils. She needed that car to leave. "Can I still drive it?"

"Nope. It's bone-dry. But don't worry, I got a friend at the junkyard. We can get you a used one for a few bucks. Gotta look for a match, though."

Oh no. That would take time she didn't have. Her fingers turned to ice. What might seem cheap to Joe would probably cost more than she could afford.

Bruce frowned and glanced out the window. "How the hell did you know about this?"

Joe shrugged. "Smelled gas and checked it out. Pretty simple."

"Well, I didn't smell anything," Bruce said.

"That's cuz you got your nose up your—"

"Excuse me." Sarah stepped to the suite landing and gripped the door handle. Her queasiness had reached critical levels.

Joe looked up. "Hey, hey. This isn't anything to get upset about. You can drive the truck 'til your car's fixed. And it won't cost much cuz Buddy owes me, and I can put it in for you."

"Th-thanks." She yanked on the door.

Bruce held a hand out to stop it from closing. "Hold on. We didn't finish talking."

"Another time." God, she needed to be alone.

Joe crossed the room and jerked a thumb at Bruce. "I'd rather eat squirrel turds than take his side, but you don't look so hot. Maybe you should sit and let Mr. Cranky Pants here get you a drink or something."

Bruce shot Joe a glare that could wither a grape to a raisin.

Sarah's stomach heaved. She rushed down the steps and into her bathroom. Taking a deep breath, she leaned back against the wall.

"Are you okay?" Bruce called from outside the bedroom.

The man was nothing if not persistent. "Yeah. Please, just go."

"Not until I get some answers."

She forced her rattled brain to focus. He'd said he wanted to discuss what had happened earlier. Maybe if she apologized, he'd leave and she could calm down and form a plan. She smoothed her hair back and made her way to the family room.

Bruce stood at the bottom of the steps with his feet planted wide, arms crossed.

She stopped short of him. If he wanted to talk, she'd talk and scoot him out. "Okay. I'm sorry about the shower comment. That's what I was going to tell you this afternoon. It was inappropriate, and we have to work together. It won't happen again." Her voice rasped from her parched mouth, yet not enough to keep her from babbling. "I mean, I wasn't wrong about you smelling good, that's true, but—"

"Sarah." He took a step closer.

Cripes, nothing she said even made sense. She pointed to the stairs, avoiding eye contact. "Can you please go now?"

"Don't care about your comment. Stop with the smoke screen. Tell me who's scaring you."

She couldn't tell him. Couldn't tell anyone. She brought a hand to the base of her throat and fingered the small hollow. "I'm just tired."

"People don't shake when they're tired."

"Well, maybe I do. Please." She pointed to the stairs again.

He came another step closer. "Staying until I get answers."

"There aren't any." That was the damned truth. No answers. No way out. No escape. No normal life again. She wouldn't give up, but she refused to drag anyone else into her nightmare.

"I'm done talking. I'll be in the bedroom." She tried to walk past him, but he snagged her arm.

"No, you won't. Who's scaring you?" His rough voice had an edge of softness. He leaned closer, his deep blue eyes willing her to answer.

"What makes you think someone is?" She glanced at the window over the couch.

"Seriously?" He waved a hand around the room. "The curtains, the locks, the way you come back pale as a ghost after a trip to town. You're terrified."

"I didn't have anything to do with the locks. Joe did that." The man barely knew her and had gone out of his way to make her feel safe. He'd even offered to fix her car. Greg always stayed a step ahead to make sure he took on the heaviest loads of work. These people at the farm cared about her, and she had to leave before *their* pictures showed up in a threatening note. Only now, she had no means to get away. A lump the size of a biscuit clogged her throat.

She tapped her foot and kept her gaze on the curtain. Maybe if she held out long enough, Bruce would give up.

"Don't nitpick about the locks. You know what I mean."

"No, I don't." She tapped her foot faster, in rhythm with her frenetic pulse.

"Stop lying."

"Lie? Why would I lie?" Her voice sounded strained, even to herself, like a person with a paper-thin hold on sanity. She attempted to go around him, but he moved in front of her.

"Talk to me." He placed a gentle hand on her arm.

"No."

"Why not?"

"I can't discuss it." She risked a quick glance at him before dropping her gaze. The maniac stalker knew no boundaries. She had to find some way to leave. Her eyes blurred with tears.

"Then I'll tell you what I think. You're running."

Bruce had already figured out too much. She pressed her lips together and shook her head. "You have to go now."

"No." He grimaced. "Damn it. This isn't just about you. Whatever has you this panicked could be a threat to the people at this farm. I won't let any harm come to my patients or anyone here. Now for the last time, tell me."

He was right. That's why she had to go, but now she couldn't with a broken car. The chill in her fingers traveled through her body. Her shoulders shook from holding back sobs, and she pressed her icy hands to her eyes. Tears seeped from the corners and ran down the inside of her thumbs to her wrists.

Bruce had let go of her arm. Maybe he'd leave. Men hated tears. He'd probably come back later as hell-bent as he was to get to the truth, but she'd have time to figure something out. Right now, that would be breathing. Tiny gasps for air teased her lungs.

"Jesus Christ, you're gonna suffocate yourself. Come here."

Bruce pulled her to him.

She pushed her palms against his pecs. "I can't—"

"Stop arguing with me." He gazed down at her and tightened his hold.

His warm, strong body encircled hers and drained her energy to fight. She melted against him. Uncontrollable tears rained down her cheeks. She buried her face in his chest and let them flow.

"Relax. You're safe."

She shook her head. "I'll never be s-safe."

He rubbed her back. "Yes, you will."

For the next few minutes, she cried and soaked his shirt. Cocooned in his arms, breathing in his clean, masculine scent, for the first time since she'd run, she wasn't afraid. When her body stopped shaking, and the tears ebbed, he eased back and bent down.

His eyes were soft. Damn if they weren't gorgeous when he let emotion shine through.

He led her to the couch, grabbed a tissue from the box on the coffee table, and handed it to her. She dabbed at her wet eyes and blew her nose. He tugged her down next to him. "Tell me what's going on."

Bruce had a right to be concerned for the people at the farm. A pitchfork stabbed at her gut. It would be safer if he knew about the whacko out there. She glanced at him.

He nodded. "Trust me."

She took a shaky breath. "You have to swear not to tell anyone."

"I won't."

"A year ago, this guy started stalking me. I was in the public eye since I performed in the ballet. He wouldn't stop, so I changed my identity and disappeared."

"What did he do?" Bruce angled his body to face hers.

"He started with flowers. I figured it was just an avid fan. Then came the notes on the windshield and voice-altered calls." She rubbed her forehead. "Each communication escalated. Before I left, he sent me pictures of my sisters out in public. Then, after he attacked me—"

"Whoa. Attacked?" Bruce's eyes widened, and he held up a hand. "Slow down. Tell me everything in order."

She told him what had happened, leaving out the parts about Mark dumping her and the cops questioning her sanity. None of that made any difference at this point. When she finished, Bruce leaped to his feet and paced.

"That bastard is done. I'll personally haul his miserable ass down to the station if I don't kill him first. What's his name?"

"That's the problem, we don't know."

Bruce fisted his hands. "What's he look like?"

"I don't know that either. I'm telling you, there's nothing you can do. The police have his DNA from the blood samples at my apartment and still can't figure out who he is."

"Why not?" Bruce's face tinged with red.

"He's not in the database, and they don't have any suspects." She held her palms up. "The cops said even if they knew who he was, stalkers don't spend much time in jail, and when they're released they start up again."

"So that's why you ran?"

"Yeah. I'm sorry. After I got an email from him at the library today, I planned to leave, but now my car is broken, so I can't." She swallowed hard and rubbed her hands down her thighs. "I don't want to bring any danger to anyone here. This is my problem, not yours. I just need to get away as soon as I can, and he'll leave you all alone."

* * *

Bruce's blood pressure climbed to the ceiling. Give him one second with that stalker. It all made sense now. The graceful way Sarah moved, her tiny stature but muscular body. The bastard had stolen the passion of her life. And here she was, ready to run again to protect everyone at the farm.

"You're not going anywhere. This geek is nothing but a coward. Terrorizing a woman with notes, emails, and voice-altered phone calls? He can hide from the cops, but he won't know what hits him if he shows his face here."

Sarah looked up at him. A little color had returned to her hollow cheeks. "He's dangerous because he's crazy."

"Well, he's going to find himself in some serious trouble if I have any say about it." The tips of Bruce's ears burned.

"He might already be here. Todd's acted funny toward me."

"I've seen the way he looks at you. I'll talk to Debbie about—"

"You promised you wouldn't say anything." Sarah bolted up.

"Debbie doesn't need him—"

"No." She grabbed his arm. "I can't be responsible for running people off the farm and taking money out of Debbie's pocket. Please, don't say anything."

He frowned. Shit. A promise was a promise. He'd just have to keep that rich prick on his radar. "All right. For now."

"Thank you." She slid her hand to the damp spot on his shirt where she'd cried. "I'm sorry. I ruined this."

Her gentle caress warmed his skin through the fabric. But more than that, she'd finally opened up to him. Trusted him enough to share her secret despite being frightened.

He placed his hand over hers. "I'm not worried about the shirt."

Her breath fanned his fingers, and he squeezed hers. So fragile and yet so strong. It had taken courage for her to forge her way across the country alone, afraid through unknown territory.

She raised her gaze. Shades of green shimmered up at him.

God, he wanted her. He started to reach a hand down, but drew it back. Not now. The urge to kiss her almost drowned him, but it wouldn't be right, and he still had his own issues. Time to leave before his body gave away just how much he wanted her.

He let go of her hand. "Thanks for trusting me. Now I can help you. Are you going to be okay if I go?"

She nodded, but he sensed her hesitation. "If you want me to stay—"

"No." Her shoulders squared.

He longed to touch her, but he knew it wouldn't end there. "I'll see you tomorrow."

She nodded again and dropped her gaze.

"Listen." He waited for her to look up. "You're safe here. I'll make sure."

"As soon as my car's fixed, I'll leave. But thank you." She gave him a sad smile and disappeared into the bedroom, shutting the door behind her.

A ball of lead dropped in his stomach.

Like hell.

He mounted the stairs, pushed the door open hard, and strode into the kitchen.

Debbie and Joe were seated at the table drinking coffee. Joe raised his eyebrow, but neither of them asked any questions.

Bruce patrolled the exterior of the suite. Sarah had done a good job. Every window had curtains. With the new locks, she should be safe.

He went back to his truck and climbed up onto the hood. As the sun dropped, clouds promised a colorful sunset. Sarah, closed off from the world, would miss it. Despite everything, the stalker hadn't crushed her spirit. She continued to fight and survive. He leaned back against the windshield for a moment. This was bullshit. He bounded off the truck, marched to the back door of the suite, and knocked.

"Who is it?"

"Bruce."

She opened the door a crack and peeked out. "What's wrong?"

"Nothing. Can I come in?"

"I guess." She stood back.

He entered the room and grabbed the blanket draped over the couch. "Follow me."

"I was going to bed. I don't think—"

"Just follow me."

The look in her eyes and stiffened back meant she'd challenge him. He blew out a breath. "Please."

She sighed. "This better be good."

He led her out to the truck, tossed the blanket on top of the hood, and hoisted her up. His hands lingered. He couldn't quite bring himself to let go. Damn it.

"I don't understand what you're doing." She tried to scooch down off the hood, but he placed his hands on either side of her hips.

He'd gotten her this far. He wasn't going to let her go now. "Has anyone ever told you what a pain in the ass you can be?"

She seemed to ponder the question. "No."

"Well, you are." He eased up beside her and nudged her shoulders back onto the blanket. "When's the last time you saw a sunset?"

Red, orange, and purple streaked across the sky. She drew her knees up, and he pulled the cover over them. "I don't remember."

"That's what I figured."

"It's beautiful."

"Yes. It is." Only his gaze wasn't on the sunset.

They didn't talk, focused on nature's show. He turned in time to see her eyes close. She had to be exhausted from the early mornings, physical labor, and stress of being on constant guard.

She must have scrubbed her face because it had a pink, clean hue. Her thick lashes fell over eyelids still puffy from crying. This time he didn't stop himself from stroking her silky hair splayed on the blanket.

He fought the strong urge to wrap her in his arms. Instead, he hopped down and came along the side of truck. He placed a hand on her shoulder and gave it a light shake. "Sarah?"

She made a small noise and rolled over to lean against his chest. Okay, he'd tried. He picked her up, and she snuggled against him, her head on his shoulder. For a moment, he held her and inhaled her sweet scent, warming his lungs.

He tightened his grip and scanned the woods, jaw set. No one would ever hurt her. Not on his watch. He carried her into the suite and slid her body down his to stand. Hell, he needed some space between them now.

"Where am I?" she murmured and opened her eyes.

"Home. I wanted to make sure you locked up."

She pulled the blanket tighter around her. "Thanks."

Yawning, she picked up the key from the table. He stepped outside and waited until the lock clicked. His shirt, still warm from her, molded against him. Now he had a real conundrum. She'd let him in. But he couldn't risk doing the same.

CHAPTER 15

RUBBING HER EYES, Sarah rolled out of bed. Saturday, her day to sleep in, and she still woke up early after another restless night of disturbing dreams. In this one, she'd been performing when a man in the crowd stood and fired shots at her on stage. She'd awakened drenched in sweat, every hair on her body standing up straight.

The scent of Bruce's cologne wafted up from her clothes. She halted midstride across the room. Oh, right, the sunset he'd taken her out to watch. She'd never been on the receiving end of caring, supportive, patient Bruce.

She closed her eyes, brought her shirt up to her nose, and inhaled. His scent, his touch, the feel of his body against hers. Heaven. But all for nothing.

Even if he did have more than platonic feelings for her, they couldn't act on them. Her life would never be normal, and he was rooted at the farm. At least he knew about the stalker. It couldn't hurt to have another set of eyes on the lookout, especially with Todd around.

Sarah moved to the dresser, opened the bottom drawer, and pulled out her pointe shoes. At last she had a little free time to dance. She tied the shoe ribbons in quick, practiced moves, and stepped to the tiny family room. Shoving the coffee table close to the couch, she made a small space to dance.

She stood in first position and did some pliés. Closing her eyes, she imagined herself back at the studio, the familiar movement of her muscles soothing her. After warming up, she attempted a leap, but her head smashed into the low ceiling. She cursed and fell to the ground, clipping the corner of the coffee table on the way down.

What a shock. The room wasn't big enough to perform ballet moves. Desperation had made her try. She rubbed the lump on her head and yanked hard to untie her shoes as a bruise colored her shin. Damn that stalker for taking away her life.

She pushed off the floor and stormed to the bedroom closet.

Stuffing her hand into her backpack, she felt around for her gun, then pulled it out. She grabbed the box of extra bullets from her dresser drawer and snagged a handful. At the library, she'd watched a video of how to load and shoot a .380 semi-automatic. Time to see how much she'd learned.

She tucked the gun and ammo into the pockets of a light, pink windbreaker, along with the hand-drawn target she'd made.

When she was outside, she glanced at the arena lot where Bruce's truck and Todd's Vette sat. Neither man was in sight. Only horses grazed in the fields.

Two cars she didn't recognize drove into the lot. She frowned and hurried to the shelter of the woods before anyone noticed her.

Something shiny in a tree caught her eye. A deflated silver balloon fluttered, tangled in the branches. She glanced back at the farmhouse porch. Maybe that's what had reflected the sun the other morning. The tension in her lower back eased.

After trekking into the forest, she found a large tree and tacked up the target. She took several paces back, fumbled to flick off the safety, and raised the gun with one hand. Finger on the trigger, she took a deep breath and shot. The recoil caused her wrist to whip back toward her shoulder. She lost balance and almost dropped the gun.

Shit. Way too loud. She hadn't gone far enough from the farm. Her breath caught as she sprinted to the tree and yanked down the target she'd completely missed. She'd have to move deeper into the woods.

A rustling sound came from a bush behind her. She spun around and tightened her grip on the shaking gun. Beads of perspiration slipped down her neck. Her frantic gaze dashed from tree to tree.

* * *

Bruce shook hands with his two new patients and introduced them to Lynn. As he led the men to the barn to meet Misty, a shot sounded from the woods. His stomach lurched. He swung his head in the direction of the gunfire and scanned the area. Sarah hadn't been around all morning and might be in trouble.

The horses in the field skittered about. Debbie came stomping out of the stables. "Someone's shooting in the woods again."

The vets looked around. Probably assessing the safety of the place. Just what Bruce needed.

He frowned. "Sorry. We get some knucklehead hunters in the area once in a while. Gimme a second to check it out."

They nodded. One of them asked, "Need any help?"

"No, I got it. Be right back."

He jogged toward the woods. More than once, he'd had to run off an idiot hunter or some kids with BB guns. That shot hadn't come from a BB gun, though.

Bruce stopped in front of a large oak. Tiny bits of paper under tacks caught his eye. Someone had probably torn down a target from the tree. He shook his head. Amateur. A bullet could ricochet back and kill the numskull. Another shot rang out from deeper in the woods. He cursed and made his way toward the sound.

Whoever was shooting hadn't tried to hide their path. Muddy footprints and disturbances in the brush made following the trail easy work. He bent for a closer look at the ground. Small shoe prints, and only one set, so no one had dragged Sarah through the woods. The tight muscles across his shoulders loosened. Such tiny feet, though. The size of a child's.

He moved quickly through the forest until he spotted a splash of pink ahead in a clearing. A girl stood with her back to him. Both hands gripped a pistol pointed at a target on a tree.

He sucked in a breath. Holy shit. Sarah. In one swift move, he leaped out of the woods and disarmed her.

"Oh my God." Sarah pressed a hand to her chest. "You scared the crap out of me. I didn't hear you."

"Good. You deserve it. What is this?" He cleared the weapon and flicked the safety on. Blood raged in his ears.

"It's my g-gun. I'm learning how to shoot it," she said, eyes wide.

"Well, it's a damned good thing I came along when I did because you were about to have your thumb ripped off when the slide came back. Who taught you how to hold a gun?"

She bristled. "I watched a video."

He shut his eyes and blew out a breath. Unbelievable. A video. She could have killed herself. "Where did you get this?"

"At a pawn shop." She nibbled her lower lip.

"I assume this isn't registered, and I know you don't have a license to carry because even I don't. The laws are strict in Maryland."

"I couldn't register it if I wanted to. Not with a fake name."

"What if Debbie called the police and they found you out here shooting an illegal gun? Do you have any idea what kind of trouble you'd be in?"

"I'm sure, but I have to learn how to use it."

His gaze went to the target. "Seriously? You were shooting at a hardwood tree?"

"What's wrong with that?"

"It's dangerous. This is why people who know nothing about guns shouldn't have them. I'm keeping this."

"No." Sarah shook her head. "It's mine and I want it back. I need it for protection." She held out her hand.

"It's not safe."

"I'm not safe," she said in a panicked voice. "Please, give me my weapon. I have to learn to defend myself."

The desperation in her eyes tore at him. She was scared for her life. He paced the area and then stopped in front of her. "On one condition."

"What?"

"You keep the gun hidden in the house and don't dare bring it back out to shoot. I'll take you to a place where I can teach you how."

"You'd do that?"

He nodded. "If you're hell-bent on learning, I'll show you the right way. There's a small range out in the boonies where hardly anyone ever goes. We can practice there if you agree to my terms."

She tugged on her earlobe. "I don't know how long I'll be here. Joe said he could fix my car tomorrow."

Bruce's stomach seized. He couldn't let her go. She'd be alone and out of his protection. "You're safer here than on the run. The suite is secure, and you have people looking out for you."

She crossed her arms and rubbed her hands up and down them. "I don't know…Todd—"

"Hasn't done anything and won't with us all around. Once you leave, all bets are off." Despite the turmoil inside, he kept his voice no-nonsense-logical.

"Well…" She eyed the gun. "I haven't found a place to go yet, and I do want to learn how to shoot. Please, can I have that back?"

"Promise you'll do what I asked and not run off half-cocked?"

"Not funny." She pursed her lips and nodded.

Relief ripped the cord and parachuted off his shoulders. He handed her the gun. Pinching the flesh under his chin, he frowned.

"What's wrong?" Sarah glanced up at him.

"Have a problem. You spooked the horses, and Debbie's back there waiting with my new patients."

"Oh no. I didn't realize you had anyone today. It's Saturday." Sarah tapped his arm. "I'm so sorry. I was too close the first time. I moved as soon as I heard how loud it was. Is everyone all right?"

"Yeah, but you've put me in a shitty spot. I don't lie to people."

"I don't expect you to." She lifted her chin. "You have a right to be angry. Tell Debbie the truth. If she fires me, it's not your fault."

"No. It won't come to that."

"What do you mean? You said you couldn't lie."

He stared hard at her for a long minute. Lying to Debbie went against his moral code.

Sarah's eyes turned glassy. "I might have scared your new patients. I know how important your program is to you. I'm so, so sorry."

No doubt from the tremble in her voice. Damn, she made things difficult. "Go back to the house through the other entrance from the woods. The one along the drive."

"But what will you tell Debbie?"

He frowned. Technically, he wouldn't be lying. "The truth. I found someone who had no idea what they were doing, ran them off, and scared them enough to never do it again." He raised an eyebrow. "That is the truth, right?"

She nodded. "Yes."

"Now go. I have to get back to my patients."

She didn't move.

"What?" he asked.

"Thank you." She stood on her tiptoes, gave him a quick kiss on the cheek, then ran toward where the woods met the drive.

He closed his eyes. His cheek tingled where her warm lips had kissed it. He had no clue what to do with her. She'd turned his world upside down. In less than two minutes, she'd made him raving mad, frustrated, worried, scared—

Whoa, scared?

He never got rattled. Not even in combat under fire. Yet whenever Sarah mentioned leaving, the chambers of his heart emptied.

That needed to change. He'd lost enough blood.

CHAPTER 16

Bruce drove into the cemetery and followed the winding road. He pulled off to the side and stopped. Rows of tombstones gleamed under the midday sun. He took a deep breath.

Emily's birthday. She would have turned thirty-two. Never thought he'd outlive her.

He'd come back to the States with a bullet wound, and Emily had been his nurse at Walter Reed. A tough lady with a big heart, she soon won his over. Her straightforward-no-BS approach worked wonders with the soldiers. She knew exactly how to treat them and earned their respect. She found a way to break through the wall Bruce had put up to survive the horrors he'd witnessed while in Special Forces. A year later, he and Emily got married. Her love filled the void left when his parents had died.

Even though he'd inherited enough money to live a life of luxury, neither of them cared about fancy things. He indulged and bought a beautiful home, but they lived a simple life, hiking and camping for fun.

He closed his eyes. She'd died two weeks before Christmas. While people celebrated with parties and gift exchanges, his entire world crashed. Now he kept the radio off through the holiday season. Christmas would never be the same.

With a sigh, he picked up the bouquet of red roses from the passenger's seat and opened the door. Head down, he marched a straight line behind a row of tombstones until he came to Emily's. Pink carnations were scattered on the grave.

Joe. He never forgot. The flowers blurred.

Bruce knelt and placed the roses in front of her headstone. His chest ached as he rested a hand on the slab and whispered, "No one could ever take your place." He stayed in that position until his legs went numb. When he stood, pins and needles pricked them.

"Happy Birthday, Em," he said softly. Painful memories flooded as he trudged back to the truck.

Every time he had entered his family room, the tree they'd cut down together mocked him. Ornaments with their wedding pictures, all smiles and full of love, hung on the branches. The gifts he picked out that she would never open glittered under the lights.

After the funeral, he and Joe went back to the house. Bruce wandered to the Christmas tree, picked up one of the wedding ornaments, and held it so tightly the glass cracked, cutting his hand. He grabbed his truck keys and drove around for hours. When he came back, he opened the door to find everything gone. The tree, the decorations, and the gifts. A short note Joe left on the counter said the presents were in a box behind the entertainment center. The next day, Bruce donated them all to a charity for battered women.

He sold his house fully furnished and moved to a condominium on the water. Like a robot, he threw himself into his job, taking on more PT patients. He lost weight and stopped going out. Friends, supportive at first, fell by the wayside when he didn't return calls.

One day, Joe showed up and dragged Bruce to the farm. Said he needed someone to train a lame ex-racehorse he'd rescued.

Bruce had argued that he didn't have time, but one look in the proud, injured horse's eyes, and he couldn't say no. Looking back, he knew they'd saved each other's lives from a downward path.

And damn that sneaky Joe. He'd known it.

Bruce got into his truck and drove through the open gates of the cemetery. When he reached the farm, he parked in the grass, away from the house and the stables. Today, he'd rather be alone as much as possible. He climbed out and leaned against the passenger door, his gaze on the horses as they grazed in the fields. The mere sight of them calmed him.

He didn't turn when the sound of random whistling and footsteps came from behind. A bottle cap hissed, and a beer entered his line of sight. He reached for it as Joe sidled up beside him and leaned against the hood.

For a while, they stood in silence sipping the beers and facing the fields.

"Lost a dollar bet yesterday on the Orioles game," Joe said.

"Yeah?"

"Damn Yankees."

"That was a tough one." Bruce ran a thumb up and down the bottle in his hand.

"Seems it's always like that. You know?"

"Like what?" Bruce glanced at Joe, who wore a frown and kept his gaze on the fields.

"Things are going great. You're moving along, thinking you have a game plan. Then bam, the Yankees come to town and kick your ass." He took a swig of beer. "And to boot, you lose your best pitcher to a career-ending injury."

"Yup."

Silence stretched between them for a while.

Joe scratched his head. "But it's not over, you know. It's never easy to find and break in a replacement pitcher, but that's what champions do. Anything to get their game back. And the fans rally to support them." He glanced at Bruce. "They love their team, and they never give up on them."

A lump formed in Bruce's throat.

Joe's gaze went back to the meadows. "Of course, the star pitcher's mad as hell he can't play anymore, but he can still watch and cheer from the stands. Cuz in the end, he wants his team to go on without him and win."

Bruce's eyes fogged.

A door slammed, and he swung around to face the house. Sarah came out onto the front porch carrying a drink. Her dark hair blew in the breeze.

Joe looked over his shoulder at the ranch. He drank the last of his beer and said quietly, "She'd want you to be happy. It's time."

Courageous, caring, beautiful Sarah. Bruce's shoulders tightened. She'd found a way in. Even after the gun incident, he couldn't stay mad at her. But if she ran or anything happened to her, he'd be alone.

Again.

"You know something else?" Joe tapped his bottle against the hood of the truck. "Only one person I can think of who was a bigger baseball fan than me."

Bruce cleared his throat. "Who?"

"Your father."

Too choked up to speak, Bruce gazed back at the fields. They used to go to the games together. Him, Uncle Joe, and his dad.

Joe pushed off the truck. "Yup. Somewhere he's got box seat tickets to this"—he waved a hand around the farm—"and he's casting his vote for you as the MVP."

Bruce blinked hard. Neither of them spoke for a long minute.

Joe dusted off his pants. "You want to get some grub?"

"No. I'm good."

"Suit yourself." He shrugged and took a step toward the house.

"Hey." Bruce kept his back to Joe and said in a low voice, "Thanks."

"Yup." Joe muttered, "Damn Yankees."

Bruce had an hour to kill before Charlie's lesson. He drove home with Joe's words ringing in his ears. "It's time."

He tried to put himself in Emily's shoes. If anything had happened to him, causing her to be the one left alone, he'd want her to be happy and move on.

When he entered his condo, he gazed around the large, open family room. Paintings of seascapes and farms graced the walls. No pictures cluttered the end tables. The stainless-steel refrigerator, bare of any snapshots, gleamed under the lights. A realtor could walk in at any time and show the place without having to remove any personal effects.

He went upstairs to his bedroom and picked up a framed photo of

Emily from the nightstand, a candid shot he'd taken of her with her horse. Right before he'd taken it, she'd looked up and grinned.

Her warm brown eyes gazed back at him. He ran a finger along the picture frame. His chest constricted. She would understand and want him to move on.

Sarah...the welcome feel of her body in his arms when he'd carried her to the suite after the sunset. The soft touch of her lips on his cheek when she'd kissed him earlier. And that, after he'd been so gruff. He wasn't upset with her for trying to learn to defend herself. Maybe not the best choice of when and where to shoot, but she had pluck. She might not be able to find the stalker, but she wouldn't sit back in a corner and cower either.

He couldn't tell her about Emily. Sarah had enough of her own problems without taking on his baggage. She didn't need the pressure of trying to measure up to a ghost. Or worse, pity him. Nope. His past, his problem to deal with.

He opened the nightstand drawer, placed the picture inside, and shut it. Nothing but lonely silence hung in the air. Maybe Joe was right, and it was time for Bruce to bring Sarah into his life. He glanced at his watch. But not today. Not on Emily's birthday. A weight pressed on his shoulders. He'd get through this one the same way he always had. Shut down the feelings. Too many, too close to the surface. He took a deep breath and stood.

Tomorrow, after his ride with Morgan, he'd talk to Sarah.

Time to take that first step.

CHAPTER 17

Sarah washed and dried her glass. Bruce had turned and looked in her direction a couple of hours ago when she'd come out onto the porch, but he hadn't waved or acknowledged her. He was probably still pissed over the gun. She'd jeopardized his program. So far, Debbie hadn't fired her. Bruce must have left out the details of *who* he'd found in the woods. Sarah would try to make it up to him somehow.

Ugh. What a mess.

Maybe she could apologize again and find out if she'd caused him to lose the new patients. She checked her watch. Charlie would be coming for his therapy soon so she'd have to wait until after to talk to Bruce.

She locked the back door to the suite and rounded the corner to find Todd standing next to her car, peering into the driver's window. Her heart jumped, and she stopped short.

"Hi. This yours?" He straightened and leaned against the side of his Vette, which was parked next to her car.

"What are you doing up here?" She glanced around, but no one was in sight.

"You answer my question, and I'll answer yours." He gave her a toothy crocodile smile.

Her pulse raced. She had to get away before he made her his next meal. She shouldn't have let Bruce talk her into staying. "I don't have time for this."

"How about I drive you down to the barn?" He patted the roof of his car. "I bet you've never been in a ride like this."

"No, thanks." She took a couple steps to go around the side of her car.

"You don't know what you're missing. One spin in this and driving that Honda of yours will feel like punishment. Come on, you deserve it."

Her stomach dropped, and she faltered a step. Punishment. *Audrey made that fatal mistake and needed to be punished for it, but I know you won't.* It could be a coincidence that he'd used the word *punishment*, or maybe he was taunting her. She met his leering gaze across the car. Alone, without her gun, she wasn't going to take him on. "I'm good. Gotta run."

She jogged toward the stables and didn't look back. His engine hummed to life, and she picked up her pace. He wouldn't try to run her over in broad daylight unless he was crazy. A psycho. Okay. Maybe he would. She reached the barn gasping for air.

Lynn led Misty out of her stall. "Something wrong?"

Sarah swiped her forehead and peered out the stable entrance. "Not sure. Do you know what Todd was doing up at the house? I found him out by my car."

Lynn frowned. "No. He was asking around for Debbie earlier. Maybe he went looking for her."

"Maybe." Sarah glanced back at the driveway.

"Be careful around that guy. I've seen him watching you."

"I'm trying. He seems to pop up out of nowhere." Her gaze followed Todd's car as it disappeared around a bend in the driveway.

"Have you seen Bruce?" Lynn tied Misty to a ring.

Sarah shook her head. "Not recently. He was with Joe earlier this morning."

"This isn't like him. He's always here early for the sessions." Lynn frowned. "Charlie's due soon."

"Need some help tacking up?"

"It's your day off. I don't want you to have to work."

"I don't mind. I'm not busy." Sarah shrugged.

"If you're sure, then thanks. I would ask Becca or Lori, but they're riding. God knows they earn the time as hard as they work around here."

Sarah grabbed a brush and tried to sound casual. "Bruce mentioned having some new patients this morning. How did it go?"

"Well, there was a little excitement with some idiot shooting in the woods, but he took care of it, and the vets are coming back next week, so I guess all's well."

Her chest lightened. Thank God. At least she hadn't lost him his new clients. It might be best to change the subject from the shooter. She didn't want to open that can of worms. "Misty's such a great therapy horse."

"I know. We're hoping to get another one soon. Morgan and Bruce have been looking."

"Morgan?" Sarah glanced up at Lynn.

Lynn nodded. "She's donating a horse to the program."

"She is?"

"I know. Shocks me too." Lynn picked up one of Misty's hooves to check.

"Why would she do that? Is she somehow affiliated with the program?"

"No. If you ask me, she's just trying to impress Bruce. He can afford to buy the horse, but he says it will make Morgan feel good to contribute." She shook her head.

"Not a fan of hers?" At least Sarah wasn't the only one.

"Nope. I don't like the way she treats the young girls. Becca and Lori bust their butts around here, and she gets on their backs if they don't have her horse tacked and ready the second she walks in." She picked up another hoof to check. "If Morgan really cared about her horse, she'd groom and tack it herself."

Sarah frowned. Coming from Lynn, who could find the good in Attila the Hun, that said a lot. "Bruce seems to like her well enough."

"I've known him a long time. As smart as he is, when it comes to women he can be a little dense." Lynn sighed. "I think he feels sorry for Morgan for some reason. She puts up quite the show around him, and she's good at it, being an actress."

"I didn't know she was."

"Yup. Used to be in a soap opera out in California. Now she does shampoo commercials in New York."

That's why she looked familiar. "Why does she live here?"

"No idea. I don't know how often she films. Clearly has plenty of spare time to ride."

Bruce entered the stables and made his way to them in quick strides. "Sorry, Lynn, I'm pushing the time today."

"Is everything okay?" Lynn cocked her head.

"Yeah. Need help with Misty?"

"No. We have it. I'll meet you by the arena."

Bruce nodded and turned.

Sarah gazed at Bruce's rigid back as he left the stables. Even when he'd been mad at her about the gun incident, he hadn't outright ignored her. And his face, so cold and detached. A frown or a scowl at least showed some emotion. He was the one who'd convinced her to stay. If she made him so uncomfortable, he should have urged her to leave.

Lynn's brows came together. "What's today's date?"

Sarah checked her watch. "May seventeenth."

"Now it makes sense." Lynn shook her head.

"What does?"

Lynn's lips compressed until they disappeared. She picked up a saddle pad and placed it on Misty. "Nothing I can talk about. Bruce wouldn't appreciate it."

"Oh." Sarah stepped away from the horse, unsure what else to say.

She glanced one last time at him. In his current mood, she didn't dare approach him. Tomorrow she'd make him some muffins and try again to apologize.

***

The morning sun shined through the crack between the suite's curtains. Sarah wrapped the muffins she'd made in clear plastic and placed them in a shallow box with no lid. They'd turned out better than she'd expected. The juicy, bright blueberries had burst and blended with the glittery sugar, swirling color through the tops. Not bad, considering her limited baking skills.

Someone knocked. "It's Joe."

He always made sure to announce himself, like he knew she would be nervous about a stranger showing up.

When she opened the door, he wiped a paint-splattered sleeve across his brow. "Finished with your car. I put a couple gallons of gas in, but you'll need to take it to the station to fill."

Her hard stomach loosened. Now she could leave if things went south with Bruce. Not that she had anywhere to go yet.

"Thanks. What do I owe you?"

"Eh." Joe waved a hand smeared with copper rust stains. "Don't worry about it. Buddy didn't charge me for the tank. Had it on the lot."

"Oh no. I want to pay for your time as well." She didn't want to accept charity, and he'd done more than he should to help her.

"Save your money. Bad news is you're gonna need it for other repairs. I looked the car over."

A nerve in her neck stung. "What's wrong?"

"Radiator's rusted almost through, tires are bald, and probably needs new brakes." His mouth twisted to the side. "Won't get many more miles out of it without more work."

Shit. She didn't have the money for repairs, and if she could only reach the next town, that wasn't much of an escape plan.

"Hey, no sad faces." He shook a finger at her. "They sell used tires, and Buddy can keep an eye out for a radiator."

Neither of those answers solved her immediate problem. And she couldn't expect Joe to keep bailing her out. "I appreciate that. All the more reason I insist on paying for the gas tank."

Joe cocked his head and sniffed. "Swear I smell cake or something."

If he was trying to change the subject, it wouldn't work. "I baked muffins. Now about—"

"How about a barter? I'll take one of them."

"That's hardly a trade." She stepped to the counter and fetched the box. "You can have all of these, but it's still not enough."

He licked his lips, and his eyes grew wide as wagon wheels. "Deal. No more money talk. Haven't ordered carryout since you showed up. Call us even."

"Okay, for now. Thanks." She'd rather pay him, but he did seem to appreciate her cooking. Maybe that meant more to him than a few bucks. She'd have to make more muffins for Bruce, but it was worth the look on Joe's face. The warmth in her chest ebbed as she eyed her last stick of butter in the dish. The new batch would have to turn out just as good.

Joe nodded and left, carrying the box like it held the triple-crown trophy.

She shut the door and pressed a hand to her chest. With no idea how far the car might go before it blew out a tire or overheated, more than ever, she needed to stay at the farm. Her heart thumped fast.

She whipped up another batch of muffins, tossed them in the oven, and headed to the shower. Joe's words about the car needing work rattled around in her head, and she lingered under the jet of water aimed at her bunched-up neck muscles.

While she brushed her hair, the stench of something burning seeped into the bathroom. Damn it. She raced to the kitchen and yanked the oven door open. Black smoke rose from spilled batter in the bottom. She snagged a dishtowel by the sink and whisked the tray out.

Steam from the damp rag she held burned her fingers. With a yelp, she tossed the hot pan onto the counter. She turned on the spigot and held her red, throbbing fingers under the cold water. A glance at the blacktopped, charred muffins confirmed her fears. Uneatable.

Her hopes for sweetening her apology to Bruce sank to the soles of her feet. She dug out a potholder and moved the tray to the sink. It hissed when it hit the water and spit dark bits of muffin onto her white T-shirt. She cursed and shut off the spigot.

Spinning on her heel, she gasped. Scorch marks marred the countertop. Her lungs collapsed like a flopped soufflé. This couldn't be happening. Now she'd damaged Debbie's kitchen. She'd owe more money than she made at this rate. With a groan, she stomped to the family room and plopped down on the couch.

Holding her head in her hands, she took a deep, shaky breath. One problem at a time. The car needed gas. She'd go to town and get whatever she needed to fix the counter from the hardware store along with a newspaper to check out the help-wanted ads. If Bruce had changed his mind overnight about her staying, she needed a place to go and a ready car.

He'd scribbled something on his calendar in the barn for noon. She could be back in plenty of time to catch him before he left for the day. Armed with a plan, she changed her shirt, snagged her purse, and headed to the Honda.

A full tank of gas later, Sarah drove past the arena and spotted Bruce's parked truck. Nervous energy revved. She might need it if he acted like he had yesterday afternoon. Cold, detached, and expressionless.

She entered her suite and opened the newspaper on the counter. If the car couldn't take her far, she'd have to hide someplace close until she had other options. A quick scan of the jobs drained her energy faster than a cellphone with too many apps open. She tore out one listing for help wanted at a produce farm not too far away. Dirt pay, hard labor, and no lodging, but if she got desperate...

She rolled her shoulders. Time to find Bruce and figure out her fate. She left the suite, locking the door behind her. Her gaze traveled the fields dotted with riders. It was a warm spring Sunday, and most of the boarders had shown up.

Bruce was nowhere in sight. He might be in the barn or riding farther out. She checked the stables. Batal's stall sat empty. Maybe she should leave a note on Bruce's truck for him to stop up to see her before he left.

A horse whinnied outside the entrance, and she turned. Morgan and Bruce stood close, holding the lead lines of Batal and Princess.

Morgan's name must have been the scrawl on the calendar that Sarah couldn't make out. Ugh. She would have to wait until the Ice Queen left to talk to him.

Moving even closer to Bruce, Morgan slid a hand up his chest to rest on his cheek. He gazed down at her, but the glaring sun made it impossible for Sarah to see his expression. Morgan eased into his arms and they embraced.

Sarah's throat closed. Of course, they were together. Just because he had some sort of attraction to Sarah didn't mean he would ever do anything about it. That was probably why he acted so hot and cold with her. She blinked fast several times. She'd been an idiot to ignore the signs that he and Morgan were a couple.

Before Sarah could get away, Morgan sashayed into the barn leading Princess. Bruce led Batal back toward the arena.

A Cheshire cat grin formed on Morgan's face. "Something wrong?"

"No." Sarah moved to pass her.

Morgan clicked her tongue. "Tsk, tsk. You're not a very good liar. Bruce and I don't keep secrets from each other; maybe you shouldn't either."

The blood drained from Sarah's limbs. Oh God. He'd told Morgan about the stalker.

Sarah stumbled and fell over a bucket someone had left in the aisle, scraping her hands on the hard dirt.

Morgan let out a throaty laugh. "Oops. What happened to those graceful moves of yours?"

Sarah shoved off the ground and marched out of the barn toward the house. Betrayal burned in her breast with every step. Bruce had probably mentioned that she used to dance and lived in California. Morgan was mocking her about being a ballerina. It wouldn't take much for her to figure out Sarah's identity with that information. Since Morgan used to live there and worked in the entertainment business, she might still have contacts. She could leak something about Sarah's whereabouts.

She'd heard that men would tell a woman anything in bed, but she'd never believed it of Bruce. He'd made her a promise. That's what she got for opening up to a man. Morgan hated her. She'd blab the secret to everyone and blow Sarah's cover.

Her head pounded in time with her swift feet.

She had no choice but to leave.

CHAPTER 18

BRUCE WALKED Batal around the field to let him cool down before he put him back in the stables. Batal needed more time than Princess to recover because Bruce had ridden him before Morgan showed up.

Morgan had seemed okay right up until they'd dismounted, and then she got weepy over the anniversary of her husband's death. Understandable. Those dates were tough.

Bruce led Batal into the stables, groomed him, and put him back in his stall. No excuse to wait any longer. Time to talk to Sarah. He hadn't dared look at her yesterday afternoon. Too many emotions were already stirred up inside of him from the cemetery visit and the talk with Joe.

Today might be the start of a new chapter in his life. His heart flexed against the cables that had held it tight for four long years. He patted Batal on the nose, then headed to Sarah's suite.

The door stood open a crack. His radar went up. Sarah always kept it locked. He stepped inside. The place smelled like someone had set toast on fire. Maybe she'd left the door open to air it out. But the window over the couch was closed.

He crossed to the kitchen and stopped short. Scorch marks stained the counter. Holy shit. They wouldn't be easy to get up. He glanced at the soaking muffin pan in the sink. Mystery solved. He narrowed his eyes. Earlier, Joe had passed him on the way to the barn, stuffing a big, fat muffin in his mouth and carrying a box. When he got closer, the crusty coot had cast a smug crumb-filled grin Bruce's way, clutching the carton possessively. Bruce could swear he'd tipped it on purpose to show off the mouthwatering muffins. Not a burned one among them.

A breeze through the open door blew a scrap of paper to the floor. He picked it up and placed it back on the counter, glancing at the title. A help-wanted ad for a produce farm. His belly balked. Sarah had no reason to cut out listings if she planned to stay like she'd said.

"Sarah?" He grabbed the ad and stepped closer to the bedroom. When she didn't answer, he poked his head through the doorway. A lumpy duffel bag sat on the bed and empty dresser drawers hung out. His blood began a slow simmer.

The door to the bathroom opened, and Sarah came out dressed in jeans and a T-shirt, carrying a full bag with a hairdryer sticking out of the top.

She gasped. "You scared the crap out of me."

"What's this?" He held up the help-wanted ad.

She glanced at the paper. "How did you get in here?"

"You left the door open. Answer my question."

She bit her lip and said nothing.

"I thought we agreed it was safer for you to stay here. Were you planning to leave?"

"It's too risky now." She crossed to the bed and dropped the bag next to the packed duffel.

"Why? Did the stalker threaten you again?" Bruce glanced at the curtained windows.

"Not since the last time." She tucked the hairdryer deeper into the bag.

"Then why run?" He clenched his jaw. "And were you even going to tell me?"

"I was going to leave a note."

"A note. Nice." That's all he meant to her. Scratch something on a sticky pad and leave it on the kitchen table like a damned grocery list. If he hadn't stopped by, he might never have seen her again. An ache split his chest in half.

He caught her arm. "You haven't answered my question. Why is it too risky?"

She faced him and raised her chin. "Because I don't trust Morgan."

"What's Morgan have to do with this?"

"Look, it's none of my business." Sarah waved a hand in the air and huffed. "I didn't realize you two were together, or I wouldn't have told you anything. She could lead the stalker to me."

So Sarah had jumped to conclusions. Made assumptions and never bothered to ask him. "Hold on a second. You think I'm involved with Morgan?"

"Well, that's what I call it when you go on picnics together, and ride together, and…I saw you with her outside of the barn today."

"Let me get this straight." His lungs burned. "You think I'm with Morgan, and therefore would obviously tell her everything you've shared with me."

"Well, I've heard that guys will talk in bed and…never mind." She dropped her gaze to the ground and tightened her lips.

Talk in bed? Christ, he hadn't even had sex in four years. "After I promised not to say anything to anyone?"

She cleared her throat. "I mean—"

"You think if I'm sleeping with someone I would put your life in jeopardy, because that's not as important as getting laid?" His head pounded. "That I, of all people, wouldn't know how to keep a secret?"

"I guess maybe I—"

"Maybe you what? Maybe you were wrong?" He yanked his hand back from her arm. "How about hell yeah, on all counts."

* * *

Sarah blinked. Bruce's eyes shot flames. Pure, unadulterated, hot-fire emotion. Wow. He did have feelings, and she'd tapped into them bigtime. Now she'd done it and pissed him off. She licked her lips. "You mean you aren't dating Morgan?"

"Bull's-eye."

She frowned. "Then what do you call it? Going on a picnic—"

"Enough with the picnic. There was no picnic. God, you're making me fucking crazy." He stabbed a hand through his hair.

She waited. Didn't dare say anything else. He might explode.

He blew out a breath and gazed at the ceiling as a muscle ticked in his jaw. At last, he looked down at her. "Morgan is nothing more than a friend. I ride with her because Princess is the only horse who can challenge Batal, and he loves to race." Bruce held a hand up. "And I don't know what you saw, but Morgan hugged me. Last I checked you didn't need a condom for that."

So they weren't together. Her heart landed a perfect grand jeté

His pupils had shrunk to tiny pinpoints.

"And that picnic? Do you know what happened?" He stepped closer, his voice controlled and calm.

Too calm.

"It's okay—"

"No, it's not okay. None of this is okay. You leaving without telling me. You assuming I'm sleeping with Morgan. You deciding I can't keep a promise. None of this is okay. So you're going to hear me out."

A vein in his neck pulsated. If he expected her to say anything, he'd wait awhile. Better to let him get it off his chest. He had a point. She'd made a lot of assumptions and some of them not very flattering about him.

"There was never a picnic. We drove together to see a therapy horse, and Morgan packed some snacks, but I told her I needed to get back." He brought his face nearer. "Do you know why?"

Sarah swallowed and shook her head. He was close enough that his breath tickled her cheeks, and the masculine scent of his cologne made her want to bury her face in his shirt.

"Because of you."

"Me?"

"Yes. You. I wanted to get back and talk to you about whatever you tried to say to me today before Morgan showed up."

Her blood ran fast laps through her veins. Heat came off him in waves, and all she could do was stare up at him, her legs pressed against the side of the bed.

"I haven't been able to think about much of anything since you set foot on this farm." His gaze dropped to her lips. "Actually, that's not true. There is one thing I can't stop thinking about."

She let out a shallow breath. "What?"

"Doing this." He snaked an arm out, yanked her against him, and covered her mouth with his.

Initial shock lasted a mere second before the kiss overtook her. He moved his lips against hers, and the pent-up fire in her body exploded. She threw her arms around him and dove into the kiss. A slight moan escaped when she opened her mouth to let his tongue inside. A primal groan came from him as he worked magic with his lips. God, the man could kiss. Her nipples hardened, and she dug her fingers into his muscular back.

He took the kiss deeper, slanting his mouth over hers. The hard length of his arousal pressed against her, sending a thrill through her body. She clung tighter.

The front door slammed and loud voices erupted upstairs.

When Bruce ripped his mouth away, Sarah almost fell over. His chest heaved and his eyes blazed. She gazed up at him, still in his arms. The room blurred behind him, his face filling her view. Heat swelled in her breast, forcing its way up to her cheeks. The small of her back vibrated under his spanned hands.

"You should have run it by me first." Debbie's gruff voice rang out from upstairs. "I'm busy enough as it is. I don't need the extra work."

"You don't have to do anything with it," Joe said.

The door slammed again, this time followed by scuffling, a howl from the cat, and a loud crash. A dog barked. Bruce cursed under his breath and let go of Sarah. A large, gangly, black dog with oversized ears bounded into the room. The mutt ran right to Sarah, tail wagging so hard it thumped the dresser beside her. She reached down, and the dog licked her fingers.

"See? Not five seconds in the house and already it's trouble," Debbie shouted from upstairs.

"Just needs some time to adjust," Joe said. "Sarah, you down there?"

Footsteps pounded on the stairs. She dropped to her knees and petted the mutt, happy for the distraction as she needed some time to regain her composure. "Yes. I think your dog sorta found me."

Joe appeared in the doorway. He glanced at Bruce and then at her. He coughed into his hand, unsuccessfully hiding a smile. "Sorry. He's gonna need a little training."

"No, he's not. He's not staying," Debbie said from the other room. "He went right after the cat."

"That's how nature made 'em." Joe shrugged and muttered, "Can't blame a guy for wanting to get some puss—"

"I'm serious, Joe." Debbie entered the bedroom. "He can't stay here. This is the most harebrained thing you've done in a long time."

The dog leaned closer to Sarah and nudged her with his nose.

Debbie glanced down at them. Her mouth pursed, she glared at Joe, then waved a hand and stomped back toward the steps. "Goddamn it. You work it out."

Sarah gazed at Bruce, who had an unreadable expression on his face as he stared at the dog.

"Where did he come from?" Sarah asked.

Joe bent over to scratch the mutt under his chin. "I rescued him from the shelter. They were gonna put him down."

"Why?"

"Cuz he isn't a puppy, and the last owner claimed he tried to bite someone who was crawling through his window. Once they get listed as a biter, no one will take them." Joe stood. "He was protecting the house. Stupid idiots."

"Since when do you go to the shelters looking for dogs?" Bruce cocked his head.

"The same time I stopped reporting everything I do to you."

They locked gazes.

Sarah broke the standoff. "Sounds like Debbie doesn't want him here."

"He'll grow on her," Joe said.

"Not if he has to go back." Sarah stood, and the dog flopped down across her feet to rest his head on the floor.

"He's sure taken to you." Joe rubbed his jaw.

"Big surprise there," Bruce said in a low voice.

Joe stroked his chin. "You know, what if he stayed down here with you when he's in the house at night?"

She'd never had a pet. "I don't really know how to take care of a dog."

"Eh. It's easy. You feed him and let him out to pee. Plenty of room on the farm for him to run. He won't even need walks."

And he'd be extra protection if the stalker came creeping around. Or Todd for that matter. Sarah glanced at Bruce. "What do you think?"

He frowned but then nodded. "I think you'd be fine with him."

"If Debbie says it's all right, we can try it out." Sarah wiggled her feet under the dog and smiled when he wagged his tail.

"Good. I have a sack of food and some bowls upstairs."

Huh. That sure was convenient. "Okay, thanks," Sarah said. "Wait. What's his name?"

"Fluffy."

Bruce snorted.

Sarah's gaze dropped to the shorthaired dog.

"Like I said. Idiot owners." Joe pushed past Bruce.

When he left, the pup rolled on his side and let out a long sigh.

"Unbelievable." Bruce blew out a breath. "I came here to ask you something."

"What?" Alone with him again, she got a case of the jitters.

"Do you like to hike?"

"Hike?"

"Yes. You've never heard of it?"

She rolled her eyes. "Of course, I mean, why?"

"I was wondering if you might want to go with me Saturday." He crossed his arms.

"I don't understand. Like on a date?"

He grimaced. "It's hiking. You know, more like a recon."

"A recon?" She squinted. That was something they did in the military to scope out an area.

"Yeah, you know. Get the lay of the land. Figure things out."

"Figure what out? I really don't understand what you're talking about." She shook her head.

He uncrossed his arms and sighed. "Fine. A date."

Her heart jumped and then sank. "I'm not dating material. I'm in hiding and can't promise any sort of future. Hell, half the time I can't plan for tomorrow. You'd be better off dating someone who could—"

"I'm aware of your situation."

She fiddled with the hem of her shirt. God knew she wanted to say yes, but it might not be fair to him, and she didn't want to risk developing feelings for someone who she'd have to leave.

"Don't overthink it." He bent down and brushed his lips against hers.

When she leaned in, he put a hand behind her head and deepened the kiss. His warm mouth covered hers, and he tasted of spearmint. He pulled back and traced a finger over her lower lip. Her entire body shivered in response. He inched his thumb down her neck to the top of her collarbone.

"So h-hike?" She couldn't think with his hands on her.

"Yes. I know a trail along the water." He stroked the sensitive area right above the bone.

"You don't play fair," she whispered.

"Not when it comes to you."

He ran his hand along her nape. The dog wedged itself between them and nudged Sarah. Bruce muttered something about Joe as she patted the dog's snout.

"I'll pick you up around ten?"

"Sure."

He smiled, gave her arm a squeeze, and sauntered out of the room.

Holy shit. That man could kiss.

And he'd smiled at her.

She ran a finger over her lips. Bruce had kissed her twice. Could have been three times if not for interference from the mutt. "We're going to have to set up some rules, Fluffy."

The dog raised its head.

"That's right. I'm talking to you." Sarah smiled to herself. Alone with Bruce in the woods. Now that she'd had a taste, she wanted him even more.

Hard to say what could happen without the dog interfering.

CHAPTER 19

Sarah checked her watch. Three o'clock. Time to head up to the house and start dinner. The week had dragged, but tomorrow was Saturday, and her hike with Bruce. Her heart skipped. Working around him had been hard enough before he'd kissed her. Now every time he came close, her body tingled. And she'd swear he found more ways to be near her than ever before. She shook her head. Better focus on cleaning up and making a meal.

She headed to the far corner of the tack room and bent over to pick up tools. Soft footsteps sounded behind her. The hairs on the back of her neck raised.

"Don't stand on my account. I like the view," Todd said.

Her stomach catapulted. She swung around and glanced behind him at the empty barn. His car hadn't been in the lot or she would have kept a better eye out. He must have just shown up.

"I have work to do." She tried to move past him, but he reached and leaned his palm against the wall, blocking her path. Damn it. He might be bigger, but she had moves and speed.

"I've been waiting for the chance to have a word with you, alone." He inched closer.

She glanced around for anything she could use as a weapon, but nothing was in reach. "We really have nothing to discuss. Now if you don't mind—"

"You can stop with the haughty act. You're a stable hand not a princess." His mouth twisted. "A little respect out of you might be a nice change. I pay good money to board here."

"You're not my boss. And I'm not on your payroll."

"You could be. Is that what it takes?" He sneered and raised an eyebrow.

Son of a bitch. Her body tensed, ready to take action.

"Don't play innocent with me. I've seen the way you parade around here. What do you expect people to think when you send out those signals? I just want a little piece of that hot ass of yours like everyone else." He slithered even closer. "Money's no object. I can make it worth your time. Clothes? A car? What's your price? Everyone has one."

He reached a hand out and brushed the side of her breast.

Bastard. She wound her arm back and slapped him hard in the face.

He staggered to the right, and she darted past him. Her hand stung as she ran out the entrance. Good. Maybe she'd left a mark.

"You're going to pay for that, whore," he yelled after her.

She ran past the horses and out into the sunlight.

Joe rounded the corner of the barn. "What's going on? I heard someone shout."

The sight of him quelled her fight-or-flight response.

Todd burst out of the stables, a bright red handprint on his cheek and blood on his lip.

Joe took one look at him and waved his shovel as he marched toward Todd. "Get the hell out of here, and don't even think of coming back."

Todd glowered at Joe and then at Sarah.

"I mean it. Send someone for your horse. If you step one foot on this place again, I'll shoot you," Joe said.

"You couldn't pay me to come back to this shithole. I'm done slumming. This dump isn't good enough for me, and neither are you." He spit on the ground in front of Sarah and stomped to the parking lot.

Greg jogged over from the field. "What's going on?"

"You okay, Sarah?" Joe asked.

"I'm fine." She nodded, her insides still shaky.

Greg's nostrils flared. "Did he hurt you?"

"No. I handled it," she said.

Bruce's truck pulled in as Todd gunned his car. The wheels churned dirt and spit up stones before the Vette thundered down the driveway.

"Shit's gonna hit the fan now," Joe said in a low voice.

The truck door swung open and Bruce barged out. His gaze flew to where they were standing, and he sprinted over to them, his mouth set. That expression didn't bode well.

Joe turned to Greg. "If you ever see Todd here, come get me. This place is off-limits now."

"I'll take care of him myself." Greg's chest puffed out.

Bruce looked up and down Sarah's body as if checking for injuries. "What's going on?"

"It's under control." Joe hefted the shovel.

"Why was Todd racing out of here? Did he do something to you?" Bruce stepped closer to Sarah.

"He tried, but no." Lucky for Todd, he'd escaped.

Bruce's eyes hardened with hot fury, and he yanked his keys from his pocket. "He's a dead man."

Joe grabbed his arm. "Don't run off half-cocked and get into trouble. He's not worth it."

"I don't give a damn. If he so much as touched her—"

"I told you it's handled. I ordered him off the farm." Joe banged the shoved on the ground.

"Not good enough. He needs a physical reminder." Bruce jerked his arm away from Joe.

"He got one already," Joe said.

Bruce swung around. "What?"

Sarah cleared her throat. "From me. I slapped him. Hard."

"Drew blood." Joe nodded as if proud. "I think he got the point."

"Wish I'd been here." Greg tapped a fist to his palm. "I'd have done more damage."

The guys were all such macho men, wanting to defend her. Her heart swelled. She waved a hand. "Let's please forget about this. I appreciate the support, but it's over, and we have work to do."

Joe and Greg looked toward the parking lot. After some grumbling, they walked back to the fields.

Bruce's mouth drew into a hard line. "What did he do?"

"Please, let it go." She took a step toward the stables.

He placed a hand on her arm. "Tell me."

She blew out a breath. "Fine. He offered to pay me for sex and tried to feel me up. I slapped him and ran. You heard the rest from Joe."

Bruce's eyes turned dangerously dark. Good thing Todd had left.

"Pay you for sex?" Bruce fisted his hands and shook his head. "Screw it. Debbie has his address. I'm getting it. He's dead."

"Oh my God. Please stop." Sarah clasped his arm when he took a step toward the house. "The man is filthy rich. If you touch him, he'll lawyer up, and you'll be in legal trouble forever. You could lose your clients. He's not coming back." She gazed up at him. "Please, I can't take any more drama."

Lynn's car pulled into the lot.

Bruce glanced at his watch and frowned.

Sarah sensed his hesitation. She didn't want any more trouble for him on her part. "Besides, the vets will be here soon, and I know you don't want to disappoint them."

Bruce sighed and nodded. "Fine. But if he steps one foot on this farm, he's mine."

Yikes. Maybe she *was* safe with all the men-at-arms surrounding her. At least she could eliminate Todd as the stalker. When he'd yelled, his voice sounded different from the stalker's. Todd was just a spoiled brat who thought he could buy whatever he wanted. And now the jerk wouldn't be hanging around anymore.

If only she could get rid of the stalker so easily.

***

Leonard adjusted his glasses and checked his email. Twenty-three days since Sarah had left, and still no replies from her. That didn't mean she wasn't getting his messages. He could picture her hunched over the computer reading and rereading them, excitement in her eyes as she realized he wouldn't give up. She'd probably rub her hands together and peek around to see if anyone noticed her reaction because she'd be in some public place, like a coffee shop or library. Even that would be fun for her. Logging on to a computer and hoping there'd be a message from him.

He frowned. If she read his emails, then she should be coming back. Someone must still control her.

She hadn't gone to Maddie's, Anne's, or her parents'. He had people watching their homes. Her sisters might be useful if she didn't come back soon. Nothing more motivating than a relative in distress. He clicked on his photo file and brought up pictures of Anne and Maddie.

His cell phone rang.

George.

Leonard's heart leaped. When he had needed a gun to kill Audrey, he'd hacked into the police computer database and found George, who came through with one. The guy had a list of offenses a mile long. Arrested multiple times. Now he was at Maddie's apartment in search of any clues that might lead to Sarah's whereabouts. Maybe he had a lead.

Leonard answered the phone. "Find anything?"

"Yeah, but I'm done being your bitch. After I give you this information, we're finished." George ground out the words.

"I don't think so. One click on the computer and everyone will know you snitched to get out of jail early. And I didn't dig any deeper, but I bet you have other secrets I could find." Leonard sat back in his chair.

"Fuck you. Squeal and I'll tell the cops about your hard-on for this chick. I'm done after this. You want what I found, that's the deal," George said in a no-holds-barred tone.

Leonard frowned. The cops couldn't do much, but he wouldn't need George anymore if he found Sarah. Besides, he could always go back on his word later. What mattered now was getting the information. He had to find his ballerina. "Okay. What do you have?"

"There's a notepad here with impressions from a torn-off sheet. Did some pencil rubbing to get an address in Maryland written under some travel dates to Pennsylvania."

Leonard stroked his chin. Pennsylvania. Maddie had booked a trip on her computer for an upcoming symposium. Everything checked out except her return flight was several days after the event ended. If Sarah was in Pennsylvania or nearby, Maddie might be staying to visit her. Excitement coursed through his veins.

George gave him the address along with a threat should Leonard contact him again, and then the line went dead. It didn't matter. He had what he needed. His pulse raced as he pulled up an online map to survey the satellite images of the area. Adjusting his glasses, he leaned closer to the screen. A horse farm in rural Maryland. Exactly the type of place someone would send Sarah to hide. Nothing but trees, fields, and country roads. Yes. This had to be the spot.

He went to his bedroom and worked his way from left to right, touching every framed picture of Sarah precisely in the middle until he reached the last one. For the first time since she'd left, his body relaxed.

When he returned to his computer, he booked an open seat on the red-eye. Perfect. He would be in Maryland tomorrow morning.

Soon, Sarah, soon.

CHAPTER 20

SARAH OPENED her eyes as the sun streamed through the crack of her curtain. She bounded out of bed, landed on the dog, and crashed to the floor.

Fluffy jerked to his feet and tucked his tail between his legs.

"Sorry, guy, I'm not used to you being here." She pushed up to her knees and petted him on the head.

The dog's soft, black snout nudged her hand, and his tongue flicked out to lick her fingers, tail drumming against the dresser.

"No worries, buddy." She let out a breath and stroked his head. Seven o'clock. Saturday. Becca and Lori took care of the horses on the weekend, so she had two days off. Three hours until Bruce came.

The hike. Her stomach fluttered. She'd been hyperaware of his presence the last couple of days. Judging from the heated looks he gave her, it went both ways.

She took care of the dog and headed back to the bathroom. So far, things were working out. Fluffy didn't chase the horses and seemed content to run in the fields or sleep in the shade. Even Debbie had come around. She pretended not to like him, but Sarah had spied her giving the dog a treat and patting his head. Sarah had ducked back behind the barn. Debbie would die if someone caught her acting like a softy.

Sarah showered, taking extra care to shave and smooth on a lilac-scented body lotion. Not that Bruce would even see her legs under jeans. Stupid. But no stupider than wearing the pink thong she'd picked up in town. It didn't matter if he never saw it. She had her sexy vibe going.

She chose a pair of jeans and a lightweight, long-sleeved white shirt. No ponytail today. For once, she'd let her hair down in more ways than one. She smiled to herself and stepped back from the mirror. Amazing what a little makeup could do. The last time she'd worn makeup was for a performance. Her chest tightened with the longing to spread her arms wide and twirl across the stage. Those days were over.

Time dragged until almost ten. She made her way to the front porch and waited for Bruce. Her gaze traveled the open fields. She had to figure out her future soon since she couldn't live at the farm forever. Correction. Hide, not live.

When she left, she'd never see Bruce again. It made no sense that he wanted to get involved. Sure, right now they had sparks flying between them and a crazy physical attraction. But he'd soon tire of the seclusion.

He didn't understand how limited their lives would be. Mark sure hadn't lasted long when the going got tough. And if the stalker really could hack into his production company accounts, nothing would stop him from accessing the therapy program. Bruce couldn't afford that risk. The vets had already suffered enough loss. She shook her head. This would never work.

Bruce's truck rumbled on the path, and she glanced up. He parked in front of the house and hopped out. At the sight of him, her pulse jumped. The wind tousled his dark hair. Muscles bulged under his light blue shirt, and his shades added a touch of cool. He mounted the steps and slid the sunglasses to the top of his head.

He frowned. "What's wrong?"

She tapped her fingers against her thigh, warring between the strong desire to go with him or to say she'd changed her mind. "I...um...am having some second thoughts about this."

"Why's that?"

She focused on the fields. If she faced him and had to take on those baby blues, she'd never say what she needed. "I tried to tell you before.

It's not fair to you. I don't want to drag you into my crazy world. There's no point in trying to start anything."

He let out a breath and touched her arm. "You're doing it again."

"What?"

"Making decisions for me. Is there some other reason you don't want to go?" His gaze delved into hers.

She shook her head. "No."

"I'm a grown man. I choose my own risks and make my own decisions. Understand?"

She bit her lip and nodded.

"I've never seen you with your hair down." He ran a hand through her hair before dipping his head to brush his lips against hers. "I like it."

Tiny shivers traveled through her.

"So are you coming with me?" He pulled back to look her in the eyes.

And she was lost. "Yes."

He led her to the truck. After she climbed in, he cranked on some tunes, and they drove through the country roads a few miles until they came to a small parking area with a wooden sign indicating a trail.

"This path runs along the water. It's not a tough hike." He slipped his shades off.

"Huh. Think I'm a wuss?" She tilted her head.

"No, ma'am. I've seen you in action at the farm."

"You did *not* just call me ma'am."

Bruce held his hands up. "No, sir. Not me."

"Hey." She play-punched his arm and laughed.

"It's nice to see you smile." He leaned closer and grazed a thumb across her cheek, resting his hand on the side of her neck. "Thank you for coming."

His fingers found the tender flesh under her ear, and her breath hitched. With the lightest touch, he rubbed the spot. Frissons of awareness rolled down her spine.

The sun shined through the window, illuminating flecks of teal in his eyes. She couldn't look away, not that she wanted to. The gentleness from a man so tough and intimidating caught her off guard. That kiss in the suite was what she expected from him. Demanding, possessive, and dominant. The kind that bruised her lips, but she didn't care.

"Sarah?" The sound of her name, almost a whisper, swirled in the air between them.

She moistened her lips with her tongue, leaning her neck deeper into his hold. "Hmm?"

"I want to start this recon right now." He inched his face closer, eyes wide open as if he couldn't break contact either. "Get to know all of you."

She parted her lips, but he brought his to her temple. Holding them there, he stroked her back. His breath fanned her hair, and she forced herself to inhale. When her chest expanded, her breast brushed against his forearm. Her nipple tightened, and he stilled.

"Better take this slow." She couldn't tell if he was talking to her or himself.

He reached behind the seat, hoisted a backpack out, and moved over to the driver's side. Blowing out a breath, he glanced at her. "Ready?"

"Mmm hmm." She was ready all right. But not for the hike. He must think she'd lost her tongue because she hadn't formed words since he'd laid hands on her.

She opened the door, and the breeze blew her hair. Birds chirped in the tall trees. They climbed out, and Bruce slid on the backpack. He took her hand. Such a simple thing, but again, a surprise. And a nice one. She'd never in a million years have pegged him to be a guy who would hold hands on a hike. Oops, make that a recon. She bit into a grin.

"What's so funny?" He cocked his head.

Uh-oh. Caught. "Nothing, I just didn't expect you to be so..."

"So what?" He let go of her hand and straightened.

Crap. She had to open her big mouth. "I don't know. Just so...gentlemanly."

He blinked and gave his head a quick come-again shake. "Gentlemanly?"

She shrugged. "I'm not complaining. I like it. It just surprises me."

He planted a hand on his hip. "I wasn't raised by wolves, you know."

Oh boy. The Bruce she knew was back. The urge to reach out and rumple his hair almost took over, but she didn't dare poke a bear with a stick. "I'm sorry. I didn't mean it to be—"

"Never mind." He shifted the pack on his shoulders. "Let's just go."

"Wait." She slipped her hand back into his and squeezed a forgive-me message.

For a moment, he stared down at her, all tension and spiky. And then his face softened. He slowly brought her hand to his mouth and kissed it, holding her gaze.

Her eyes must have registered her shock, or he'd noticed her knees wobble, because the hint of a satisfied smile formed, and he led her to the trail with a strong grip. Oh yeah, his swag was back, and hot damn he had her attention.

They trekked along the narrow path, stepping over roots and fallen branches. A squirrel scurried across and climbed up a tree. The earthy scent of pine and moss hung in the air.

"Tell me about your family," he said.

Her throat tightened.

When she didn't say anything, he stopped. "Unless you don't want to talk about them."

"No. It's okay. I just miss them." She lowered her gaze to the ground.

"I'm sure."

"It is what it is." She took a breath and resumed the hike. "I have two sisters. We're close even though we're all different. Maddie's a year older than me, Anne two. She can be quite the mother hen. But honestly, I don't know if I could have pulled this off without her help. She's my rock."

"I'm glad she's there for you."

"Maddie can be a bit much. I think it's the red hair. She's an archaeologist and definitely in the right field." Sarah shook her head. "I'll never forget the time she called Anne and me into the basement. Maddie was around nine. She dug into her pockets and dumped the contents on top of my dad's workbench. Buttons, Barbie doll limbs, Happy Meal toys, and a bunch of random stuff. Next, she tells us to bury them."

Bruce climbed over a fallen tree and kept hold of Sarah's hand as she followed. "Did you?"

"Yup. She ran around and had them all dug up within minutes." Sarah smiled. "That little twerp. She marched us out to the garden where we'd buried some of them and read us the riot act for not smoothing out the soil. Said we made it too easy."

"That's hilarious."

"It wasn't to my mother. She loved her gardens." Sarah brushed back her hair from the wind. "We raced out to find my mother standing next to her garden, which now looked like a minefield gone bad. She gave us the scariest stink-eye ever."

A sound came from the woods, and Sarah stopped short. "What was that?"

Bruce craned his neck and peered into the woods before shaking his head. "I know what a person sounds like moving through the woods. That was an animal, probably a rabbit. Nothing to worry about. I'm right here with you."

She had to stop being so jumpy. He was right. No one would attack her with him around.

He tugged her hand and led again. "I take it you all survived the garden digging?"

Sarah glanced at the woods but followed him, picking the story back up. "Until Mom went out front to the landscaping." She grinned. "The garden wasn't the only place we dug."

"Tactical error."

"It kind of went from there. I don't think Maddie ever thought of doing anything but archaeology." Maybe she should tell him about Maddie's upcoming visit. He'd find out soon enough when she showed up at the farm. "She's coming here next week."

"What?" He froze midstride and turned around.

"She has a conference at Penn State, and she mapped out a route taking busses to get here. I'm going to pick her up in town."

"You look worried about it."

Tension bunched the back of her neck. "I am. I mean, I want to see her so badly, but what if somehow the stalker follows her?"

"How?" He held a hand out palm up.

"I don't know. Anne seems to think it's a good plan, and she's cautious, so I'm probably being paranoid. But still—"

"What if I pick Maddie up in another town? If anyone was following her, they wouldn't see you."

Hmm. Not a bad idea.

"And I'd make sure no one tailed us back."

"You'd do that for me?"

Bruce stepped close and cupped her chin, raising her head until she met his eyes. "That and more."

The woods quieted, fading into the background as all the air seemed to leave her lungs. Her gaze traveled over his tanned face, pausing on the lighter-colored jagged scar. All lines and planes, with a square jaw, his features exuded strength. No studio makeup or pampered skin on this man. He was pure, unadulterated male. And yet, earlier, he'd pressed those full, sexy lips against her hand with enough tenderness to make her melt.

"I like you this way." He traced her lower lip with his thumb.

Blood rushed to her belly and then farther south. "How?"

"Not arguing with me."

When she opened her mouth to protest, he placed a finger across it. "Shh. Let me finish."

As long as he kept touching her like this, she'd let him talk until the leaves fell.

He settled a hand at her waist. Moving his finger from her mouth, he ran it along her cheekbone. "You're like a prized racehorse. Spirited, proud, and beautiful. Sensitive to my every contact."

She trembled and gazed up at him, mesmerized by the soft cadence of his voice. His eyes caught the filtered sunshine and changed color to reflect the deep hues of the green forest. Never mind that he'd just compared her to a horse; to him, that was the highest compliment.

"And inside..." He skimmed his hand down the column of her throat to the opened top button of her blouse. Pausing, he slid his palm to the left, over the fabric, and pressed it flat. "...beats a strong heart full of courage, love, and kindness."

No one had ever spoken to her this way. His words were a balm to the all the craziness in her life. Somehow, despite her desperation, he saw beneath the surface, and it humbled her. His hand warmed the skin under her shirt. He had to feel the erratic thumping of her heart.

Leaning down, he brought his lips to within a breath of hers. He shifted his hold from her waist to the small of her back, pulling her up against the length of him, fully aroused.

Pleasure swam through her to know she had that effect on him. She tipped her face higher, craving his lips.

A soft breeze blew between the fraction of an inch that separated them.

"Hey. Wait for me." A child's voice rang out, followed by the sound of footsteps running through the woods.

Bruce cursed and stepped back.

The separation jolted her body. She'd shut out everything but him and forgotten where they even were. Her surroundings came back into focus.

A little boy ran past them chased by a smaller girl, who continued to yell, "Wait."

From across the path, Bruce's eyes burned hot enough to scorch.

"Sorry, excuse us." A woman wearing a backpack hurried past.

Their footsteps grew fainter, and Bruce glanced at the trail. "Ready to get moving again?"

She'd rather pick up right where they'd left off, but they were in public. Maybe he'd lost track of that as well. "Sure."

They hiked in silence for a while, which gave her a chance to cool down. A calmness settled over her as she inhaled the piny scent of the woods. Aside from her crazy hormones, spending time with Bruce talking and hiking was fun. She could get used to this. "So do you have brothers or sisters?"

Bruce's hand froze on the branch he held to the side for her to pass. "My parents died years ago, and I don't have siblings." He stepped over a mushy spot on the ground. "Watch the mud."

He couldn't mean he had no family. "Wait."

Bruce stopped. "What?"

"Is your uncle Joe the only relative you have?"

"Yes."

Her breath stalled. "I'm sorry. That must be—"

"It's fine." He swiped at another branch in the path and led again.

Okay, that topic was off-limits. She frowned and followed. He sure could wipe his face clean of emotions when he wanted, but she'd seen plenty of feelings before when he'd almost kissed her. Maybe he'd talk about something else. "What was it like growing up on a farm?"

"Cool. I got to spend a lot of time with horses."

"Greg told me about how you saved all of them from a barn fire. He said you have some sort of—"

"What? When did he tell you that?" Bruce swung around to face her.

"After the incident with the runaway horse."

"Christ." He plodded on. "It wasn't a big deal."

"Sure sounds like a big deal to me." She stifled a laugh when he smacked a branch out of the way. "Greg said you were only fifteen, and they wrote about it in the papers, and people started calling you a horse whisperer."

He pivoted on his heel. "He told you that too?"

She nodded.

"It was a long time ago." He shook his head.

"Well, it made an impression on him. He thinks you're a legend." She placed a hand on Bruce's arm. "I've seen you with the horses, and you have a gift."

He looked to the sky and blew out a breath. After a few seconds, he asked, "You getting hungry?"

Changing the subject. Typical. She grinned. "Sure."

"There's a spot up ahead we can eat."

They stopped by a cluster of flat rocks next to a running stream.

"It's gorgeous here." She raised her face to the warm sun while Bruce shrugged off the backpack.

He pulled out a couple of waters and two subs. "Italian or turkey?"

"Turkey, unless you prefer it."

"Nope." He handed her one.

Sarah unwrapped her sandwich. While they ate, Bruce pointed out a red-tailed hawk soaring over the woods and told her about the various fish native to the stream.

She rested her back against a rock, and her bones melted. The gurgling stream, the warm sun, Bruce's rich, deep voice. She could lose herself in this peaceful setting. But she wanted to know more about the man beside her. At last, she had the chance to ask some questions. "How did you get into hippotherapy?"

"Joe showed up one day and told me he'd bought an ex-racehorse and needed someone to train him."

"Batal?"

"Yeah." Bruce took a sip of water.

"Does he work with your patients?"

"No. He's way too spirited for therapy. I only use horses like Misty. But if I hadn't come to train Batal, I never would have seen the program." He took another sip. "A woman at the farm ran it, but she worked with cerebral palsy kids. I couldn't believe the results. I looked into setting up a program for the vets. Timing was perfect because she and her husband moved, and Debbie had space for me at the farm."

Bruce waved a hand at her. "What was it like growing up as a dancer? Did you have to go to special schools?"

Ballet. Her heart turned inside out. Every morning she ached to slip on her shoes and dance again. "I went to New York when I was fourteen. The theater company became my surrogate family."

"Must have been hard to leave home so young."

"Yeah. Besides missing everyone, I didn't have a social life outside of the studio. No proms or football games."

"I spent all my time at the ranch, so I get it."

She glanced at him. They had more in common than she'd thought. "I'm not complaining, though. Dance is all I ever wanted to do." She shrugged. "The rehearsals are intense, but it's all worth it when you perform. It's like my body and soul are extensions of the music. For that space and time, nothing exists but the dance. I don't know if you can understand…"

He nodded. "Sounds like riding for me. No way to describe the feeling. It's all about trust and connection with the horse. I forget about everything else."

"Then you do understand. Nothing can replace it. All my life I worked so hard, and I finally had my dream. The sacrifices my family made to put me through the school… They were so proud when I earned the position of principal dancer." The acute pain that came whenever she faced all she'd lost crushed her chest. She closed her eyes.

*** * * ***

Bruce mentally slapped himself. He'd invited Sarah out to have fun.

Instead, they were tripping down a sad memory lane, talking about his lack of family and the fact that she couldn't perform anymore. He slid closer and put an arm around her.

"You'll dance again. I promise." He squeezed her shoulder, and she leaned into him.

Stroking her hair, he kissed the top of her head. She raised her face to look up at him. Her soft breast pressing against his ribs stirred something low and primal. He shifted and lowered his mouth. "I didn't get to finish this."

"What?"

He didn't answer with words. Instead, he grazed his lips across hers and scooped her onto his lap. Maybe not the most strategic move, considering his condition.

"Oh." The corners of her mouth turned up.

With the lightest touch, he kissed each side. A tiny sigh slipped from her, and he rubbed a hand down her back.

His growing erection pressed against her outer thigh. She blushed. God, she was beautiful. Ever since their first kiss, he'd craved touching her. He'd forgotten what it was like to allow himself to feel. The world dropped away whenever he held her.

Her breathing turned shallow, and he closed his eyes. He couldn't get enough of her. His cock throbbed under the pressure of her weight, and he stifled the urge to rock her against it.

He slanted his mouth across hers. Her soft lips moved under his. When she darted her tongue against his teeth, heat blazed through his body. He gripped her tighter and worked his tongue into her mouth, exploring her sweetness.

Plop. Plop. Plop.

He pulled away. Damn distractions.

Next date was going to be someplace private. He scoped the area. His gaze settled on a tall oak across from the stream.

He stilled.

Sarah looked up. "What's wrong?"

Bruce stared at the heart he'd carved in the tree years ago after he and Emily had picnicked under the oak. It glared at him from across the narrow stream as he held Sarah in his now-stiff arms.

She pushed off his lap and twisted to follow his gaze. "I don't see anyone."

He was hiking the same trail he had with Emily. They'd sat together on these rocks as well as the ones under the oak. He'd told Emily at her grave no one could replace her, and here he was, trying to do exactly that. He brought a hand to his forehead.

"Bruce? What's wrong?" Sarah squatted next to him.

Too many things. Her scent, her warmth, the way she melted into his arms. The strong longing he had to pull her close and let her in warred with his guilt.

Sarah's packed duffel bag flashed in his mind.

She was unpredictable and too independent to rely on him. If threatened, she'd run. And she'd take his heart with her. Or what was left of it. He couldn't afford the risk. And if she didn't run, she'd be stuck with someone who couldn't commit and was haunted by a ghost.

"I think it's time to get going." He stood, tossed the trash into the backpack, and stuffed his arms through the shoulder straps.

"Why? I don't understand."

He poured ice into his veins. His detachment might hurt her at first, but in the end, she'd be better off. He carried around way too much shit. She deserved better.

"I'm sorry. You were right this morning about this being a mistake."

Her mouth dropped open. "A mistake? But why? I—"

"It's not you. I'm sorry."

She flinched. "Seriously? It's not you, it's me?"

That sounded horrible, but it was the truth. "Like I said, I'm sorry."

She swallowed hard and picked up her bag.

He started down the trail.

She kept up with his quick pace back to the truck and climbed in when he hit the Unlock button.

After tossing his pack in the back, he glanced at her. Lips pressed together, hands gripped in her lap, she blinked as if fighting back tears.

Fuck. He'd really hurt her.

Nothing he could say would change the fact she was better off without him. She leaned her head against the passenger window and closed her eyes as he drove. He ground his molars, forcing his gaze on the road.

When at last they reached the farm, he stopped the truck and made a move to open his door.

"Don't bother." She yanked hers open.

His insides twisted. He'd caused her so much pain. Fucked everything up. "Sarah, I'm sorry. I—"

"Please, just stop." She held up a hand then all but ran to the back entrance of the suite.

CHAPTER 21

LEONARD HIKED through the woods with sweat pouring down his back from the afternoon sun. As usual, his planning had paid off. After pulling up the satellite images of the farm online and noting the surrounding woods, he'd purchased camouflage clothes and gear to bring on the trip.

His gun had been another matter. Since he couldn't take the weapon on the plane, he'd accessed the underground black-market sites and found a guy in Baltimore who would sell him one. If only Sarah could see how daring he'd become. He'd met in alleys and traded with thugs. All for her.

He held back a tree branch as he stepped over a root. His brand-new boots made his feet sore even though he hadn't hiked far. From studying the layout of the farm on his computer, he'd found the perfect place to set up surveillance. He'd left his car tucked between some trees well off the road. The distance from it to the point he'd chosen was 0.32 miles. According to his calculations, the farmhouse, stables, and arena should all be visible from that vantage point.

When he reached the tree line, he pulled out his binoculars from the backpack. He'd paid top dollar for the high-end, special zoom model with range finder. Nothing was too good for Sarah. He eyed the large house not far from where he stood. Maybe she was living there. Oh, to see his beautiful ballerina at last after twenty-four agonizing days. His pulse raced. Life would be right again.

He checked his watch. Two o'clock. Still plenty of light and time for him to scope out the farm. He pulled out a perfectly folded, cut-to-precision piece of tarp from the right top pocket of his shirt and spread it on the ground. Making sure he still had a clear view of the house, he sat on top and propped his back against a tree. Not the most comfortable arrangement, but he'd endure anything for the chance to find his Sarah.

Unfortunately, she'd have to be punished when they got back. He'd cleaned, vacuumed, and painted the closet in his bedroom. He would lock her inside for the same amount of time she'd been missing. She had to understand that as much as they loved each other, they shouldn't be apart for so long. Of course, he'd let her out for meals and to use the bathroom, but that would be all. And he'd be near her at night when he slept, so she wouldn't be alone. She'd learn her lesson and not leave again.

At the sound of a truck's engine, he took off his glasses, stored them in their case, and raised the binoculars to his eyes. A pickup drove the dusty path to the house and parked near the front. A woman got out and hurried to the back door.

Dark hair shorter than Sarah's, but the way she moved, it had to be her. He zoomed in on her face. His heart leaped into his throat. Yes, he'd found her.

But she was crying. He held his breath and focused. Her shoulders shook as she unlocked the door and swiped at her cheek. He'd been right. She missed him. Probably had spent the last weeks in tears. What a waste of time. They could have been together. Obviously, someone was still controlling her.

A couple of girls came out of the stables and jogged toward the fields where horses grazed. An older man rounded the corner of the house and got into a beat-up truck. Leonard frowned and lowered the binoculars. Too much activity. He'd have to conduct surveillance and note people's schedules. Not a problem. He was very good at that. On leave from work, he had all the time in the world to figure out a plan. He'd get to Sarah when she was alone and bring her back with him.

The search was over. The hard ball in his stomach melted. Tonight, he'd go on his computer and change the color of her hair on his pictures to match her. She shouldn't have dyed it without his permission, but he'd let that go for now. When they returned home, he'd make her change it back.

He drew out his tablet. Time to make some notes. Maybe he'd return after dark for a closer look at the house.

CHAPTER 22

MORGAN PULLED down the small fireproof box from the top of her closet and unlocked it. She took out a yellowed newspaper clipping and twisted her mouth into a sneer. The worst day of her life had been when Pete had called her five years ago with news about her sister.

Emily.

Morgan had been sitting by the pool, her ancient husband inside, napping as usual.

"I have an update for you," Pete said.

"What?"

"Emily's engaged. They posted an announcement in the paper. I'm mailing it to you along with my bill."

Morgan bolted up. "Engaged? To whom?"

"Some rich physical therapist named Bruce Murphy."

"Name doesn't mean anything to me. Who is he? What's his deal?"

"Comes from a wealthy, prominent family in Maryland. They owned a horse farm and won the Preakness a couple of times. Major money. Parents died and left him everything. He went into the Navy to become a SEAL and then came back after an injury to finish school for physical therapy. Met Emily at the hospital."

Morgan's belly roiled. Damn that Emily. Just when Morgan had her right where she'd wanted. Broke from school loans and living with their aunt in a small apartment. Emily never should have landed someone like Bruce.

"Check your email. I sent you a picture of them. I gotta go. Keep you posted."

Pete hung up, and Morgan clicked over to check the message on her phone. She gaped at the image. Bruce was a woman's wet dream. While her geriatric geezer husband pawed her every night, Emily had somehow managed to snag a filthy-rich, smoking-hot fiancé.

Morgan picked up a vase of flowers and threw it to the marble floor. A glass followed and then everything else within reach she could smash.

Five years and the rage still blazed. Morgan unfolded the newspaper clipping and laid it on the top of the box. Bruce's smiling face mocked her. His arm wrapped around Emily, her left hand, sporting a huge diamond ring, rested on his lapel. A fairy tale come true. Bruce had married Emily, paid off her debts, and bought her a huge house.

She'd won again. Since Emily had died and couldn't pay, Bruce would.

Morgan placed the wedding picture back in the box and slammed the lid shut. She planned to emotionally destroy him. Oh, he'd be fuckable all right. Nothing like the other men she'd tolerated. She'd seduce him and relish the fact that every night she'd be screwing her sister's husband.

When the time was right, and Bruce had fallen for her, she'd hit him with her little secret. She licked her lips in anticipation of the shock and horror he'd feel. He'd earned it when he messed everything up and came in like a knight in shining armor to save the day. Emily, always the princess, even to the end. Now Morgan would have the last laugh.

Time to find out what Pete had uncovered.

Morgan drove to the PI's office and pulled into a spot in front of a tired brick building. She entered the small hall and knocked on the first of three shut wooden doors. Pete called for her to come in.

"Have a seat." He gestured to one of the two brown upholstered chairs with gold buttons down the arms. She sat across from him and the medium-sized wooden desk with files stacked on both sides. Sun shined in from the window behind him, lighting a beam of dust particles to illuminate the otherwise barren, dark room.

The lack of décor didn't bother Morgan. His office, like his looks, could be deceiving. Dull brown eyes that matched his hair peered at her from behind bifocals. He had the body of a mid-fifties, sedentary man. He wore a cream, button-down shirt with yellow stains under the arms and a tan tie that had served as a ketchup catcher in the past. No one would look twice at him. Probably how he wanted it.

"Like I said on the phone, I've found out who your missing person is." He handed Morgan a flash drive. "You can access everything through this on your computer, but I have a paper report as well."

"Good. Enlighten me." She sat back and crossed her legs.

"Her name is Sarah Cooper. Facial recognition matched her to a picture from the missing person reports in California."

Morgan blinked. Well, well. A fake last name. No shock there. And she had been right about California. "What else?"

"She was a professional ballerina. Didn't show up for work one day. Disappeared, according to the news." He picked up a paper. His gaze scrolled down as he rattled off Sarah's family history, education, and dance companies with which she'd performed.

Morgan tapped her fingers on the arm of the chair. "Did she have a boyfriend?"

Pete adjusted his glasses and glanced back at the paper. "She'd been dating a guy for a while named Mark Sherman. He's a stage-play producer. Some pics showed up of them together at various places. Don't know if they're still an item."

"Maybe he was abusive." And Sarah was running from him.

"It's possible, but I don't think so." Pete dropped the paper on the desk. "I did a quick check, and nothing came up as far as domestic violence or restraining orders. His record is clean as a whistle." He leaned back and folded his hands over his belly. "But there is something you might find interesting."

"What?"

"I had to phone a friend. This information wasn't readily available." He rolled his fingers together in the universal sign for money.

"How much?"

"Double."

Morgan's pulse sped up. He must have something good to ask for twice the price. She nodded. "Better be worth it."

He shrugged. "Only you would know."

"Go on."

Pete shifted in his chair and leaned forward. "I know a guy, who knows a guy on the force—"

"Get to it." Morgan snapped her fingers.

"He said Sarah reported being stalked."

Now it made sense. That's what had her so freaking paranoid.

Pete scratched his head. "According to what I could find out, it's typical of a crazed-fan stalker."

Not shocking. That stuff happened a lot in Hollywood. "Did they catch him?"

"Nope. At first, there was some talk about Sarah's mental health. The police questioned some things."

"What do you mean? Like what?"

"She'd reported stuff had been moved around in her dressing room, and she'd smelled cologne in her bedroom." He picked up a pencil and tapped the eraser on the desk. "She saw a therapist for a while."

Sarah had been thought to be unstable or paranoid. Interesting. "And they never figured out who the stalker was?"

"Doesn't look like it. The last report the police had was of her being attacked by him in her apartment, and then she disappeared."

"Huh." Morgan nodded. "Anything else?"

Pete held out his hands. "That's it."

"Very well." She pulled out two envelopes, took some bills out of one, and added them to the other before handing it to Pete. "Feel free to count it."

"I'd say I trust you, but in my business, I don't trust anyone." He picked up the envelope and thumbed through the bills.

Morgan stood. "If you find out anything new, there's more where that came from."

"Nice doing business with you." He raised his bulk out of the chair and shook her hand.

She smiled the entire drive home.

Time to cause some trouble for the Tutu-Tease.

CHAPTER 23

Sarah stared out the suite window, stalling. She'd managed to avoid Bruce the rest of the weekend, but that wasn't so easy on a Monday. He had clients, so he'd be around all morning.

Anger coursed through her veins. She'd had it with his hot-and-cold treatment. One minute kissing her senseless, and the next, swatting her away like a pesky horsefly. No more. She'd told him the whole thing was a bad idea, and he'd still insisted they go on the hike. Mr. I-Make-My-Own-Decisions had failed to mention that they might change on a whim. Well, too bad. She wasn't playing that game anymore. The ranch served one purpose for her—to stay safe. She hadn't come there to find romance.

And now, with her and Bruce avoiding each other, she'd be just as safe somewhere else. She picked up her phone and dialed the number on the help-wanted ad for the produce farm. Before it rang, she hung up and brought a hand to her forehead.

Working somewhere else meant lying all over again, and Bruce hadn't taught her to shoot yet. But they weren't even on speaking terms, so she wouldn't go if he asked. She'd figure out another way to learn.

Fluffy picked up his tug rope and bounced across the room. He nudged her hand.

She'd have to leave him behind. Her heart wrenched. She bent down and hugged him hard. "I'm sorry, guy. I'll miss you."

But she had to do this. She couldn't stand being around Bruce with his cold-shoulder treatment. Not after she'd fallen so hard for him. Every time she looked at him, she'd remember how her body came alive when he kissed her.

She stood back up, took a deep breath, and dialed the number again. Her pulse quickened with every ring, but she firmed her resolve. She had to leave.

A man answered. "Hawkins Farm."

"Hi. I'm calling about the ad in the paper for the job—"

"Sorry. We filled it yesterday. You can try back in the fall."

Damn it. She'd waited too long. Her shoulders slumped. "Okay. Thanks."

Hiking with Bruce had cost her the job. Now she'd have to deal with seeing him until she found somewhere else to go. And she still had the problem of a car she couldn't drive far. She made a mental note to check with Joe on his progress finding a used radiator and tires.

She closed up the suite and headed to the barn.

When Bruce showed up, she focused on sweeping and kept her head down. Maybe he'd take the hint and leave her alone.

"I need to talk to you." The sound of his voice reverberated through her bleeding heart.

She stiffened. Damn him. She swept harder, keeping her head down. "It's not necessary. You were clear the other day. Let's move on."

"Not about that. I told you I was sorry."

"Sorry for how it ended or sorry we went out?" She raised her head to meet his gaze.

"Both."

Just twist the knife deeper. She couldn't read his expressionless face. Those eyes of his that had blazed with heat and raw desire on the hike were flat and cold. She shivered. He might as well be wearing an iron mask. And as much as it hurt, she still wanted to reach out and touch his cheek or kiss him. Anything to break through, but there'd be no more touching. She had to protect herself.

"I need to know when and where to pick up your sister."

Crap. They did need to work out the plan. It made sense for him to get Maddie, but she didn't want any favors from him. Maybe she could ask Joe. "I'll make other arrangements."

"No. I said I would get her, and if there's any trouble, I'm the most equipped to handle it." He folded his arms.

She hated to accept anything from him, but Maddie's safety and keeping the stalker at bay mattered more than Sarah's pride.

Shit. He was right. If he'd managed to pull people out of covert operations while under fire, he could probably handle bringing her sister to the farm. She nodded. "Okay, for Maddie's sake, but I'll pay you for the time and gas."

"Don't insult me." He shook his head. "You know I won't accept that."

Of course, he wouldn't. She was being petty, but he'd earned it. "Fine. She's supposed to arrive Friday. I'll know more about times in a couple of days."

"I'll clear my calendar."

She went back to work but glanced up as he walked away, his broad shoulders stiff. Her hands had gripped them when he'd held her in his lap. The hard muscles rippling under her touch when he moved. She shut her eyes and ignored the ache in her chest.

The rest of the day, he worked with his clients, and Sarah steered clear. Only, she couldn't help but hear his voice in the arena or catch him from the corner of her eye as he passed by, causing every cell in her body to yearn for him.

As she mucked out a stall, Lynn rounded the corner.

"What's up with Bruce?"

Sarah paused with the rake in hand. "What do you mean?"

Lynn shrugged. "He hasn't been himself. I'm worried."

Sarah shook her head. She forced a matter-of-fact tone. "Can't help you. He really doesn't talk to me much anymore."

CHAPTER 24

Morgan parked in the lot by the arena and scanned the fields. Sarah and Greg were out with the horses. Perfect. She'd timed her arrival early enough in the morning not to run into Bruce. Unless he'd changed his schedule, Tuesday patients came later in the day.

She pulled a new bridle out of the trunk and made her way to the tack room. Should anyone ask, she'd say she came to check the size of the new one against the old.

Happy to find the room empty, she went to Sarah's backpack in the corner. One day she'd passed by when Sarah had plucked out a set of keys from the front zipped pocket. Morgan glanced around and dug out the keys. She checked her watch. Sarah didn't head to the house before noon most days, so Morgan should have plenty of time. She returned to her car and drove to the hardware store to make copies.

A short time later, she pulled back into the lot. With luck on her side, everyone was still out in the fields. She grabbed the bridle again and hurried to the stables. As she rounded the corner to the tack room, Joe came out. Her gut lurched.

He made no bones about his dislike of her. His gaze went to the bridle in her hand. As much as it killed her, she held her hostility in check. Couldn't have him bad-mouthing her to Bruce.

She plastered on a smile. "Hi, Joe."

He didn't bother with pleasantries. Most times, he ignored her. He nodded, but his eyes narrowed. She strolled into the tack room and hurried to Sarah's backpack to return the keys. Seconds later, Joe entered. Morgan pulled down Princess's old bridle from a peg and made a show of holding it up to the new one.

Too close.

The lame-o fence fixer had almost caught her.

Too bad, old man. He'd never outwit her. She smiled. Now the real fun would start.

* * *

Leonard slid his binoculars down from his eyes to make a timed entry in his tablet. The fourth day of surveillance, he hoped to establish a clear pattern of activity from Sarah. After she'd come home crying on Saturday, she'd spent the rest of the weekend in the house. Obviously, she was too upset over missing him to do anything. His heart swelled. She loved him so much.

He sat in the middle of the tarp he'd placed on the ground. A gnat buzzed in his ear, and he swatted it. For the third time in twenty minutes, he and pulled out bug repellent. He stood, closed his eyes, and pressed the trigger to spray in a fluid motion from his head to his boots. When the mist settled, he sat. Later, he would scrub his face to remove the poisonous DEET and wash his clothes in the tub he'd disinfected with bleach. He never used laundromats. They were fraught with bacteria from people's sweaty clothes.

He hated the forest. The bugs that crawled onto his towel. The birds that screeched in the trees. Complete chaos over which he had no control. But he'd endure it. For her.

After researching horse farms, he understood their schedules, which included early feedings. Leaving the hotel by four in the morning gave him enough time and the cover of darkness to set up for his surveillance. He'd parked his rental car off the road behind a large tree near the woods.

When Sarah came out of the house at six o'clock, his breath hitched.

Like yesterday, she wore boots, jeans, and a T-shirt. Clearly, she wasn't dressed to dance. So graceful, her every move. She all but floated across the yard.

He focused his binoculars on her as she led horses into the fields, lugged buckets out of the barn, and filled them with water. His ballerina shouldn't be performing menial tasks. Unacceptable. He'd convinced himself she'd just been helping out yesterday, but now it seemed she might work at the farm.

Calluses would form on her smooth, perfect hands. The stench of manure would cling to her hair and clothing. He wrinkled his nose. They would have to throw out everything she wore at the ranch. He'd order new outfits for her online and have them delivered to the hotel. Then, he'd wash them and store the garments in his suitcase so they never touched any other part of the room. At least he'd be returning the rental car, so the dirt and smell wouldn't ever be in his own vehicle.

While making more notes, he shook his head. This had to end. So many people came in and out of the farm and house. He had to get her alone. For now, he'd have to wait and establish the patterns of the farm's daily routines. No rush. He could be a patient man now that he had his love in sight. Planning was everything.

He brought up pictures of her on the screen of his iPad. Since he wasn't home, he couldn't keep to his routine of counting paces through his bedroom to tap her photos. His shoulders tensed. He swiped his finger across the display to bring up the next shot. After running through them four times, he took a deep breath. Better. Everything would be all right. He had his ballerina in his sights.

Soon, he'd find a way to get to her alone and take her back.

CHAPTER 25

Midday, a rap sounded on the suite door. Sarah had come back for lunch and wasn't expecting anyone. "Who is it?"

Fluffy jumped up from his bed and scampered to the door barking.

"Bruce."

Her heart started at his voice, a kneejerk reaction before the pain of their situation flooded back. It had been two days since he'd talked to her about picking up Maddie. She'd managed to avoid him, but every time she caught sight of him, her chest grew tight. If only he'd never kissed her. Or smelled so good. Or made her crazy with wanting him from one look.

On the way over to unlock the door, she glanced at the empty couch and stopped short. Her purse was missing. Earlier, she'd counted the money in her wallet and left the handbag on the sofa. Her gut rolled. Joe said he'd found a radiator and tires. She had just enough to pay for them.

"Sarah?"

She flung open the door, hurried back to the couch, and searched behind the pillows.

"What's wrong?" Bruce asked.

"My purse is gone." She gazed around the room then beelined to the bedroom. Everything was as she'd left it, with no purse in sight. Her pulse galloped in the base of her throat.

She pressed her fingers to her eyes. A feeling of déjà vu crept over her. The stalker used to hide and move things around in her dressing room to prove he could get to her anywhere. He liked to mess with her. Somehow, he must have been in the suite.

Her lungs seized, and her hands turned ice-cold.

The whole thing was starting over again.

She flung open drawers and rifled through them. Panic overcoming logic, she headed to the bathroom and checked the shower.

Bruce gripped her arms and held them firmly until she opened her eyes. "Calm down. You aren't acting rationally. It wouldn't be in the shower."

"What?"

"Think. When's the last time you had your purse?"

"This morning. I ran up here between chores at ten to call Maddie and count my money. I know I left it on the couch."

Bruce's eyebrows shot up. "Why were you counting your money?"

Like she'd tell him that. It was none of his damn business. "What difference does it make? If the purse is gone, so is the money."

Fluffy wedged himself between Bruce and Sarah. He nudged her hand and whined.

Bruce's gaze dropped to the dog. "Was he in here when you came up earlier?"

"What?" She glanced at the vanity top. Nothing appeared to be in a different spot.

"The dog. Did he come in with you?"

"Yeah, he follows me most times. Why?"

Bruce let go of her and went back into the family room. He bent down and looked under the sofa. Fluffy shoved his head under Bruce's arm and licked his face like they were playing some sort of fun game.

"What are you doing?" Sarah asked.

"Thinking like a dog." He crossed the room to Fluffy's bed, picked up a corner, and then snatched her purse from under it. "I found the thief."

"Fluffy?" She let out a breath.

Bruce handed the bag to her.

"He must have taken it when I was in the bathroom." The tension in her muscles uncoiled. Her gaze rested on Bruce's chest. She wanted to bury her head in it and feel his arms around her. Kiss those sensual lips that worked magic and made the world fall away. No. None of that would happen again. She slapped the desire aside and placed the purse on the counter out of Fluffy's reach.

Bruce took a step back. "I stopped by to check on the arrangements to get Maddie."

"Right." Of course. Reliable, responsible Bruce. He hadn't come to see her. All business, he wanted to fulfill his obligation. She tucked a stray hair behind her ear, and his gaze followed her movement. His jaw set. She could swear his eyes flashed, but it happened too fast for her to be sure.

She picked up a piece of paper from the coffee table and handed it to him. "I gave Maddie your cell number. This is hers. She said she'd call when she got into the next town on Friday. She's going to be at their library."

He tucked the note in his pocket and glanced at her purse. "Okay. Listen, about your money situation, if you need—"

"No, thanks. I don't need anything from you aside from a ride for Maddie."

He stared at her for a long moment, nodded, and let himself out.

Her tongue grew thick in her mouth. He had to think she was a paranoid mess. He'd accused her of being irrational. Probably questioned her sanity like the cops had when she'd told them things had been moved around in her dressing room. Bruce had to be patting himself on the back right now for getting away from her and her craziness.

She sat on the couch and rubbed her forehead. He may not be interested in her anymore, but she couldn't shut down her emotions like he could. He'd awakened feelings and sensations she'd never experienced. All the logic in the world didn't stop her from aching for his touch. The way he looked at her with those cold, detached eyes hurt too much. She'd have to leave after Maddie's visit. The car should be fixed by then, and any job she could find, she'd take.

* * *

Finally, Friday night. Sarah checked her watch. Six o'clock. Maddie would be here soon. The last couple of days had been sheer hell working around Bruce and yearning for what she couldn't have. Seeing her sister would be the bright spot in her week. Hell, her life at this point.

Maddie had texted her that they were a few minutes away. Sarah waited on the porch until Bruce's truck arrived.

He pulled a suitcase out from behind the seat as Maddie hopped down. She had dressed for the warm weather in jean shorts and a yellow tank top. Her red hair blew wild in the wind.

Sarah ran down the steps to greet her.

Maddie threw her arms open for a hug. She squeezed Sarah so hard she couldn't breathe. After a long embrace, Maddie took a step back. Her gaze traveled up and down Sarah, and she nodded. "You look good. I was scared of what I might find."

"Thanks for the flattery. I won't let it go to my head."

Bruce picked up the suitcase. "I'll take this inside for you."

"I can get it," Maddie said. "You've done enough."

Sarah faced Bruce. "Thank you."

"No problem."

Sarah turned back to Maddie. She couldn't take those cool eyes of his.

"Nice meeting you, Maddie." He opened the truck door and got in.

Sarah's gaze followed the pickup as he drove away. Her insides compressed.

"Holy shit. I'm here one minute and there's major drama," Maddie said.

"What?"

"You. Him. Now it all makes sense."

"What makes sense?" Sarah squinted. Nothing had happened that should send up any red flags.

"The two of you. Sheesh, you could have given me a heads-up."

"About what?"

"That he's got a thing for you." Maddie ran a hand through her curls. She sighed. "No wonder he didn't bite when I tried to flirt with him."

"What?"

Maddie waved a hand. "What do you think? You send this smoking-hot guy to pick me up and don't mention you're involved. That's like handing matches to a pyromaniac."

"God, Maddie. Do you ever stop? I have to work with him."

"Relax. I wasn't going to sleep with him. I just like to flirt."

Sarah frowned. "What makes you think we're involved?"

"The way he looked at you. Did you have a fight or something? When we pulled in, I glanced over at him, and his eyes were tortured when he saw you. Then, he iced over when you spoke to him. What's going on?"

Huh, so maybe he did still have feelings. But he was determined not to act on them, so it made no difference. Sarah shook her head. "Grab your suitcase. We can talk inside."

They climbed the steps, and Sarah led Maddie to the suite.

Fluffy jumped up from his bed and raced over to them.

"Oh, look at this cutie. He's so sweet." Maddie bent and petted the dog while Sarah poured iced tea.

She gave Fluffy a chew toy, and he scrambled to a corner and went to town on it. "That will keep him busy while we catch up."

After handing Maddie her tea, Sarah took a seat next to her on the couch.

"Now clue me in. What's up with you and Smoking-Hot?" Maddie asked.

"First things first. Is there any news on the stalker?"

"No. It's been all quiet. Maybe he's given up."

"I don't think so. I can't count on it, that's for sure."

"How are you handling things?" Maddie glanced at the curtained windows.

"I'm doing the best I can. Tell me what's going on with everyone." Sarah sipped her tea and sat back.

Maddie leaped to her feet, yanked an envelope out of her suitcase, and handed it to Sarah. "Mom mailed me a letter to bring to you."

The sight of her mother's handwriting made Sarah's eyes blur. She ate up every word of the note like a starved child handed a loaf of warm bread. "God, I miss them. I'm so glad you're here."

"Me too." Maddie sniffed and cleared her throat. "You've stalled long enough. What's going on with Bruce?"

"Nothing. We went hiking together one time, and halfway through the date he ran for the hills." Sarah shook her head. "No pun intended. He made it clear he's not interested in me."

"That's total bullshit. I saw the way he looked at you when you had your back to him. Like you were the prize in a big gumball machine and he didn't have a quarter."

Sarah smiled. "Strange analogy."

"It fits. He wants to eat you up." Maddie let out a low whistle. "I'm telling you, when he pulled up in that truck and I saw those biceps..." She held a hand to her chest. "That guy is sex on a stick, and that's a lollipop I'd love to lick."

"For God's sake." Sarah had forgotten that Maddie had no filters.

"Relax. It's hands-off from now on. I didn't know he was taken."

Sarah huffed out a breath. "We are *not* involved. That's what I'm trying to tell you."

"But you want to be."

"No, I don't." Only she did, in the worst way.

"Yes, you do."

"Don't."

"Stop lying to yourself. Now back up. What happened on the hike?"

Sarah's cheeks warmed. Sitting on his lap, his hot lips on her mouth.

"Holy shit. You're blushing." Maddie scooted closer. "OMG. You did him!"

Sarah jerked her head back. "No. We just kissed."

"Oh. Well, that's a start. How was it?"

"Good. I mean, I've never experienced such chemistry before. He sure acted like he felt it too." Right up until he'd ditched her.

"Did he have a boner?"

Geez. She wasn't about to discuss Bruce's...anatomy. "This conversation is over."

"Sorry. I forget how shy you are about guys. I meant was he into it?"

Sarah sighed and leaned back. "I thought so. But it doesn't matter. We had lunch, and then he got this weird look on his face. Date over."

Maddie frowned. "I know what I saw. This is far from over."

"Well, it is for me. I don't want to talk about this anymore."

"Okay, for now." Maddie glanced around the place. "What do you do around here for fun?"

"Fun?" Sarah shrugged and pointed to a book on the table. "I read. Debbie let me borrow her library card."

"Seriously? When's the last time you've been out?"

"I went to the store the other day."

"No. I mean for real out. Like someplace fun."

Sarah shook her head. "I don't. I can't risk someone seeing me. I stick to the library and food store. I wear a hat and keep a low profile."

"We're in the middle of nowhere." Maddie waved her hand. "You don't know a single person within five states of this place. And I don't mean to insult you, but it's not like you're a major movie star. Who's going to recognize you?"

"Still, I can't chance it. I'm sorry, Maddie. I know this is going to be boring for—"

"Oh, shut up. It's not about me. I figured you were going to say this, so I came prepared." She marched over to her suitcase and unzipped it.

"What are you talking about?"

She dug around for a second, and then tugged out a long auburn, curly wig. "This way you won't look like the old you or the new you."

Holy shit. Sarah choked on her tea. "You're crazy."

"No, I'm not. You've been holed up for too long. Haven't heard a peep from your computer creeper in over two weeks. We're going out. I even brought you a dress to wear." She produced a small strip of red, silky fabric.

"That's a dress? It looks like a Fruit Roll-Up."

"And you're going to look sensational in it."

No way in hell she'd wear that. "I really don't—"

"Look, I ran it by Anne, and even she said it should be all right with the disguise."

"She did?"

Maddie nodded. "Yes. Call her if you don't believe me."

"That's not necessary."

"There's a cool-looking bar not far from here I found online. We could—"

"Online?" Sarah tensed. "Oh no. Did you google that on your computer?"

"No. Relax. I did it at the library." Maddie squeezed Sarah's arm. "I know how freaked you are. I don't do anything related to you on my computer. Neither does Anne."

"Okay. Sorry."

"Anyway, the website said the bar used to be a warehouse. People left comments about it being the happening place to go in this small town. What do you think?"

Sarah rubbed her chin and willed her nervous stomach to calm. Maddie had a point about the disguise, and it might get her mind off Bruce for one night, but they'd have to find a way to get there. Joe had fixed her car, but driving with stolen plates was too risky. "Maybe if Debbie says we can take the truck. I hate to ask, but it's not like they need it at night for anything, and I could offer to pay for gas."

Maddie fist-pumped the air. "Hot damn. Now we're talking."

"If we go, I'm not wearing that red, slinky thing. I can't draw attention to myself."

Maddie held up the dress and shook her head. "Damn shame. You would have had the guys drooling over you."

"Exactly my point."

"Okay. And I can drive so you don't have to worry about getting pulled over and flashing that fake ID."

"Well—"

"That's it. Go find this Debbie and ask." Maddie shooed her away, like her bossy little self. "We're hitting the town, girl."

CHAPTER 26

SARAH SQUEEZED her hands together in her lap as Maddie drove the truck. "I really don't think this is a good idea."

"We've been all through this, and you're going to have fun. Wonder what Lollipop Man would say if he saw you now. I like you with the curls."

"He wouldn't say anything. I don't exist to him, apparently."

Maddie waited for a car to pull out of the packed parking lot of the bar and took the space. She glanced over at Sarah and frowned.

"What?" Sarah met her gaze.

"If you want to go back, it's okay. I just thought this might cheer you up. I'm not trying to—"

"No, I'd like to feel normal again, you know, for one night. You were right. I'm tired of being a recluse. No one will recognize me. Let's go."

Maddie smiled and patted Sarah's arm. "That's the spirit."

After they got out of the truck, Maddie smoothed down the front of her skirt. When Sarah had mentioned not wanting to draw attention, Maddie chose a brown mini and a cream clingy top that showed off less cleavage than her usual going-out attire. She'd sighed, as if in pain, when she'd tossed aside her stilettos in favor of lower heels. Nothing too sexy, but she'd get hit on wearing a trash bag.

After much debate, Sarah also had worn a miniskirt, but black. They'd compromised on the top. A silky red button-down. Sexy in a conservative way. Maddie liked the color, Sarah, the coverage.

Neon beer signs flashed in the windows of the large building. Sarah swung the door open and surveyed the mobbed room, noting the hall across from it with restrooms and another exit. Always good to have an escape route.

Band members plucked strings and tested the mic in a corner behind a small dance floor. High-top tables with metal clips holding drink-special cards surrounded the rectangular bar. Wooden steps led to a second story with pool tables and another bar.

Maddie weaved through the crowd, and Sarah followed. All the tables were taken, and people stood behind the occupied seats at the bar.

Maybe upstairs wouldn't be as packed. Sarah pointed to the steps. Maddie nodded, and they made their way to the stairs. Maddie stopped. "Hey, there's Bruce."

No way. Sarah glanced at the table ahead where sure enough, Bruce and another man sat with a couple of beers in front of them. Her heart battered her rib cage.

"Hmm. This is an interesting development." Maddie smiled. "We have to say hi."

They would run into Bruce. Of all things. Totally mortifying. Sarah yanked on Maddie's hand, but she forged ahead in the direction of the table.

"Hi, Bruce," Maddie called.

Bruce glanced up, and his eyes widened. His gaze darted around the people next to Maddie and right over Sarah. He grabbed Maddie's arm and stood. "Where's Sarah? Is everything okay?"

Too late to avoid him now. Sarah raised her chin. "I'm right here."

Bruce's head snapped back, and he scanned her from head to foot. His jaw went slack.

Maddie patted Sarah's shoulder as if pleased. "See? Even Bruce couldn't tell it was you."

"What are you doing here? And what's this?" He waved a hand at her wig.

Before she could answer, he stepped to the side, boxing her in against the table, his body a shield to anyone passing.

"I drove the farm truck, and this is Sarah's disguise." Maddie grinned. "Pretty sweet, huh?"

Bruce turned to Maddie. Under his scrutiny, her smile faltered, and she shifted from one foot to the other. Of course, she wasn't used to the killer looks he leveled, but it took a lot to rattle Maddie.

Heat rose to Sarah's cheeks. He might be shocked at seeing her there, but what she wore and where she went was not his concern.

"You gonna introduce your friend?" Maddie glanced at the other man at the table.

The guy stood. Tall, with dark hair, green eyes, and masses of muscles, he flashed a smile. Bruce glanced at Sarah and introduced his friend as Scott.

"This place is packed. We can't even get to the bar," Maddie said.

"Why don't you join us?" Scott snagged a chair from the table of three beside them.

"Sure, thanks." Maddie took a seat.

Sarah glared at Maddie. She had to know how awkward this was after their conversation about Bruce. Sarah fingered the strap of her purse. She glanced up to find Bruce once again eyeing her from top to bottom.

He yanked the chair out next to him. "Here. Sit."

A waitress stopped at the table, and Maddie ordered a cosmo. Not a bad plan. Sarah needed something to help her get through the night. She ordered one as well, and the guys asked for another round of beers. Maddie launched into full flirt mode and chatted with Scott until the drinks came. Playful hand slapping of his arm. Leaning close to talk. Sarah couldn't help but be jealous of how easy it was for Maddie. Having spent most of her time with ballet dancers, the majority of them girls, Sarah lacked those skills.

Every cell in Sarah's body screamed awareness of Bruce, the anything-but-a-ballet-dancer, beside her. She sneaked a peek at him, all grumpy and bear-like. He was staring at her but quickly picked up his beer and took a swig. His musky male scent filled her nostrils, causing her lower parts to tighten.

When the drinks came, Sarah downed half of hers. The cool, sweet liquid soothed her throat.

As the band warmed up, Sarah swirled her glass. A bead of condensation dribbled down the side. She rubbed her finger up the streak and licked it. Bruce sucked in an audible breath, shifted in his seat, and looked toward the band. Maddie continued to chat and flirt until their drinks were almost gone.

"Hey, you guys wanna play pool?" Maddie asked.

Sarah choked on the last of her cosmo. Maddie must have lost her mind. They were wearing miniskirts.

"Sure," Scott said with a grin.

"I stink at pool." Sarah narrowed her eyes at Maddie, hoping she got the message.

"Come on. It's just a game." Maddie stood.

She would die a slow death later. A very slow death.

The band started to play as Sarah said, "I really—"

Maddie tapped her ears, shook her head, and pointed to the steps. Scott took her hand to lead the way. Left alone with Bruce, Sarah glanced at him. They couldn't talk over the music even if he wanted to, which was doubtful. She grabbed her purse as he stood and slid her chair out. He waved a hand for her to go ahead and followed so closely his body heat warmed her back.

When they reached the top, she spied Maddie at the end of the room by a pool table. She waved to them and pointed at Scott, who stood in line at the bar against the wall. Sarah's gaze traveled over the pool tables. Beyond them people clapped and booed from another area with dartboards.

"I'll go help Scott," Bruce said.

Any excuse to get away. Fine by her.

She had to pass by a rowdy group of men with ball caps and T-shirts stretched to the limit over their guts. Several empty plastic pitchers and half-full mugs lined the windowsill near them. One of the men let out a loud whistle. The others looked in Sarah's direction. Their gazes never made it to her face.

She tried to walk past, but the whistler made a quick move to block her.

"Wanna play with us?" He ran his hand up and down the pool stick, and the guys behind hooted.

Crap. She didn't need this when she was trying to blend in with the crowd. She shot a glance at the bar, but Bruce and Scott had their backs to her.

Her nose crinkled at the scent of sweat and body odor.

The man took a step closer, his gaze on her breasts. "I like a woman who wears red. Would Little Red Riding Hood like to play with the Big Bad Wolf?"

She caught sight of Maddie storming up behind him, a pool stick in hand. Oh no. This was gonna be trouble. Her sister had a protective streak a mile wide.

Sarah had to defuse things before they caused a scene. She pointed to Maddie. "Sorry, I don't roll that way. I'm with her."

Maddie thumped her stick on the floor. "Is there a problem?"

"Aww...shit." Wolfie's posse guffawed as he waved a hand and backed off. "Never mind. Fucking waste."

"Let's go." Sarah slung her arm around Maddie's shoulder.

Maddie huffed and glared back at the guys but went with Sarah. "I had that."

"I know." Sarah's racing pulse slowed back to almost normal. "Thanks, but low profile. Right?"

"Sorry." Maddie squeezed her side. "I just can't stand assholes, and you were—"

"Fine. I was fine." Sarah smoothed her skirt. Crisis averted. A little voice inside of her applauded.

"You were." Maddie rested her hand on the pool table and gave Sarah an assessing look. "That was quick thinking. You are...I don't know...different. Edgy...in a good way, though. Street-smart almost."

Sarah rolled a pool ball under her hand and glanced up at Maddie. "I'm learning to do what I have to. Maybe I need to channel a little more of you."

Maddie gave her a suffocating hug. "No, sis. You got this. And *we* got this. I'm with you."

Sarah glanced at Bruce and Scott, approaching them. "The last thing I want to do is play pool with Bruce." She put a hand on her hip. "Or for that matter, do anything with him. He clearly can't stand to be around me. Didn't say a word to me the whole time you were flirting with Scott."

Maddie shook her head. "You must be blind. That man is so hot for you, his insides are fried. I'm trying to give him a chance to show you."

"You don't understand, Maddie. He's made it clear—"

"I don't care what he's said. I know men, and I'm telling you he's got it bad for you."

"No, he doesn't. And—"

"Hey, thanks." Maddie took a glass from Scott, who returned with Bruce. She nodded to Sarah with those give-him-a-chance eyes.

Bruce handed Sarah her cosmo. She thanked him and took a big sip. Forced to rub elbows with the Terminator, she needed a drink. Maybe it would numb her rebellious, raging hormones. This night had turned into a mess.

* * *

Bruce took a deep breath and a swig of beer as Sarah leaned over the table to make a shot. Her skirt hiked up, right to the edge of her shapely little ass. The way the material clung to her curves made him crazy. She probably thought she'd dressed conservatively, given what other women wore in the place, but it only teased him into wanting to see more.

The band downstairs started a new number, and Maddie grabbed Scott's hand. "I love this song. Wanna dance?"

Sarah shot her a look, but Maddie waved and waltzed toward the steps with Scott, calling over her shoulder, "We'll be back."

Bruce stared at them. He couldn't ask Sarah to dance. As hot as she had him right now, if he touched her, he'd lose it. He pointed to an empty high-top by the dartboards, needing to get away from the pool table and the miniskirt. "Do you want to sit down?"

"I guess." She took a sip of the cosmo and followed him to the table.

Sarah glanced at the stairs and ran her fingers around the rim of the glass. "So how do you know Scott?"

Bruce gripped the beer bottle tighter. "We grew up together."

"Oh." Sarah tugged her blouse away from her neck, drawing the material in the front snug against her breasts.

His shaft came to life beneath the table. Damn it. He didn't need this. "Maddie seems to like him."

"Yeah." Sarah shifted in her seat. "Look, I love my sister, and I'm not going to apologize for her, but Maddie is kind of—"

"Don't worry about it. Scott just got burned by a woman. That's the only reason I'm here. I dragged him out." Bruce faced her. "He's not looking for anything serious."

"Fair enough." She shrugged, finished off her drink, and stood. "I'm gonna head downstairs now. I'm sorry Maddie left you stuck with me. You don't need to be my babysitter."

Shit. He couldn't let her go down there alone. Not in a miniskirt and heels with those make-his-mouth-water, toned legs. "Wait." He pointed to the dartboard. "You ever play?"

She shook her head. "Nope."

"Wanna try?" Sensing her hesitation, he stood and waved a hand. "Come on, I'll teach you."

She cocked her head and nibbled at her lower lip.

Damn, she made him crazy when she did that. Control. He had to stay in control. After the hiking fiasco, he'd learned his lesson. Hands off, or he'd get lost in her.

She shrugged and sauntered over to the dartboard. Her swinging hips and the way her skirt clung to her ass aggravated his condition.

"No." He pointed to the line of tape on the floor to distract her as well as buy himself some time. "From back here."

"Oh, I see."

"You can throw from closer if you want."

"Nope. I'll play by the rules."

He handed her a dart. She threw it, and the arrow hit the metal rim of the board.

"Crap." She shook her head. "I can do better than that."

He picked up the fallen dart and handed it to her.

This time she missed the target altogether. She huffed out a breath and planted her hands on her hips.

Figures. Of course, she'd be a competitor. He'd goad her if he had to.

Anything to keep her from traipsing around alone in a bar full of men on the prowl. "Ready to give up?"

Her eyes narrowed. "No. Give me another."

He handed her a dart and failed in his attempt to ignore the incredible shape of her legs. "Let's play trivia."

Her eyebrows raised. "Huh?"

"It's a new game." Total lie. Maybe he could distract her focus from winning. "Before you throw, ask me a question, and after I answer, you toss it."

"Okay." She cocked her arm back. "Favorite color?"

"Green."

She threw, and this time the dart hit inside the outer ring, but still fell to the ground.

"Better. You're moving your shoulder, though." He came up behind her and placed a dart in her hand, covering it with his. "Try again. It's all in the release." As soon as his body touched hers, hot desire raged through him. He took a quick step back. "Keep your shoulder still, and use your arm."

The tip stuck in the outer ring.

"Woohoo." She pumped a fist. "Your turn."

When she bent over to pick up the darts, he sucked in a breath. He had to stop looking at her ass. She handed the darts to him, and he cocked back his arm.

"Trivia, remember?" She tapped his shoulder.

"Oh, right. Favorite band?" he asked.

"Bon Jovi."

He threw and hit the bull's-eye.

"Hey, you didn't tell me you were a ringer." She thrust her hands on her hips.

"I might have played a few times, but we won't keep score. It's just for fun."

"Okay." She moved back out of the way. "You get two more, right?"

He nodded and picked up the next dart. "Favorite movie?"

"*Dirty Dancing.*"

The image of Sarah's body pressed against his in a sexy, hot dance flashed in his head. He threw the dart, and it dinged off the wall, missing the board.

"Come on. Don't blow it to make me feel good." Sarah pursed her lips.

Like hell. He picked up his last dart. "Favorite all-time actor."

"Harrison Ford."

He hit the bull's-eye again.

Sarah snickered. "The Force was with you on that one."

"Smart-ass. Take one more shot." He yanked a dart from the board and held it out to her.

Her smile wavered, but she cocked her head and took the dart. "Okay. One last question."

She drew her arm back. "Ready?"

"Go for it."

"Why did you end our date?"

CHAPTER 27

SARAH HELD her breath and glanced at him from the corner of her eye.

"Because of the heart," Bruce blurted out, then froze.

Sarah slowly lowered her arm. Her fuzzy brain scrambled to make sense of what he'd said. She twisted around to face him.

His lips pressed together, and he checked his watch.

"Your heart? I don't understand."

"We should find Maddie and Scott. It's getting late."

The cosmo burned in her stomach. "No. I want to know what you're talking about."

"Just let it go." He met her gaze. His brows lowered, and his eyelids tightened as if he was in pain.

She reached for him before she could stop herself. Placing a hand on the side of his face, she smoothed the wrinkles next to his eyes. If only he would talk to her.

He covered her hand with his and gave the smallest shake of his head.

Goose bumps ran down her arm. The stubble on his rugged jaw tickled her palm. She slipped her tongue out to moisten her lips, and his gaze followed.

He could shake his head all he wanted. His eyes told another story.

She might not have the most experience with men, but she knew desire when she saw it.

A muscle in his jaw twitched. He fought so hard for control all the time. Maybe he worried about letting that heart of his go. And her own heart leaped. Maybe he cared about her more than he'd admit.

She inched closer, and he didn't back off. The fire in her belly worked its way up to her face. Inhaling his clean, all-male scent, she reached her other arm up to his shoulder and pressed against the length of him. Her libido did a victory lap as his arousal pushed into the flat of her stomach.

His nostrils flared, and his hand stiffened over hers.

He wanted her. No matter what he said or did. With heels on, she stood tall enough to almost reach his face. His breath blew across her hot cheeks. Her stomach tittered like an eight ball on the rim of a corner pocket.

The muted lights above shimmered, cut by the slow-turning blades of a fan. She slid her hand behind his neck, closed her eyes, and pulled herself up inch by inch for a kiss.

She could almost taste the malty beer on his lips when his hand locked around her wrist, and he took a step back.

She opened her eyes and sucked in a breath. Something exploded in her chest, crashing down a brutal reality check. Once again, she'd made a fool of herself.

The man didn't want her. He might have a physical attraction, but clearly, that's as far as it went. And he'd demonstrated he could control his urges, unlike her. Barbs of humiliation ripped open the still-fresh scab from his rejection on the hike.

She yanked her wrists from his grip. "You win, Bruce. Game over."

Stomping to the stairs, she cursed him and the horse he road in on. Ha.

When she reached the bottom, she glanced around the mass of people. It might take a while to find Maddie. She found a seat at the bar and ordered another cosmo. In three big gulps, she downed the drink and wiped her mouth with a cocktail napkin. She scanned the room again and spotted Maddie and Scott dancing. That's what she'd come for, to have some fun.

A tall man in a white polo shirt and jeans eased onto the seat next to

Sarah. He rested his forearms on the counter. Nice biceps. Big ones. Like Bruce's. Sexy, hot, off-limits Bruce, whose biceps she couldn't touch. Probably this guy would let her. Unless he didn't want her either.

"Would you like to dance?" he asked.

Or...maybe he did. She turned to face him. Light brown eyes, dark hair, and a friendly smile.

Her body hummed with a nice buzz. "Do you know how much I want to dance?"

He cocked his head. "No."

"Lemme tell you. More than anything in this whole wide world." She spread her arms wide. "That's how much."

"So that's a yes?" He raised an eyebrow.

She nodded and placed a hand on his arm as she stood. Squeezed it for a second. Touched his biceps!

His smile widened.

Two for two. She'd touched a man, *and* he hadn't run away. And a hot guy too. Not some mousy wimp. So Bruce, Mr. Snow-Miser, could put that in his blower and—

Whoa. She slipped as her foot hit the floor. The man grabbed her before she fell.

"You okay?"

"Yup." She regained her balance and nodded.

He led her to the dance floor. The guy had moves. Might not be ballet, but so what, at least they were dancing.

The song ended, and the lead singer called out, "Gonna slow it down for this next one."

Good. Her feet were a little unsteady. Maybe downing that last cosmo hadn't been such a great idea. Her dance partner took one of her hands, wrapping his arm around her waist. They swayed to the music.

"I'm Anthony. What's your name?" he asked in a smooth voice.

"Sarah." She focused on his face because the background began to spin.

"You're beautiful and a great dancer." His fingers stroked the side of her waist, sliding the silky material of her blouse up and down her skin.

If the guy were Bruce, dancing this close, she'd be on fire. But with Anthony, nothing. A warm body and a nice smile. No sparks, no passion.

Damn it. Doomed for life to moon over the Abominable Snowman. She shut her eyes and leaned against his chest in defeat.

* * *

Bruce's gaze followed Sarah until she disappeared down the steps. He stabbed a hand through his hair. Goddamn it. He'd hurt her again. The pain in her eyes when he'd pushed her away sliced through him.

They'd even been having fun playing darts. Something he'd never done with Emily. He rubbed his temple. Sarah was nothing like Emily. He'd hiked with Sarah, but even that had been different. When he'd met Emily, he'd come home from his stint overseas wounded, scarred, and burned out. Her tough get-back-up-on-the-horse attitude was exactly what he'd needed. She'd seen him through a bumpy time and helped him heal. He'd always love her for that.

But things were different now. He didn't need his protective armor anymore to get through a day. Sarah had a softness about her that called to him. Brave, caring, graceful, and beautiful. She had it all. And having feelings for Sarah didn't take anything away from Emily. She'd always be a part of him. But that part was in the past now.

He flattened his hand on the table and glanced at his fingers. The tan line from his wedding band had long ago faded, but he still had the ring in a drawer. That was what he needed to do with his memories. Keep them tucked away, but make some new ones. With Sarah.

All week he'd been tortured working around her. It had taken every ounce of his energy to keep up the cold front. With one touch, she melted him faster than ice in a shot of Jack Daniel's. He couldn't protect himself from loss anymore. She'd stolen his heart. If he wanted it back, he'd have to share it with her. If it wasn't too late.

After being rejected twice, she'd have every right to tell him to shove it. His pulse quickened.

He pushed away from the table, took a deep breath, and strode to the stairs. No turning back this time. All or nothing.

When he reached the first level, he surveyed the room. She wasn't at the bar. Maybe she'd found Maddie and Scott. His gaze stopped on Sarah, out on the dance floor, in the arms of a man. The guy rubbed up and down her sides as she smiled up at him. He pulled her closer, and she rested her head against his chest.

Bruce fisted his hands, and hot blood raged through his body as something snapped inside. Spots appeared before his eyes. Another man holding and stroking Sarah. Like hell. Breath ready to burst from his lungs, he pushed through the crowd until he reached them.

He tapped the guy's shoulder hard. "Take your hands off her. She's with me."

The man stood eye-to-eye with Bruce. He tightened his arm around Sarah. "You know this guy?"

She blinked and looked at Bruce but kept leaning against the man, as if for support. "Yes. And what I do is none of his business."

The guy shrugged and kept Sarah in his embrace. "You heard the lady. She's with me. Take a hike."

Sarah snorted. "That's how this all started."

"Time's up." Bruce gripped the man's arm and brought his face close. He narrowed his eyes and squeezed hard on a pressure point. In a lethal go-ahead-and-make-my-day tone, he said, "Let go of her right now."

The guy winced, and his eyes widened. "What the fuck?" He drew his arm away from Sarah and backed off. "I don't need this."

"Who the hell do you think you are?" Sarah poked Bruce's chest. She teetered and waved her hand. "What was that about?"

She was drunk all right. And spitting mad. With a right to be. He'd lost his mind at the sight of her with another man. He reached for her arm. "Come on, let's go outside and get some fresh air."

"No. I came here to dance, and I intend to." She jerked away and gazed around the bar. "Now where did Anthony go?"

He had to get her outside. "You've had too much to drink. I'm trying to help."

"I didn't ask for your help. I don't need a big bully following me around scaring away my dates." She glared up at him. "And what do you care anyway? You don't want me, so why do you give a damn if anyone else does?"

Shit. She couldn't possibly think he didn't want her, but she was too drunk to reason with. "Look, let's discuss this later. You need some air."

"No. I don't. I need to dance. I'm not leaving, so go away." She wobbled.

Damn it. Stubborn woman. "Fine. Then I'll dance with you."

He pulled her into his arms, but she stiffened.

"You don't want to. I'll find someone else." She tried to worm out of his grasp, but he held her tighter and waited until she looked into his eyes.

"I do want to dance with you." He rubbed her back and guided her into his embrace, moving with the music.

She shivered and melted into his arms. "I hate you right now."

"You should." He sighed. At least she'd stopped fighting him.

"I don't feel so great," she said in small voice.

"I know. Let's go." He steered her through the crowd to the front door and out.

She sucked in a breath of air and leaned against him. "Hey. Guess what?"

"What?" He guided her toward his truck. The best thing for her would be to get her home to sleep it off.

"I don't want to kiss you." She hiccupped. "I feel like shit, but at least I don't want to kiss you."

"Okay."

She stopped walking and attempted to cross her arms, but with only one free, it ended up slung across her waist. "No. You don't get it. I always want to kiss you. All the time." She shook her head and pouted. "But you don't want to kiss me. And I have to work. I don't think I could kiss you all day at work."

Holy shit. She was really ripped.

Before he could say anything, she added, "But I still want to."

"Let's keep moving." He tried to drag her along, but she stood firm.

"And ya know what else?" She faltered, and he tightened his grip on her waist. "I don't wanna kiss just anyone. Nope. Only you." She poked a finger again at his chest. "I didn't even wanna kiss Anthony, and he was pretty hot and a good dancer." She squinted. "I thought I wanted to kiss Mark, but that's cuz I'd never kissed you. And he didn't ever wanna kiss me either. Unless we had sex, and that wasn't even very good." She frowned. "But he was a jerk. Do you know how long we dated?"

"It's none of my—"

"Two years. Then the stalker came and poof." She snapped her fingers, or at least tried. "Done with me. Too hard. I wasn't worth it."

Bruce shook his head. Asshole. She deserved better. "Come on, let's keep going."

"I tried to kiss you tonight, you know."

A hammer drove a spike in his heart. He'd hurt her.

"But you didn't want me to. So I give up." She waved her one free hand in the air. "I have to leave. It's too hard to be around you."

Sarah leaned against the side of his truck. He pulled her from it to face him. "You promised you wouldn't run."

She sighed. "You don't want me cuz I can't be normal, and you think I'm paranoid. So I'm outta here."

"No. Damn it, Sarah." He had to make her realize none of that was true.

She pressed her stomach and took a couple of steps to the woods at the edge of the parking lot. "I'm gonna throw up."

Bruce held the hair from her wig back as she vomited. At least some of the liquor would be out of her. She dry-heaved and shook.

"Let me help you to the truck." He slung an arm around her and hoisted her into the passenger seat. From behind the bench, he grabbed a tissue and a bottle of water. "Here, you can rinse your mouth out."

She did, spitting the water out on the ground. He shut the door, went around to the driver's side, and climbed in. She looked over at him, her eyelids heavy.

"You held my hair back." A sad smile formed on her face. "No guy does that. Yup. I gotta leave."

"No, Sarah." His gut bottomed out. He put a hand on her cheek. "You're dead wrong about everything. I want you more than anything in my life."

The truth hit him hard. He stroked her face, and her eyes started to close again. This conversation would have to wait until morning.

He tugged out his phone and dialed Scott's number. On the fourth ring, Scott answered. The bar noise all but drowned out his voice.

"Scott, can you hear me?" Bruce asked.

"Hold on," Scott said.

He must have stepped outside because the background noise faded.

"Where are you? Maddie and I have been looking for you guys."

Bruce glanced at Sarah, now asleep. "Sarah's not feeling too well. I want to take her home. Can you make sure Maddie gets back to the farm safely?"

"No problem. We were ready to leave anyway. I'll follow her. It's on my way home. See you there."

"Thanks, bro."

Bruce fastened Sarah's seat belt. Gorgeous even in that ridiculous curly wig. She thought he didn't want her. Might have left without telling him. He'd fucked up so badly. Tomorrow they'd have a talk, and God willing, she'd give him another chance.

CHAPTER 28

BRUCE PULLED up to the farmhouse. Sarah was asleep with her head against the window of the passenger door. He grabbed her purse and shook it. A smart man never reached into one of those booby traps. Guaranteed to pull out a tampon. A jingle came from the front pocket, and he fished out the keys. He unlocked the house and came back to the passenger side of the truck. "Come on, Sleeping Beauty, time to get to bed."

Sarah opened her eyes and blinked. "Where are we?"

"Back at the suite. Let me help you."

She put her hands on his shoulders and slid down. "Mmm, you're warm."

"Let's get you inside." He tried to lead her, but she clung to him and didn't move her feet. "Never mind. We'll do it this way." He picked her up, and she buried her head in his chest.

"You smell so good. I might want to kiss you again. But you—"

"Maybe tomorrow, if you still want to." They were *not* going through the whole kissing conversation again. He smiled despite the situation.

When he unlocked the door, the dog ran over and whined.

"Hey, guy. Gimme some room here."

Bruce carried Sarah into the bedroom. The scent of cologne hung in the air. Probably Maddie's, although not very feminine.

Fluffy ran up to him and whined again, blocking his way to the bathroom.

"What's wrong with you?" He glanced around but didn't see any messes on the floor. Maybe the dog had been lonely or was jealous because Bruce was holding Sarah and not petting him like usual.

He took Sarah into the bathroom and set her on her feet, keeping an arm around her for support. "Do you want to clean up or just go to bed?"

She squinted under the lights. "There's two of me."

Someone was going to hurt in the morning.

She gave the wig a hard tug and it came off, scattering a bunch of pins. Her hand shook as she reached for the mouthwash on the counter.

"Here." He poured a bit into the lid and handed it to her. She managed to get some in her mouth, swished it around, and then spit into the sink.

"Okay. Night, night." She stumbled to the bed and flopped down on top of the covers.

Good enough. He opened the window to let air into the stuffy room and then went upstairs to make sure she'd locked the door to the main house. When he came back to the bedroom, he gazed at her, now curled into the fetal position. His shoulders dropped. He'd hurt her so many times. Unable to resist, he bent down and kissed her cheek.

She murmured something and shifted.

He closed the window and twisted the lock.

An engine hummed and gravel crunched up the drive. Scott and Maddie must be returning. Bruce went outside and held a hand up to shield his eyes from the headlights.

Maddie jumped from the truck and sprinted to him. "What's going on? Is Sarah all right?"

"Yes, but she had too much to drink."

Scott got out of his car and came to stand beside Maddie. "You guys need help with anything?"

"No. Everything's under control now, thanks," Bruce said.

"This is all my fault. I made her go out. She doesn't drink much. I just wanted her to have some fun. Damn it." Maddie stamped her heel in the dirt. "I knew if she was with you, it would be fine. I mean, she's obviously…"

Bruce raised an eyebrow. "What?"

"Never mind." She gazed at him with fierce eyes. "Sarah wasn't drunk when I left her. What happened?"

The woman had missed her calling as an interrogator. "I don't know." He shrugged. "She went downstairs, and when I caught up to her, that's how she was."

"What do you mean when you caught up to her? Why did she leave you?"

Shit. He'd had enough for one night. "Look, it's late. She's safe, and that's all that matters. Tell Sarah I'll be over tomorrow morning."

Maddie placed a hand on his arm. "I'm sorry." She gave him a soft squeeze. "Thanks for taking care of her. I'm mad at myself, and I didn't mean to take it out on you. I got so scared when we couldn't find her. I thought the stalker—"

"It's okay. I promise no one will get to her here. Make sure you lock up."

"I will." Maddie waved to Scott. "Thanks for following me back."

He gave her a warm smile and nodded. "Anytime."

She hurried into the house.

"Stalker?" Scott raised an eyebrow.

Bruce frowned. "It's a long story. I'll explain tomorrow. I'm sorry. I owe you for tonight."

Scott shook his head. "Like hell, I owe you. Maddie gave me her number. She's something."

* * *

Sarah opened one eye as sunlight poured through the crack in the curtains. She half raised, then put a hand to her head and sank back down. Throbbing pain. Not good. The night came back in bits. Cosmos. Dancing with a strange man. Throwing up.

Ugh. No.

She covered her face with her hands. Bruce had been with her. He must be so disgusted. Nothing worse than being around a puking drunk.

As if things weren't bad enough before, now he would avoid her like roadkill. She tried to sit up, slower this time. Better. His scent clung to the blouse she still wore. Well, they had danced together at least for a little while.

She shuffled to the bathroom, splashed water on her face, and brushed her teeth. Hairpins littered the floor and counter around the wig next to the sink. She shook her head. Not a clue what had happened. She plodded to the kitchen to find Maddie brewing coffee and toasting a bagel.

"I heard you get up. Thought you might like something in your stomach."

Sarah smiled. "Thanks. I need carbs."

Maddie took a step closer and brushed a strand of Sarah's hair back. "I'm sorry. I take the blame for this."

"Not your fault. You didn't force the cosmos down my throat."

"But I should have stayed with you. I thought you and Bruce would, you know, be better off if I left you alone."

"You don't get it, Maddie. We're done. I tried to kiss him, and he shoved me away. Can't get much clearer than that."

Maddie poured two cups of coffee and handed Sarah a mug. "You're wrong about him."

"How so?" Sarah pulled the bagel out of the toaster.

"He's crazy over you. He drove you home, tucked you in bed. No guy does that if he's not interested."

Sarah wrinkled her nose and glanced up. Another piece of the night slipped into her memory of him holding her up in the bathroom. "You don't know Bruce. He thinks he's responsible for everyone."

Maddie shook her head but didn't argue further. "How do you feel?"

"Like shit." Sarah took a sip of coffee and picked up a glass from the drying mat. "I should drink some water." She filled the cup. "Thanks for cleaning up. I meant to wash these before we left."

"Huh?" Maddie cocked her head.

"The dishes. Thanks for cleaning them."

"I didn't."

Sarah choked on her water. "What do you mean? If you didn't, who did?"

"Dunno. Maybe you did before we left. Don't worry about it."

"I don't remember doing that." Sarah's stomach balled.

Maddie rubbed Sarah's arm. "Sweetie, I'm sure there's a lot you don't remember about last night."

"Yeah. I guess." Sarah glanced at the empty cup on the drying towel, and took a deep breath. Maybe Bruce had cleaned up.

Maddie said, "Want to go get a warm shower? You might feel better."

"Okay." Sarah took a step toward the bathroom, breakfast in hand.

"Wouldn't hurt to put on a touch of makeup so you don't look like death when Bruce shows up."

Sarah spun around. "What?"

"He said to tell you he'd be by this morning." Maddie stuffed a piece of bagel in her mouth.

"Why?" Nerves fluttered in Sarah's stomach.

Maddie pointed to her full cheeks and shrugged.

Sarah shook her head and made her way to the shower. Damn Maddie. She knew more than she was telling.

* * *

At the sound of Bruce's truck, Sarah's heart jumped. Apparently, that organ hadn't gotten the memo last night. She rinsed with mouthwash and swiped on some lipstick.

When she trudged back to the family room, Maddie sat in front of her laptop.

"Give him a chance," she said.

"What?"

Maddie smiled her annoying know-it-all smile. "He's hot. He cares about you. Don't miss out." She stood. "Think I'll take a walk. Come on, Fluffy."

The dog leaped up and chased his tail.

Maddie laughed. "Leave a towel on the doorknob if—"

"That's not funny." Sarah scowled and crossed her arms. Bruce sure as hell wasn't coming for any action after last night. But at the same time, he was the one who'd insisted they play darts, and she hadn't asked him to bring her home. She'd tried to get away from him, so it really wasn't her fault.

Maddie opened the door and said hello to Bruce, who stepped back to let her pass. He bent down to rub the dog's head and accept a lick.

Fluffy trotted off after Maddie.

"Hi, Sarah." Bruce entered and shut the door behind him.

She shot a glance at him, and her hormones came to life. He wore a cool blue T-shirt that matched his eyes.

"Thanks for bringing me home. I'm sorry about last night."

"I'm not," he said.

"What?"

He came across the room and stopped in front of her. "Sorry about last night."

"I don't understand. I—"

"You said a lot of things that weren't true. I'm here to set them straight."

Oh God. Her mind raced, but she came up with nothing. "What did I say?"

The corners of his mouth turned down. He placed his hands on her shoulders and rubbed his thumbs under her collarbones.

Her unsettled stomach fluttered. She hadn't expected him to ever touch her again.

"You told me about Mark and how he thought you were too much work."

She winced. "I'm sure you didn't want to hear about that."

"Actually, I did." He moved a hand to the side of her neck. "I'm not him."

Her head hurt. He couldn't possibly mean he thought they had a shot at anything together. But his warm hand on her skin was giving her other ideas. "Look, I don't need you to feel sorry for me. I'm over it. He was a jerk. So don't—"

"Agreed. Only a dick would let you go."

She gazed into his eyes and wrinkled her brow. He wasn't making any sense because twice he'd kicked her to the curb. And on that subject, he'd lost the right to touch her. Her traitorous body heated up from the smallest contact. She tried to step out of his reach, but he tightened his grip on her shoulder.

"I'm not done."

"Well, then talk with your hands off me because—"

"Point taken." He let go of her, and she backed up, crossing her arms. "Let's get this over with. What else did I blurt out last night?"

"That you wanted to kiss me all the time."

Shit. Those cosmos had sure loosened her tongue. She blew at her bangs. "I don't see what purpose this is serving. I babbled like an idiot. I've apologized. Can you please go now?"

"No. Not until I ask what I came to." He moved closer.

She dug her nails into her arms, his proximity making her pulse speed up. "What?"

"I don't deserve it, but I want another chance with you." His eyes burned with intensity.

She stared into them and fought for control of the feelings warring inside her. He couldn't be serious, yet he'd come to talk, and the grave lines on his face screamed of sincerity. A little voice squelched the hope in her soul. Been there and done that. She uncrossed her arms and rubbed her neck. "Why? What's different now than the last *two* times you've told me this?"

"I realized I fucked up and made you think the wrong things."

"Like what?"

He extended his hand but stopped short of touching her arm. "May I?"

The room seemed to shrink, and the space between them charged with energy. The sound of her own breathing filled her head. She should say no. She should step away and tell him to leave. She should give him a push right out the door. Only, her hands ached to touch him. And all she wanted was to wrap her arms around him and take the leap. She gave him a tiny nod and held her breath.

His eyes lit, and he stepped closer. He brushed her cheek with his knuckles, sliding them down to her jaw. Her skin quivered under his touch.

"You told me you thought I didn't want you." He circled her waist with his other arm and pulled her close.

His hard length pressed against her.

Oh.

"Don't ever think that again."

She rested a hand on his soft shirt and pushed back, raising her gaze to his. "I don't doubt your attraction. But that hasn't been enough before to keep you from shutting down."

His eyes pleaded with her, and a tiny vein jumped in his cheek. "It's not just physical. I see who you are. You're caring and kind. Generous and beautiful." He rubbed his fingers up and down the curve of her waist. "Last night when I saw you with that other guy, I lost control."

She winced. She'd never seen him so unhinged. "Yeah, about that—"

"You had a right to be pissed." He shook his head.

"I don't understand. I thought this whole stalker thing was too much for you. You told me on the hike I was right about it being a mistake for us to go out."

"It didn't have anything to do with you or the stalker."

"Then what?" She frowned. "You said it was a bad idea for us to be together."

"Doesn't matter now. I was wrong. And I promise, if that bastard comes near you, he'll regret it."

The fierceness in his eyes caused her to blink. "I don't know."

"Please." He threaded a hand through her hair. "Can you give me another shot?"

His warm breath caressed her cheeks. He pressed a soft kiss on her forehead and stroked her side.

She wanted to believe him. She'd be risking it once again, but she couldn't walk away without knowing. Resting her head on his chest, she sunk into him. "Okay."

He let out a breath and squeezed her tight. "You won't regret it. I promise."

When Fluffy barked outside the door, he loosened his grip.

His mouth curved with a smug smile, and he traced a finger along her cheek. "Now that you told me how much you want to kiss me all the time, I'm going to find it hard to hold back."

Ugh. She had talked his ear off last night.

"You're gorgeous when you blush." He ran his thumb over her lips. "When does Maddie leave?"

"Wednesday. Why?"

"Because I want to take you on a real date. How about Sunday?"

"You know I can't do a real date out in public." She bit her cheek.

"How about going out on my boat? We'd be alone."

Alone. That conjured up all sorts of possibilities. Her insides warmed. "You have a boat?"

"Yes. I live by the water and keep it at the marina next door."

"I had no idea."

"Are you up for it?"

"Sure." As long as they weren't in public, she'd be fine.

"Great. I'll come by around nine?"

"Okay."

"Promise I won't hurt you again." He touched his lips to hers. "Sorry I ever did."

She swallowed hard.

The doorknob jiggled for a few seconds. Maddie giving notice.

"I better get going." He crossed to the door and stopped. "You might want to get a bathing suit. Or not. We're going swimming with or without one."

He gave her a heated look and let himself out, saying goodbye to Maddie on his way.

Sarah blew out a long breath. Bruce stripped down to bare skin. She could barely control herself with him fully clothed.

Her knees went soft.

CHAPTER 29

MORGAN SAT at her computer and tapped her fingers on the table. From what she could tell, things had cooled off between Sarah and Bruce. All week they'd danced around each other, not even talking. But Bruce still shot heated looks at her behind her back. Time to get the ballet whore the hell out of town.

Sarah had gone out with her sister last night in some disguise, giving Morgan the perfect opportunity to dig around in the suite. And it had paid off. She'd found a letter from Sarah's mother with a return address that was about to come in handy. Also, Sarah's real license, with the last name, Cooper. Figures, after Morgan had just paid Pete for that information. No matter, she had what she needed. Morgan's mouth curved into a wicked smile as she typed.

Dear Hugh and Jennifer,

I've found your daughter, Sarah. It's impossible for her to hide from me. See how easily I've located you? I'll use whatever means I need to get my ballerina back. Parents, siblings…Don't worry. Soon it will all be over.

Morgan slipped on gloves, printed out the letter, and tucked the license inside as proof she'd been in the suite. Sarah would freak out. That and the postmark from the town should be enough to send her packing.

Of course, Morgan could send the note directly to Sarah, but that was no fun. Let her fear for the safety of her sappy parents and crank up the tension.

Morgan opened her phone calendar. Saturday, less than two weeks away, she and Bruce would be taking a trip to North Carolina to see a horse. That would require an overnight stay. If she timed it right, the letter would arrive while they were gone, and Sarah would leave when Bruce wasn't around to stop her. Morgan had plenty in mind to keep him busy on their trip. He'd never be able to resist her. No man ever had. When they returned, she could at last reap her ultimate revenge with the ballerina bitch out of the picture.

She ran her tongue over her lips.

Time to go shopping for the trip.

CHAPTER 30

SARAH PULLED a pair of shorts over the bottoms of the black string bikini she'd purchased in town. The only bathing suits left on the rack had been skimpy. If not for Maddie, she might not have even bought one. Her sister had only been gone a few days, but Sarah already missed her. At least the boat trip would take her mind off it. She waited for Bruce in front of the house.

He drove up and hopped out of the truck. She lowered her gaze to his muscular thighs under red swim trunks. Her blood surged to lower parts.

"What are you looking at?" He stopped in front of her.

"Nothing. I've just never seen you without pants."

He grinned, and her face heated.

"That didn't come out right. I—"

"I know what you meant." He stroked her arm. "Try to relax. We're going to have fun today."

Fun. With a hot guy. On a boat. She could do this.

They drove to the marina with the windows open. Sarah let the wind push her hand up and down as she held it out the window. Beach music from Bruce's iPod played through the speakers. She sighed and leaned her head back against the rest.

"This is the first time I've seen you relaxed like this." He squeezed her leg. "It looks good on you."

"I'm actually excited. I've never been on a boat. Have you always had one?" She glanced at him as a shadow crossed his face.

"No. I bought it a few years ago. It's my getaway from the world. I sleep overnight on it sometimes." He kept his gaze on the road.

"Do you take a lot of people out?"

He shrugged. "Not really. Everyone's always busy. Scott and Joe have gone fishing with me a couple of times. That's kinda it."

"Oh, just guys." Good. He'd never slept with anyone on the boat. Warmth spread up her neck.

He glanced at her and hitched an eyebrow. "Why are you blushing?"

Shit. He knew exactly what she'd been thinking. She shifted in her seat.

"There's a first time for everything." His mouth curved.

He pulled into the marina and grabbed the cooler. "Can you bring those bags?"

"Sure."

Seagulls screeched and dove to the water, snatching out crabs and fighting over them in midair. The cool breeze blew her hair and tickled her toes in flip-flops.

She followed Bruce down the long pier. People waved and said hi as they passed. Some were loading their boats while others sat in chairs drinking coffee and chatting. A couple of kids and a man at the end of the dock cast fishing lines into the water and reeled them back.

"We're here." Bruce set the cooler down next to a big, white-lidded box with the name *Escape* on top in big, black letters.

She eyed the large, shiny boat. With sinks, lounges, and carpet, they wouldn't be roughing it. A door led to what had to be a cabin beneath a long expanse of a bow with a window in the middle that popped up. Kind of like a mini-house.

"Wow. How big is this?"

"Twenty-eight feet." He jumped onto the swim platform and unsnapped the cover.

"What can I do to help?" Sarah glanced around.

He reached up to graze his hand along her ankle. "Just stand there and look gorgeous."

She smiled down at him. Not a bad view from her vantage point.

His biceps flexed as he pulled off the cover. He'd donned shades. The man screamed cool and sexy. After tossing the cover on the dock, he hopped out and stuffed the canvas into the white, hinged box. He leaped back onto the platform. "Ready?"

"You're like a Mexican jumping bean. All over the place." She laughed.

He held a hand out. She took it and stepped onto the boat.

"Ah. The first place for a kiss." He tapped a foot on the deck.

His lips brushed hers, and they tingled.

"We're going to work our way around the boat," he said in a throaty voice against her mouth.

Confetti exploded in her stomach.

He stepped aside. "Go ahead."

She went through a half-door, passed the seating area, and stood by the steering wheel, out of the way. He reached up and grabbed the cooler from the dock. Bulging muscles. So hot.

The engines fired to life. After checking some gauges, he pointed to steps leading to the front of the boat.

"Can you climb up there and undo the ropes when I tell you to?"

"Sure." She kicked off her flip-flops and stepped up the stairs.

"Mostly, I just wanted to watch you do that," he said loud enough for her to hear.

She smirked and untied the ropes. After she climbed down from the top, he backed the boat away from the dock.

"Where are we going?"

"Out into the Chesapeake. I know a place we can anchor and swim." He pulled his shirt over his head and tossed it onto the seat next to her.

Oh God. Ripped. As if she'd expected anything less. From his well-defined pecs to the six-pack abs and the dark trail of hair that led farther south, he was sex on a stick. She bit her lip as Maddie's words came to mind.

Then she spotted the bullet wound, inches from his heart.

She caught her breath. Multiple jagged scars hid beneath his curly chest hair. Something terrible must have happened, like torture. Her eyes blurred.

He fiddled with the GPS before turning to her. "Once we pass the marker we can..."

His gaze followed hers, and he stiffened. In a matter-of-fact voice, he said, "Some souvenirs from my tour. Sorry. Didn't mean to—"

She wrapped her arms around his neck and kissed him. Deep inside, she ached for whatever he must have gone through and thanked God he'd come back. A tear trickled down her cheek.

He pulled back and ran a hand down the side of her face. "Don't. It's okay."

"No. It's not. What if you'd—"

"But I didn't." He cupped her chin and looked into her eyes. "Let it go. Please, I brought you out to have some fun today."

She nodded. He must be fighting his own demons, and her sympathy probably only added to the pain. Talking about it might cause him to relive things he'd rather forget. To lighten the mood, she waved a hand at the gauges. "Can this thing go fast?"

"Hell yeah, but we need to pass the no-wake buoy first. If you're warm, you can take that off." He tugged at her T-shirt. A slow, predatory smile formed.

Her pulse raced. Bruce, in his element on the water, was seductive. Sexy, bold, and unreserved, he defined smoking-hot. Not another boat in sight. No wonder he liked it. And she didn't have to worry about the stalker or anyone else seeing her. She leaned up and kissed his cheek, running her hand over his broad shoulders.

He lowered his head and found her lips. "That's three places. Next kiss on top."

When he wrapped an arm around her, she pressed her cheek against his bare chest. She resisted the strong urge to slip her tongue out for a taste of his hot skin. A lollipop she'd like to lick. Damn that Maddie. This was what she was talking about.

They passed a marker and Bruce said, "Ready to go?"

She nodded.

He pushed two levers forward, and the engines roared. The front of the boat rose out of the water, and they picked up speed. Wind whipped at her face as they bounced over the waves. Holding on to the back of his seat, she quickly learned to keep her knees soft and roll with the bumps. "This is amazing."

Bruce grinned and cranked the levers farther to send them flying across the water. She glanced back at the white foamy trail they made as the power and energy of the boat coursed through her body. What a rush. He brought his mouth close to her ear to yell over the noise of the engines as he pointed out places along the shore. Her body shivered in response.

They reached a point where he slowed the boat and steered into a narrower path of water.

"This inlet has a cove. It's not too shallow for my boat. I anchor overnight here sometimes."

Trees lined both sides of the deserted shore and blocked the view from the bay. Sarah glanced around. "It's certainly private here."

"That's what I was shooting for." He climbed up the steps and went forward to drop the anchor. When he came back down, he shut off the engines. He flicked a switch, and music played through the speakers.

"Cool. You have a stereo?"

"Yup. Want to see the cabin?" He pointed down a set of steps.

"Sure." She descended, glancing around. "Holy crap. You have a full kitchen down here?"

"Yes."

She stopped in front of a large V-shaped bed. Complete privacy. In the mirror above it, she met his gaze, and her cheeks blazed.

"You wanna swim?" he asked.

"Sure." But not really. She was in a room with a bed and a half-naked man who made her blood hot.

"I'll be up top if you want to change and leave your clothes down here. Remember what I said about kissing you in every part of this boat?" He leaned down, bringing his mouth close to hers.

She held her breath and parted her lips in anticipation, but he moved to whisper in her ear, "Later. That's a promise." He climbed the steps. "Don't linger."

She took a deep breath. Time to dive in.

CHAPTER 31

BRUCE STOOD on the swim platform when Sarah came out of the cabin. His gaze raked up and down her body, and he found it hard to swallow. The all-black string bikini covered little. Nothing connected the front and back of the bottoms but a small tie. Her nipples poked through the thin material on top. One tug of a string and he could have at that gorgeous body.

She cocked her head. "What?"

He blew out a breath and stepped from the platform to run a hand down her side. Curves. Sexy as hell. "You're a goddess in that bathing suit."

She fidgeted with one of the ties. "I bought the cheapest one."

"It paid off." Blood rushed to his loins as he stroked her soft, smooth skin. He had to get in the water or he'd burn up. Grabbing her hand, he led her to the swim platform. "Come on."

She dipped a toe in and made a face. "That's cold."

"Yup." He jumped in.

When he surfaced, she stood above him, hands on her hips. "Hey, you splashed me."

"It's water. Get in, wimp." That should do it.

Fire lit in her eyes, and he laughed.

She opened her mouth, shut it, then took the plunge. "Cold. Cold. Cold," she sputtered when she surfaced and swam toward the front of the boat.

"What did you expect?" In a few quick strokes, he caught up to her.

"Not this cold." She swam away again.

He smiled. A challenge. Good. He went around the back of the boat to meet her on the other side. The water reached his shoulders, which meant he could touch, but she couldn't. He stopped a few feet in front of her. She must have had her eyes closed because she swam right into him. He grinned at her shocked expression and picked her up. She grabbed hold of his shoulders as her legs wrapped around him.

The contact of her body sent shock waves through him. "I think I know how to warm you up."

Her gaze went to his lips, and he brought his head close for a kiss. She opened her mouth for him. Cool and salty. He deepened the kiss. His tongue explored the inside of her mouth, causing her nipples to harden.

Floating in the water, with her legs wrapped around him, she bounced against his arousal. She moaned and tightened her thighs. God, she made him hot. Too damn hot. He could make love to her right there in the water, but he didn't want to rush things. She needed to know he wasn't in it just for sex. He forced himself to break the kiss. "Warmer?"

"Mmm..." She wiggled against him, and he groaned.

"Okay. Me too." He spun and pulled her arms around the front of his neck to carry her piggyback style to the boat. She didn't protest, but her breasts bouncing against his back did nothing to improve his current situation. "Up you go."

He hoisted her onto the platform and climbed up the ladder. From under the seat, he grabbed a couple of towels and handed her one. As she dried off, her gaze flitted to the bulge in his bathing suit.

"You have that effect on me." He shook his head, and she blushed. "You ready for some grub?"

"Sure. I wish you would have let me bring something."

"Nope. You make meals for everyone all the time. I got this one."

He pulled a cooler out from under the sink and set two sandwiches on the table along with a couple of iced teas. Sarah wrapped the towel around her waist and sat on the lounge.

"Maddie would love this." She waved a hand toward the shore. "Lots of places to dig and explore. Anne says that girl will never settle down. Always traveling from one place to another. My parents are starting to give up on ever having grandkids to spoil."

"Do you think about that? Having a family?"

"Sure. I mean, I used to." She toyed with her napkin. "Dancers retire pretty young. I had it all planned out. Open my own studio, get married, have kids." Her face fell. "That's all changed now."

Bruce placed a hand over hers. No one had the right to take her dreams away. "It's not going to be like this forever. He's going to make a mistake and get caught."

"Let's not talk about him anymore. I don't want to ruin a perfect day."

"Fair enough." When they finished their lunch, he put the trash in a bag. "You wanna soak up some rays on a float?"

"Sounds like fun."

"Wait here." He grabbed a raft from the cabin and brought it up. "Come on."

"Okay. You're the program director." She followed him out to the swim platform. He jumped into the water with the float and held it out for her.

"Climb aboard."

She scooted onto it and lay down on her back. "Where's yours?"

"Don't need one. I'll take you for a ride."

"You don't have to do that. I'm—"

"Just enjoy it."

He towed her around the cove to where the water became shallower. His gaze traveled over her body. Her perfect, creamy-white skin contrasted with the black bikini. Tiny scraps that barely covered her, but hid the secret parts he ached to touch. To caress. To drive her to the brink with his tongue and teeth. Already hard, his cock throbbed and chipped away at his control.

He couldn't stop his hand from skimming down the length of her.

Starting at the outer curve of her breast, to the flare of her slender hips, along her lean thighs.

She shivered and took in a shaky breath.

Satisfaction rocketed through him at her response. Nothing mattered but bringing her to orgasm. He'd waited so long and fought so hard against the attraction. He intended to savor every second, teasing and taunting her until her beautiful body climaxed.

Lowering his head, he brought his lips to hers. He drew the kiss out, gentle at first, and then sucked on her lower lip until she opened her mouth. Their tongues tangled, and he slid his along the side of hers, eliciting a small moan from deep in her throat. His cock grew harder.

Her cool hands flattened against his pecs, graceful fingers digging in as she kneaded the muscles, sending ripples of awareness across his flesh.

He broke the kiss and gazed into her eyes. Cobalt, dark, and glossy with desire. His swim trunks tightened to the point of bursting the seams.

"I wondered what you would feel like." She continued to roam her fingers along the contours of his pecs.

An electric current buzzed under her splayed palms. The tentative, shy way she explored him ignited something hot and primal. He had to keep the focus on her before the inferno inside took over.

With his finger, he traced from her stomach to the dip of her belly button, then followed the path with his mouth. He feasted on her smooth, soft skin, licking his way lower and lower. Like an exotic, tropical island, she smelled of coconut and sunshine. An all-consuming hunger for more caused blood to pound in his head.

When he dipped his tongue into the hollow of her navel, her abs tensed, and she whimpered, tilting her hips up. The demand for release warred with his longing to taste and feel every inch of her.

* * *

Sarah wallowed in sensations. The cold water lapping onto the raft, and Bruce's mouth, hotter than the sun, inches from her sweet spot. The bristle of his whiskers teased the sensitive flesh of her stomach. Pressure built between her legs until she ached.

He rested his hand on her hip bone and glided his thumb under her bikini bottom. With the lightest touch, he slid his finger over her sensitive nub. She jolted and caught her lip with her teeth.

Still working magic with his fingers, he raised his head and swooped in for a kiss. His tongue probed her open mouth as his damp hair dripped on her collarbone. She snaked her arms around his neck and dove deeper into the kiss, mating her tongue with his. He tasted of salt, sex, and everything she'd denied herself for too long. She dug her fingers into the thick muscles of his back, and a thrill spiked low in her belly.

Crests of pleasure rose from where he stroked her. Closer and closer, he brought her to the edge. Her thighs quivered, and her breath caught. She squeezed her eyes shut, prepared to ride the next wave.

But he drew his hand away. "Oh no. Not yet."

She gasped, but he covered her mouth with his, swallowing her protest. This kiss, demanding and urgent, stole her breath. When he pulled back, she panted, and her pulse jumped at the heat and lust in his eyes.

His broad shoulders blocked the sun. Outlined by the bright background, he loomed large. Buff and ripped, his sheer size should intimidate her, but he'd never been anything but gentle. The wild part of her craved the challenge of making love to such a man. God knew he had her wet enough.

"So much to explore…" The rasp in his voice and the anticipation of what might come next shot excitement through her.

He scooped water with his hand and held it above her to drip the cool liquid onto her already-hard nipple. She trembled as he slid aside the triangle covering her breast.

Keeping his gaze on hers, he brought his mouth to her breast and sucked the peak, tugging with his teeth. She dug her nails into his biceps and arched her back. He freed her other breast and filled his hand, squeezing and toying with the nipple. She'd never experienced anything so erotic. Bright sun, floating on a raft, every fiber of her body aflame. Each time he touched her, a coil of passion wound tighter.

He nuzzled the inside of her breast and worked his way up to her neck while he untied her bikini bottom and yanked the fabric off. God, she was naked outside and too far gone to care.

"I wasn't quite finished here." He drifted his hand up her inner thigh. Higher and higher until she eased her legs apart, silently begging him to touch her *there*.

His words, whispered against the tender skin of her throat, vibrated in her chest.

He slipped a finger inside her. "Now you're ready."

That was an understatement. Desperate to feel him, she reached out her hand and fondled the bulge in his swim trunks. He had to be close to exploding, his erection huge and hard.

He sucked in a sharp breath and slipped another finger inside her, using his thumb to stroke her clit.

In and out, he thrust his fingers and continued to stroke her. Liquid fire burned through her veins. He dragged his mouth up the length of her throat and kissed under her ear. With his teeth, he caught the lobe and nibbled, unleashing something feral and primitive in her. His hot breath scorched the side of her face. She turned her head to offer her mouth, and he claimed her lips.

Every muscle in her body shook, begging for sweet release. She slid a hand down into his bathing suit and fisted his swollen cock. "I need you inside me."

Face flushed, the corded muscles in his neck taut, his eyes burned with his thirst for her.

"The condoms are on the boat," he said, his breath ragged.

She couldn't hold out much longer, the friction of his fingers driving her to the precipice. "I'm on the pill. Please, *now*."

For a gut-wrenching second, she feared he'd say no, but he yanked his swimsuit down and hoisted her off the raft. Yes. Sweet Jesus, yes.

Cupping her ass, he crushed her against him. She hooked her legs around his waist and pressed herself down on his arousal. Wanting, needing, yearning, she gripped his shoulders. Inch by inch, she stretched to accommodate his thickness.

A growl reverberated in his chest as he pushed the last of his length into her. He held her still. Fully connected, she gazed into his eyes, and the incredible emotion in them stopped her heart. Bruce, deep inside her. Holding nothing back.

She loved him. The realization filled her as much as he did. She could never ask for more. He'd given her all of him.

Heat blasted upward, and she nodded to his unasked question. Yes, she was ready for more. He eased out and thrust back in. She moaned and clenched her insides around him.

"God, Sarah." His hoarse voice made her half-crazed with need.

He pumped faster, water splashing around their bodies, driving her out of her mind. The lines blurred between where she started and he ended. She threw her head back and closed her eyes. A final wave of ecstasy unlike any she'd ever known rolled through her, and she cried out, letting go. Her body rhythmically squeezed him as he thrust one last time, stiffened, and groaned in his own release.

She melted against him.

His heartbeat thumped under her cheek, and she locked her arms around him. Her swollen nipples still tingled, and sensations continued to shimmer, lighter and lighter. As her pulse slowed, she breathed in the salt air and clung to him, brimming with emotions.

When he slid out of her, she whimpered at the absence created.

He leaned back to look at her. "I'm sorry it didn't last longer but—"

"My brain would have short-circuited if it did." She sighed and buried her head in his chest.

He stroked her back and held her. Content, she relaxed against him. Whatever might happen down the road, her memories of this one magical day would last forever. He'd given her the gift of freedom. Her first taste since the stalker entered her life, and she loved him for it.

She loved him.

No point in fighting it anymore. She could fill a book with the list of reasons why. His care and concern for the vets, the way his eyes steeled when he was in protective mode, everything he'd done to get Maddie to and from the farm. And now, the mind-blowing sex.

A seagull called out overhead, and awareness of her naked state crept back. She shifted. "We should get dressed."

"If you insist." He let go of her and pulled up his swim trunks.

She snatched her bikini bottoms from the raft and retied them. If only she had the rest of her life to share with Bruce. A heaviness sank from her stomach to her feet.

"Hey. Why so sad?" He framed her face with his hands.

She leaned her cheek into his palm. "I don't want it to end."

"Oh, it's not over." He brushed his lips across hers. "I have plans for the V-berth."

CHAPTER 32

SARAH CLIMBED the ladder to the swim platform on legs still a bit shaky from their close encounter.

"I like the view here." Bruce said from behind her.

She grinned and called over her shoulder, "Down, boy."

"Boy?" Water splashed her ass, and she whipped around.

He hitched an eyebrow. "Do I need to drag you back out here and prove something?"

Her belly flipped, and she blurted out the first thing that came to mind. "Thank you, sir, may I have another?"

The sound of his laughter tickled her ribs. She liked this playful and fun side of him.

"Grab a towel, and I'll meet you up top." He pointed to the deck in front of the windshield. "We can catch some rays."

"Where are you going?"

"I have to find the raft."

She snatched a towel from the seat and wrapped herself in it, scanning the water behind him. "What happened to it?"

He shrugged. "Dunno. Wasn't exactly paying attention once I, uh… got you off."

Someone was proud of himself. She waved a hand at him. "Shoo. I'll be on the top."

A roguish smile formed on his face. "I think I'd like that."

And her knees wobbled.

He pivoted, heading toward the shoreline.

She couldn't drag her gaze away from his upper body, all tanned skin and brawny muscles, flexing as he moved through the water. Saliva pooled in her mouth.

Raising her hand, she shaded her eyes. Like hell she'd wait up top and miss the view of him coming back. If he never wore a shirt again, she wouldn't mind. And damn if he didn't look like a god as he waded back, dark hair gleaming, his strong thighs contracting with each step. Okay, maybe more like the devil because the thoughts he evoked were downright sinful.

When he reached the boat, he tossed the raft next to her on the swim platform and hoisted himself up. Rivulets of water streamed down the hard contours of his pecs.

And lower.

She swallowed hard, her gaze stuck on the path to—

"Hello? My eyes are up here," he said in a caught-you-looking tone as he reached for a towel.

God, she had no control around him. She needed to get a grip.

"I thought you were going up top." He rubbed the towel over his stomach, and she developed a case of towel-envy.

"I was...waiting for you."

"You didn't have to."

Oh yes, she most certainly did. Heat rose to her face.

He grabbed her hand along with a couple of dry towels. "Come on. Let's chill."

Yeah. That's what they should do. Not go down to that mysterious V-berth, the name alone full of sexual innuendo.

They climbed up top, and he spread the towels on the deck. She stretched out on one and shoved her libido to the side. The sun warmed her as a slight, cooler breeze blew, rocking the boat.

"Hmm, this is nice." She closed her eyes.

He twined his fingers through hers, and she sighed. A sleepy, warm feeling took over.

Bruce holding her hand.

This man was a keeper.

* * *

Sarah opened her eyes and blinked at the bright light.

"Have a nice nap?" Bruce leaned over, blocking the sun.

Still on the boat. Hot sex in the water. It hadn't been a dream. She smiled up at him. "Yes."

He lowered his mouth to hers. Soft and gentle, he kissed her.

"Mmm. This is a nice way to wake up." She wriggled closer to him.

He stared down at her for a long moment, then cleared his throat. "You've gotta be thirsty."

Before she could ask what he'd been thinking about, he yanked her to her feet. "Let's get something to drink."

They climbed down to the main deck, and he disappeared farther below into the cabin. When he came out, he handed her a bottle of water and a menu.

"There's a restaurant nearby we can order from. Do you like crab cakes?"

"I don't know. Never had them." She shrugged.

"What? That's a criminal offense in Maryland. This place has the best crab cakes in the state. Call in two platters, and pick out something you know you'll like as well."

"We don't have to order extra food. I'm sure it will be—"

"Don't argue." He put finger over her lips and wrapped an arm around her back. "I need to keep my strength up."

Eating was the last thing on her mind. And the finger on her lips, the only thing. Well, not the only thing. There was *that* thing pressing against her.

He brought his mouth to her neck and feathered it with kisses, sending hot shivers through her body.

"What do you think?" he whispered in her ear.

Hard to say when she couldn't breathe.

"Can you pick out something from the menu?" He glided his finger down the column of her throat.

Her brain scrambled to figure out which menu he was talking about. Because right now the options in front of her were more than tempting. "Do you mean..."

"Oh yeah." He inched back. "Later. There's no rush."

He should speak for himself.

His intense gaze burned her as he massaged her back. In a husky voice, he said, "Anticipation can be powerful."

Her nipples tingled in agreement.

He kissed her with just enough heat to leave her wanting more, then paused, his lips inches from hers. "Sarah, whatever you want. It's all about you. Say the word and we can—"

"No." As if she'd back down from a challenge. And sure as hell not this one. Bruce gave new meaning to the word foreplay. But most of all, she trusted him. Whatever he had in mind, she'd go along for the ride because she might never have this chance again. "I'm in."

He blazed her with another kiss, then nodded to the table. "Call an order in while I bring up the anchor."

When he turned, she flung a hand out and cupped his erection. "I think the anchor's already up."

His nostrils flared, and his lips curved in a tortured smile.

She grinned. Two could play this game.

* * *

The wind blew in her face as they cruised across the bay, chilling her body and her rebellious hormones. Bruce had given her an extra T-shirt to wear as a cover-up. It whipped around her legs and smelled of him. A sensual combination she tried not to think about.

And failed.

He guided the boat into a slip in front of a large restaurant with decks, umbrella tables, and a band playing. He tied the ropes to cleats along the dock and vaulted onto the pier. "I'll be right back."

The sound of laughter and music filled the air. People milled about, and children played in the sand surrounding the outdoor tables. A crowded tiki bar kept drinks flowing in the far corner. A weight dragged her spirits down. She couldn't go to places like this with Bruce.

He came back with a brown bag, jumped into the boat, and dropped the package on the table. "What's wrong?"

"Nothing."

"Not nothing. Talk to me." He stepped closer.

"I can't do this to you. It's not fair. You deserve to be able to go out in public." She glanced over his shoulder at the restaurant.

"That's what this is about." He sighed. "You don't get it. We're going to ride and find a quiet private spot to have dinner on the water. I'd rather do that a million times more than sit in some loud place." He touched his lips to hers. "And there's a hell of a lot better chance I'll get laid in my scenario."

"Typical guy." She smirked, but the steamy look he gave her sent a surge of heat to the spot beneath her bikini bottoms.

He started up the engines, untied the ropes, and drove the boat for a short ride before slowing down. They anchored in yet another private cove where trees blocked the wind. She sucked in a slow breath. Her mind wasn't at all on the bed in the cabin below or the man who turned her legs to JELL-O with one look.

"I'll grab some plates." Bruce dug around in a cabinet under the sink, and her gaze fixed on his tight, perfect ass.

Anticipation did build excitement. She'd lost all concentration since that little warm-up he'd done on her.

He handed her two plates and dug a bottle of wine from a cooler.

"What the heck? Is this boat like a clown car? More and more things keep coming out."

"Lots of hiding places. You have to tuck it all in storage." He smiled and opened the bottle. After pouring a glass, he handed it to her. "See if you like it."

She took a sip and nodded. Crisp, cool, and just the right touch of sweet.

"I'm starved. Sit." He pointed to the table.

They emptied the bag, and Sarah forked a piece of crab cake. She took a bite and rolled her eyes. The flaky broiled taste of butter and Old Bay seasoning melted in her mouth. "This is delicious."

"Glad you like it."

When they finished, Bruce gathered the trash, refilled their glasses, and came to sit beside her. He threw his arm around her, and she nestled against his shoulder. She inhaled his salty, fresh scent. If only she could bottle it.

They sipped wine as soft music streamed through the speakers.

* * *

Bruce kissed the top of Sarah's head. He'd taken her like a wild animal in the water earlier. The way she'd responded to him had driven him out of his mind. Sure, it had been a long time since he'd had sex, but something told him that had nothing to do with it. She drove him to the point of losing all control. And that rarely happened to someone with his training.

If only he could freeze time and stay with her forever in their sanctuary. She'd relaxed against him, the tension gone from her body. But soon enough, they'd have to leave, and the worry lines would come back to her face.

He rubbed the inside of her palm with his thumb. "Do you have to be back any certain time? I have more plans for tonight."

"Oh?" She glanced up at him, and he didn't miss the light of hope in her eyes.

"I mean after we're done here. Unless you want to spend the night at my condo?"

Her brows drew together, and after a few seconds of what had to be a debate, she sighed. "No, I better not. I need to be awake early to make breakfast, and with Debbie right upstairs, I feel sorta funny having you stay at my place. I mean, it's not like I'm a prude or anything, but—"

"Shh." He brought her fingers to his lips and kissed them. "You don't have to explain. I understand. You can stay at mine another time. I want to wake up with you in my arms."

"That would be nice." She rubbed his thigh.

"So you never answered me. Do you need to be back anytime soon?"

"Nope. I'm yours until the carriage turns into a pumpkin."

He squeezed her shoulder. "Good."

"Wait, what kind of plans do you have later?"

"It's a surprise. You'll see."

Her soft breast pressed against his side, and the image of her rosy peaks hardening under the cold water popped into his head. That caused a hardening of another kind.

"Umm...speaking of a surprise?" Sarah glanced down and raised an eyebrow. "Does this signal the end of the anticipation phase?"

"You ready to check out the V-berth?" He smoothed her hair back from her face.

A spark lit in her eyes, and she rubbed a hand over his erection. "I've been ready."

He led her down into the cabin. She stripped the T-shirt off and leaned back against the pillows.

One look at her near-naked body, and he had a throbbing hard-on. He took a deep, long breath, and climbed onto the bed.

Slow. Slow it down. Treat her the way she deserved. Cherished, tender, with love.

Love? He froze.

"What's wrong?" Sarah reached a hand up and stroked the side of his face.

Warmth filled his heart. Yes. He loved her, and this time guilt didn't flood him. He had something unique with Sarah. Courageous, sweet, willing to take on anything, she continued to amaze him. No denying the intense physical attraction, but his feelings went much deeper. He was ready to take their relationship to the next level. Emily would have wanted him to be happy. He smiled and brought his head down to kiss her. "Absolutely nothing."

She wrapped an arm around his back as his tongue explored her mouth. The sweet, unique taste of her filled him. Nibbling her neck, he untied the bikini top and slipped it off. Her skin warmed under his touch, fanning the fire between them.

He eased back and gazed at her puckered nipples. Blood burned through his veins. He'd never tire of looking at her. Bringing his mouth down to suckle her breast, he skimmed a hand along her inner thigh and up to her hip. He yanked the bikini-bottom tie and ripped the piece off her. Palming her soft mound, he slipped a finger into her. Christ, he'd barely touched her, and she was ready for him.

She whimpered with need, arching her back and making little noises that caused his cock to pulse against the constraints of his swim trunks.

Her hands tugged at them, her voice husky. "Take these off. I want to feel you on me."

"Not so fast." He caught her wrist, brought her hand to her own breast, and placed his over the top of it, squeezing. Her eyes grew wide, and something hot and wild battered in his chest. "That's it. Touch yourself. You're beautiful."

He slipped his hand from hers. As if he were in an erotic dream, he stared as she continued to fondle her breasts. His cock swelled to the point of agony. The boat swayed, or maybe he did.

He kissed her stomach and slid his mouth lower and lower until he reached the softness of her curls. A squeak came from her as she raised her hips and spread her legs apart, hands still on her breasts. Sweet Jesus. Hot demand fisted his cock.

Moving into position, he brought his mouth between her legs. The sweet scent of her arousal intoxicated him. He buried his face in her wet warmth and slicked his tongue in circles around her clit. She gasped and undulated her hips, providing him better access. Her thighs quaked.

"That's it. Let it go, baby."

Faster and faster, he flicked his tongue over the tip of her core. She seemed to fight for air, gulping between tiny squeaks. Her hands clenched the sheets, and she let out a high-pitched moan that nearly had him coming in his shorts.

"Bruce, yes! Bruce..."

He thrust his tongue into her and sucked as she squeezed against it. On and on, she moaned and writhed, amplifying his own hot desire with the sheer knowledge he could bring her to this point.

When her legs slacked and she let out a long sigh, he glanced up at her.

Eyes glassy, face flushed, she bit her lower lip. "Holy hell, Bruce."

She sat up and brushed her mussed hair from her cheek. After shaking her head as if to clear it, she gazed at his groin. Hard to miss considering it was granite-hard and pointing at her.

"Get that suit off now. It's your turn." She licked her lips and shifted to her knees.

Lust exploded in his belly. He yanked off the swim trunks.

She lowered her head to take him in her mouth inch by agonizing inch. He inhaled sharply, the room blurring. When she flicked her tongue against the engorged head of his cock, his thighs tensed. She reached a hand around to grip his ass while she slid her lips down his entire shaft, sucking him deep into her throat and moaning. The vibration sent shock waves through him. Wouldn't last another second if she did that again. The carnal need to be inside of her overcame him.

He grabbed her shoulders and settled her onto her back.

Her lips, shiny and wet from him, curved into a come-take-me smile. She opened her legs.

He positioned himself and rubbed the tip around her opening. The muscles in his abs constricted, his entire body tense.

As he slid inside her, she stared up at him, her luminous eyes filled with emotion. They belonged together. She fit him perfectly. Love for her wrapped around his heart and squeezed it tight. No holding back anymore.

For a second, he closed his eyes and got lost in the hot, tight feel of her. He pumped in and out, picking up the pace as she met his thrusts with small moans of pleasure. The smell of desire and everything Sarah filled his lungs.

Their breath came in bursts as the room rocked, and she gave all of herself to him. Higher and higher they climbed the ladder, each thrust taking them to another level. The air between them sizzled. Beyond sex, beyond need, beyond anything, he wanted to be one with this woman who had broken through his wall of defenses and shown him love again.

"Oh, Bruce..." Her rib cage raised off the bed and she called out again as wave after wave compressed his raging shaft.

The sight of her up-thrust breasts and the sweet sound of his name from her lips drove him over the top. He pumped one last time, threw his head back, and with a guttural growl, emptied inside her.

She whimpered and reached for him, pulling him down on top of her. Muttering words he couldn't make out against his chest, she threaded her fingers through his hair. Heat rose off her slick body.

Not wanting to hurt her with his weight, but too full of emotion to speak, he raised onto his elbows, gently kissed her, and eased onto his side. She snuggled against his shoulder, resting a hand on his breastbone. An after-sex shudder shook her body, and fulfillment washed over him.

In a soft voice, she said, "I didn't know it could be like this."

"Neither did I." She'd awakened feelings he'd never experienced. He tightened his arm around her and pressed his lips to the top of her head. Content, happy, satisfied. A couple of months ago, he would have sworn he'd never be any of those things again.

"I'll always remember this day. No one can take it away from me." She gazed up at him. "Thank you."

Something was off. That sounded like a goodbye. "I'm not selling the boat. We'll come back out."

"I hope so." She rested her head on his shoulder.

His gut wrenched. Not hope so—know so. No one would take her away from him. He put a hand under her chin and lifted her head to gaze into her eyes, still laced with the remnants of their passion. "I won't let him get to you. I wasn't there last time."

"I thought we weren't going to talk about this today."

She must not think he could do anything about the bastard. "Damn it, Sarah. Promise me you won't run off."

"I don't want to argue with you."

Nerves pinched the back of his neck. "Then promise."

"I can't let him harm anyone at the ranch." She shook her head.

"Trust me. If he shows up, he's the one that's going to be hurt. I mean it. I want that promise." He couldn't lose her after falling in love again.

"Why?"

"Because I lo—"

Her eyes grew wide.

Damn. He couldn't tell her this soon. He'd scare her away. "Lose you. I don't want to lose you. We're just getting started."

She pressed her lips together, leaned up to kiss him, and then lowered her head back onto his shoulder.

Unease settled in his chest. Nothing he could do for now except keep his eyes open and make sure that asshole didn't get anywhere near her.

The cabin darkened as the sun fell, and Bruce shifted. "We should probably get going."

"This has been the most magical day ever. I hate for it to end." She snuggled under his shoulder.

"It's not over yet. I still have that surprise for you."

"What is it?" She drew her head back to face him.

"I would say the best is yet to *come*, but I'm pretty sure nothing tops the mind-blowing sex."

"Can't argue with that, but you have me wondering what you're up to."

"Not for long. Time to pull up the anchor."

They headed back to the marina. In the cabin, they changed into shorts and T-shirts. After they unloaded the boat and snapped the cover on, Bruce drove the truck into town.

"Seriously? Where are we going?" she asked.

"You'll see." Excitement brewed in his stomach. He pulled into a strip mall and went around the back to park in a spot behind a metal door.

"What is this place?"

Instead of answering her, he opened the glove box and pulled out a key. He got out of the truck. "Come on."

She followed him to the metal door, and he slipped the key in the lock. He took her hand. "Close your eyes."

"Why?" She glanced around the dark lot.

"Just do it."

She did as he asked and took a few steps as he tugged her along.

"Okay. You can open them now."

She did and gasped.

CHAPTER 33

SARAH'S GAZE dashed around the empty dance studio. Mirrors lined the walls, with a barre embedded along one of them. A large observation window on the right overlooked the room from the second floor. Black speakers were mounted near the ceiling in the corners. She turned to Bruce. "I don't understand."

"I rented it for you."

"You wh-what?" She brought a hand to her chest.

He shrugged. "I knew you'd need privacy. They close at seven thirty, so it's yours for as long as you want after that any night but Saturday and Sunday when they sometimes have evening classes."

Her heart threatened to burst. She could put her slippers on and dance again. The space, the mirrors, the perfect floor. Her muscles quivered with pent-up energy.

"I figured the timing was perfect with the summer help at the farm and you only needing to do the housework and a couple hours in the stables." He stroked a hand down her hair.

She glanced around the room. Renting a private studio had to be expensive. As much as she wanted this, she couldn't accept it. Her lungs whooshed out a breath of air. "I-I can't afford to pay you back for this."

He grasped her hands and pressed the key in one. "I have more money than I know what to do with. It means nothing to me. This. *This* means something."

"It's too much."

His gaze burned into hers. "Let me give you back a little of what that bastard took from you. Please. For me."

Tears misted her eyes. Dance. She could dance again.

"Hell. Don't cry on me now." He wrapped his arms around her.

"I'm sorry. It means so much to me. I—"

"Shh." He pressed his lips to the top of her head. "Just promise me one thing."

"What?" She clung to his shirt, one hand fisted with the key inside.

"That you'll let me watch you. I want to see you dance."

She nodded against his chest.

Yeah. She loved him.

* * *

Bruce drove Sarah back to her suite and kissed her at the door. "I'll see you tomorrow, bright and early."

"You coming for breakfast?" she asked.

"Do you want me to?" He cocked his head. "I can't promise not to touch you."

She snaked her arms around his neck. God, he smelled amazing. Like the fresh, salty sea. "I don't care what anyone thinks."

"But you said you didn't want me to stay because of Debbie."

"I meant overnight. People knowing we're dating is different than them hearing us having sex."

"Okay." A smile played at the corners of his mouth.

"What?"

He leaned down, his lips brushing the lobe of her ear. "Think I'm about to ruin Greg's day tomorrow."

Sarah laughed and drew her hands back. She pulled out her keys, went to unlock the door, and tensed.

"What's wrong?"

Her stomach knotted. "It wasn't locked."

"Maybe you forgot to lock it."

She shook her head. "I never forget."

"Stand back." He opened the door and flicked on the lights.

Fluffy jumped up and ran over to him. He whined and sniffed around the room, snout to the carpet.

"Stay here." Bruce entered the suite and checked the rooms. "All clear. It's safe to come in."

Sarah shut her eyes. She'd left from the front of the house.

"It's okay." Bruce stroked her arm.

"I don't remember when I used this door last."

"Maybe Joe let the dog in through it and forgot to lock up. No one's here."

She glanced around. Sometimes Joe did take care of the dog. "Everything looks the same as when I left."

"So relax." He took her hand. "Do you want me to stay with you?"

"No. I'll be fine." She rubbed her arms and glanced around the room again. "I have Fluffy with me."

"All right. Then I'll see you tomorrow."

He brought his lips to hers for a soft, tender kiss. "Thanks for coming today."

"Which time?" She raised an eyebrow.

"Naughty girl." He gave her butt a playful slap. "I better go."

She followed him to the door and locked up.

Sleep didn't come easy, but at some point, she must have drifted off because her alarm awakened her bright and early.

She topped off a bowl of fruit for the breakfast she'd prepared in the main kitchen. Her gaze shot to the door every time someone opened it.

Joe sauntered in and went to the coffee maker. The man had his focus on caffeine first every morning.

Greg had already loaded his plate with food and ate at the table.

Debbie had some paperwork out and wrote notes while drinking her coffee. She glanced up when Bruce entered, and went back to writing.

Greg yelled out a hello as Bruce crossed the room. Bruce nodded to him and stopped next to Sarah.

Her stomach flipped and sizzled like a pancake on a hot griddle.

"Morning. You sleep well?" he asked.

She cleared her throat. "Yes, and you?"

"I was *up* all night, after leaving you," he said low enough that no one else could hear.

Oh God. Maybe she wasn't so ready to let the world know about them.

"I warned you." He leaned over and kissed her.

Silverware clattered to the floor. Sarah shot a glance at the table. Greg bent down to pick up whatever he'd dropped.

"About time," muttered Joe from his station at the coffee machine.

Bruce snatched a plate and serving spoon. "This looks awesome. I'm really, *really* hungry this morning."

Debbie slapped her pen down and stood, grabbing her empty coffee mug. "For God's sake. Get a room, you two."

Joe snorted.

Bruce's mouth twitched as he piled food on his plate. His gaze darted to Sarah, and she fought the urge to smack that smug look off his face. Good thing he was so freaking amazing in bed, or she'd kill him.

He picked up a strawberry. "These look fresh. Did they come from the farmers market?"

Sarah tapped her foot. Prickly heat singed her face. Now *he* was swapping recipes and having fun quizzing her about the food while everyone stared at her.

"Yes, as a matter of fact."

"How about the maple syrup? Looks like a new—"

She kicked her foot against his. "Could I have a word with you?"

"Sure. Which one?"

Another snort came from Joe.

"Out there." She pointed to the porch and stomped past him. When he followed her out, she whirled around to face him.

"What do you think you're doing?" She crossed her arms.

"You're gorgeous when you're angry." He swaggered over, and she took a step back. "Why are you so upset?"

"You know damn well. Why don't you wear a T-shirt that says, 'I slept with her'?"

"I would if I could." He smiled. "You told me you didn't care if they knew."

She frowned. "Well, I didn't realize how embarrassing it would be."

"Sorry." He put a hand on her arm. "I've wanted you for so long. I can't act like nothing happened, and they were going to figure it out sooner or later anyway."

"I suppose." She had to get used to them as a couple.

He brought his face close to hers.

"I wasn't kidding. I barely slept." He traced a finger along the line of her neck, and she shivered. "All I could think about was making love to you again."

His arms came around her, and heat blasted through her body.

He covered her mouth with his for a long, sensual kiss. "Better get used to this. I intend to do it a lot."

The door opened, and Debbie stepped onto the porch. Sarah tried to move away, but Bruce had her in a vise grip.

Debbie waved a hand in their direction and shook her head. "Geez. I'm heading to the stables."

Bruce's lips curved, and Sarah took a deep breath.

He kissed her again. "My trip is this Saturday. We'll have to make the most of our time this week before I leave."

She frowned. Morgan. Alone with Bruce for two days.

"What's wrong?" he asked.

"I wish you weren't going with Morgan. She...bothers me." Sarah's jaw tensed.

"We're just friends, and this horse looks really promising. It's exactly what we've been searching for from what I can tell, or I wouldn't go so far to see it." He stroked her cheek. "I can take on more patients if I get another horse. I already have two more vets interested in the program."

That mattered much more than her jealous peeve with Morgan. "I'm sorry. I really hope it works out."

"I am worried about leaving you, though." He frowned.

"It's only for one night." She shook her head. "I'll be fine. I haven't heard from the stalker in over three weeks. Besides, you don't sleep here anyway. What's the difference?"

"Well, I asked Joe to stay here the night I'm gone."

She winced. "That wasn't necessary. Now I feel stupid. Like I need a babysitter. I'm surrounded by people all the time, and I have the dog."

"Joe sleeps over sometimes anyway. Just an extra precaution. Debbie has a shotgun, and they both know how to use it."

"Okay." She would feel safer. "Thank you."

He smiled. "Now are you done chastising me so I can get some food? You did invite me."

"Yes, but go easy on the PDA."

"You wanna start tossing around acronyms? That's a battle you'll never win against a military man." He brought his lips to hers and she smiled against them.

* * *

Leonard placed the tarp on the dirt, knelt, and pulled out his binoculars. All weekend with no sight of Sarah. His eyebrows twitched. Since it was Monday, she'd be back to her routine and he could keep track of her.

After drawing a tissue from his pocket, he dabbed at the sweat under his eyes. He raised the binoculars and trained them on the front porch where Sarah stood in front of a man. The guy stepped closer to Sarah, *his* Sarah, and kissed her.

Leonard flinched and gripped the binoculars tighter. His heart jackhammered in his chest. The rubber lens hoods dug into his eye sockets. No. She didn't fight or slap the man. Impossible. She appeared to kiss him back, letting him hold her like a lover. Leonard's stomach lurched. This man must have seduced her. He'd soiled her. Ruined her. Somehow made Sarah forget how much she loved Leonard.

Tiny, bright pinpoints of light appeared before his eyes, and he became dizzy. He lowered the binoculars and leaned against the tree. He'd warned her. Told her how much he loved her. She'd had the chance all along to come back, to admit her love. He shook his head and dragged a hand down his face.

Traitor. A complete fake. He couldn't allow her to live and be a walking reminder of his misplaced faith. They would have been perfect together, only she was flawed. His world crashed down around him. He gasped for air and bent over, squeezing his eyes shut as he rocked. No way out. She'd left him no choice now. He wouldn't need the closet or the locks.

She'd made a fatal mistake in betraying him.

Just like Audrey.

CHAPTER 34

SARAH GAVE Bruce the stink-eye as he managed to slide a hand along her thigh when he passed her leading a horse out of the stall. It had been almost a week since the breakfast fiasco, and still, every time she came anywhere near him, heads turned. To make matters worse, he seemed to be enjoying the whole thing. He found creative ways to brush against her and keep her body humming.

She'd gone to the ballet studio the last five nights, and between that and the sex, every not-normally-used muscle in her body ached. As if he hadn't done enough, Bruce bought her an iPod, downloaded the music from her solo performances, and pumped the compositions through the sound system.

The first night, after running some errands, he'd returned to watch her practice. At the end of the piece, he'd framed her face with his hands and told her he could see her soul when she danced. He'd taken her back to his condo and made tender love to her, worshipping every part of her body.

She shivered at the memory and forced her focus back to cleaning buckets.

Bruce approached and stopped in front of her as Morgan's car pulled into the lot behind him.

"Sorry you got stuck working on a Saturday. You have to be tired," he said.

"Becca never calls in sick. I'll be fine." Sarah shrugged. "Besides, I won't dance at the studio again until Monday."

"True. Morgan and I are leaving soon."

One day without seeing him shouldn't seem like it would be forever, but it did. Maybe his travel companion had something to do with that.

Sarah wiped her hands on her jeans and tried to keep his goal of helping more veterans in mind. "I hope this horse works out."

He held his palm to the side of her face and kissed her. Soft and slow, with the promise of more to come. When he pulled away, he stroked her cheek. "Want to go out on the boat when I get back?"

"For a repeat?"

"Hell, yeah. We never made it to the aft berth where the other bed is," he said with a glint in his eye. "I intend to get on the road early. Rest up for me."

Sarah went back to work but kept glancing at Bruce. Morgan laughed and put a hand on his shoulder. The Ice Queen always had her paws on Bruce. Sarah slammed the bucket down.

She lugged the pail inside and brought out another. After Bruce drove off in his truck, Morgan sauntered across the lot and stopped next to her. Sarah kept her head down and squirted water into the pail.

"Well, well. A little workplace romance going on?"

"It's none of your business," Sarah said.

"I like to keep up. You know, I'm going to be spending the night with Bruce, and that man has stamina you wouldn't believe." Morgan sighed. "Wait, maybe you would know."

Sarah wiped an arm across her forehead and huffed out a breath. "You can cut the act. Bruce told me you're just friends."

"Oh, we are, dear. Friends with…benefits." She winked and strolled to the stable entrance.

Sarah's stomach bottomed out. Lie. It had to be a lie. Bruce wouldn't do something like that. She shut her eyes. Morgan's hand on his shoulder, the familiar way she touched him, she acted like his booty call. No. The witch lived to mess with her. Probably jealous. Still, Morgan had a clear interest in him and a body that screamed sex.

"You okay?" Lynn asked.

"What? Sorry, I didn't see you come over."

"I saw Morgan talking to you, and you looked kinda upset."

"She has that effect." Sarah glared at the stables. "She was suggesting she and Bruce...well...never mind."

Lynn's eyes narrowed. "She wishes. She's been after him since the second she came here."

Ugh. The last thing Sarah wanted to hear.

"Don't worry about her." Lynn placed a hand on Sarah's arm. "Listen, as long as I've known Bruce, I've never seen him happier."

"Well, that's something, I guess."

"You're good for him. I was starting to worry he'd never date again. Four years is a long time to mourn."

Sarah's heart froze and then jump-started. "Wh-what?"

"His wife. You didn't know?" Lynn's eyes grew large. "I just assumed—"

"I can't believe this." The blood drained from Sarah's head. This couldn't be true. He would have told her.

"I shouldn't have said anything. He's so private." Lynn squeezed Sarah's arm. "I'm so sorry."

If he'd kept that a secret, God knew what other ones he had. Maybe friends with benefits. Sarah's world spun. She'd shared the most intimate parts of herself, and he'd kept something so huge from her. "I need to know. Please, tell me."

"Come, sit down." Lynn went to a bench in front of the stables and sat.

Sarah took a seat next to her and forced a deep breath. "What happened?"

"His wife was a nurse. One night, driving home, she was killed in an accident. He never had the chance to even say goodbye. It crushed him." Lynn tugged at the neckline of her shirt. "Everyone here knows about it. I figured by now you would too."

Wonderful. Common knowledge to everybody. Except her. A wave of nausea rolled in her stomach. He knew everything about her life, but she didn't really know too much about his. He'd mentioned his parents were dead, but he never talked about them or how they died. In fact, he didn't discuss much of anything about growing up. And forget about his time in the service, although she couldn't blame him for not wanting to relive those experiences.

God, it all made sense now. The hot-and-cold treatment. He must have been battling with guilt. She lowered her head into her hands.

"Please, Sarah. Don't overreact. He's a good person, and I can see how much he cares about you." Lynn rubbed her back. "You know how guys are. They don't like to talk about feelings."

"Thanks for telling me." Sarah stood on shaky legs and dusted off her pants. "I should get back to work."

Lynn ran a hand through her hair and blew out a breath. "Shit, I'm sorry."

CHAPTER 35

LEONARD PARKED in the lot of Mario's Pizzeria & Restaurant across the street from the strip mall that housed the ballet studio. He checked his watch. Eight thirty, Saturday evening. Sarah should be there. For the last five nights, she'd shown up at eight o'clock, driven by her lover from the farm. He twisted his mouth and shook his head.

Last Monday, after he had witnessed Sarah's betrayal, he'd followed them to the studio. He couldn't risk being spotted as a tail, so he'd parked across the street to watch on Tuesday. Sure enough, they'd shown up at the same time.

Every night of the week, they'd followed the same routine. The man parked around the back of the building. He always came to the front and yanked on the door, as if checking the locks. A few minutes later, he would leave and return within an hour or so. Perfect. Leonard wouldn't need much time for what he had planned. Same routine, all week. Except they weren't here tonight.

Through his binoculars, he scanned the face of the building. A glass door and windows provided a view of the interior. To the left of a counter was a hall with restrooms at the end. The studio itself had to be behind the door to the right of the desk where people came in and out. The reception area remained unoccupied at certain times. Leonard wrote down when and for how long. Each entry on a separate line, evenly spaced, in military time for accuracy. At nineteen-thirty each night, everyone left the building, and a woman locked the door.

Tonight, more people kept arriving, and it didn't appear the place would be closing at the usual time. Leonard got out of the car, crossed the street, and strolled along the sidewalk in front of the stores. He paused at the dance studio. A flyer on the window advertised beginner classes Saturday and Sunday nights from seven to nine. No wonder Sarah hadn't shown up. She must only come on weeknights.

As he plodded back to his car, the tension in his shoulders made him hunch. He stretched before getting back in, but it didn't help. Over and over, the gut-wrenching image of Sarah kissing that man replayed in his head.

From the glove compartment, he pulled out the satin pointe shoe ribbons. He wrapped and unwrapped them around his left index finger six times and again six times around his right. At last, his muscles loosened, and the image faded.

The wonderful life he'd planned with Sarah had ended with that kiss. Weak. She had let another sway and control her. Now she'd pay for it.

He tucked away the ribbons.

Something nagged at him. Sarah's lover had left the farm in the morning and never come back. Not his usual behavior. With him out of the picture, Sarah stood a better chance of being alone. Leonard tapped his fingers on the steering wheel. Finally, this might be his opportunity.

* * *

Morgan lit candles and fluffed her hair. So far, things had gone as she'd hoped. Bruce had loved the new horse. After tonight, she wouldn't need the excuse to take trips with him. She had him right where she wanted. A laugh bubbled in her throat as she glanced at the bed. Well, not quite yet.

Her gaze swept around the suite. She'd booked two but had to change the reservation when Bruce insisted he stay in a regular room. With all the money he had, it made no sense, but she didn't care. He'd be in her bed most of the night anyway.

The champagne she'd ordered sat on ice in a silver bucket. He wouldn't refuse a toast to the new acquisition. At least she'd get him to her suite that way. After he took one look at her, the rush of his blood from one head to the other would do the rest.

She rolled on black fishnet stockings and snapped them to a lacy garter belt. A crotchless thong and a black underwire cupless bra, exposing her breasts, completed the look. She dabbed on some candy-apple–red lipstick, then stepped into a pair of silver stilettos. Standing in front of the mirrored closet, she admired herself. Victoria's Secret models had nothing on her. She slipped on a satin robe and picked up her cell phone.

"Hey, Bruce. How about stopping in for a celebratory toast?"

"Thanks, but I have some work to do."

"Always working. Phooey. I have a bottle of champagne chilling. I hate to waste it, but I'm not going to drink alone."

He didn't answer right off, then said, "I need a half hour at least."

"No problem. I'll be waiting. Room 602."

"Okay. But just one. I wanna get to bed early."

"Me too." With him.

CHAPTER 36

BRUCE STIFLED the urge to call Sarah. Damn he missed her, but she got nervous when her phone rang. Work had been brutal with her gorgeous body making him crazy. Hadn't helped that he'd touched her at every possible chance. He shook his head. Better finish up the notes on his patients' sessions and check in with Morgan. He'd rather skip the whole drink thing, but she'd come all the way to North Carolina. The least he could do was stop in for a few minutes.

He closed the computer and grabbed his room key. When he knocked, Morgan opened the door and stepped to the side. She wore a silky pink robe, the room behind her dark.

His gut waved a warning flag. "Am I too early?"

"No. I just wanted to be comfortable. Come in." She held the door wider.

He frowned but entered. The scent of vanilla filled the room as candles flickered on the coffee table, TV stand, and bureau. Everything about the setup screamed ambush.

"You have the wrong idea here."

"What? We're just having a toast to celebrate." She sashayed to a silver bucket on a stand, pulled out a bottle of champagne, and opened it. Foam oozed from the top, and she poured him a glass.

With the room so dark, he couldn't read her eyes. She sounded normal enough. One drink and he was out of there. "How about putting on some lights."

"I prefer candles. I bring them when I go to hotels. Makes it homier, don't you think?" She smiled and picked up a champagne flute, which she poured to the brim.

The women he'd worked with slept on the ground and packed what they could carry to survive. He probably shouldn't compare Morgan to them. So she liked candles. She wasn't in the military and had a right to live any way she wanted.

"To finding the perfect horse." She raised her flute and clinked his. "Let's have a seat."

Shit. It would be rude to take one sip and leave. He hit the Light button on his watch to check the time. "Just for a minute."

She sat in the love seat, and he chose a chair across from her.

When she crossed her legs, her robe opened to reveal fishnet stockings and a garter belt.

Fuck. His stomach hit the Eject button. He sprang to his feet. Should have trusted his first instinct. No idea what game she was playing, but he was out of there. "Whoa. You definitely have the wrong idea."

Morgan put down her glass and stood. "No, I don't. Whatever we do is our private business." She untied the robe and let it slide to the ground.

Her bare breasts gleamed in the candlelight.

His blood pressure rocketed, in the bad way. He shook his head and took a step toward the door. "I'm leaving."

Morgan yanked on his arm. "Look me in the eyes and tell me you don't want me."

"Don't do this. Not interested."

She moved to stand in front of him, snaked her arms around his neck, and pressed her breasts against his chest. "What happens here, stays here." She ground her hips against him. "Come on, you know you want to."

Jesus, he was living a cheap porn flick. Her perfume choked him and coated his lungs with the sickening smell. He dragged her hands off his neck and held her arms in front so they covered her breasts. "Stop. I'm going."

Morgan pouted and fluttered her lashes. "I-I've wanted you for so long." Her gaze dropped to his crotch, and her mouth gaped open. "I thought it was mutual."

"Nope."

He strode through the door and downed the stairs two at a time while his mind ticked through all their interactions. He'd never led her on. She had to be unstable or something. The long ride back home tomorrow would be a shit sandwich. He'd never be able to look at her the same.

His phone rang on his way to his room.

Morgan.

Better answer or she might show up at his door half-dressed.

"It's me. Look, I'm sorry. I feel so—"

"Forget it. This is done."

"You made that clear."

He unlocked the door and tossed his key on the bureau. "You left me no choice."

"Well, I'm sorry. I hope we can still be friends."

She and the elephant would never fit in the same room. Best to be direct. "You can't put the bullet back in the chamber once you fire the gun."

She sniffled. "Can you at least forgive me?"

More acting. Not buying it. "I need to go now."

"Okay. I'll be ready by seven tomorrow." She sounded chipper, like he'd said no to turn down service instead of being serviced.

"Make it six, and meet me in the lobby." Fully clothed, for Christ's sake. He hung up.

Sarah had been right about Morgan. Sure, she flirted, but until now, he'd assumed it was harmless, filling some need she had for attention. He'd related to her because they'd both lost their families, she didn't seem to have many friends, and their horses challenged each other.

Him-Morgan-Sarah. All together at the farm.

What a clusterfuck.

If Sarah found out what happened, she'd flip. She already couldn't stand Morgan. He blew out a breath. No point in telling her. Morgan sure as hell wouldn't run around announcing what happened. He'd take her home. Pretend none of this had happened. Over and done. Time to move on.

* * *

Morgan yanked off her heels and threw them across the room. She jerked the champagne bottle out of the bucket and chugged it until her throat burned, stomping around the suite.

No man had ever turned her down. Bruce had to be blind. That bimbo ballerina had nothing on her. Broke, dirty, and smelled like manure. Damn the bitch. She'd better be gone when they returned.

A red haze blurred Morgan's vision. She gulped more champagne. In front of the bathroom now, she hurled the bottle against the ceramic tub, where it shattered with a satisfying crash, sending glass shards flying through the room.

"Fuck you!" She stabbed her fingers through her hair and squeezed her head.

Fuck them both. They'd pay. She took a deep breath. Time for plan B.

After stripping off her lingerie, she shoved her arms into the robe, sat on the couch, and kicked the lacy pile with her foot. No hot-blooded straight man could resist her outfit. Goddamned goody-two-shoes. No wonder her stupid sister had fallen for him. Two peas in a pod. Took the man four years to get over Emily, then he picked Sarah, another pitiful loser.

Morgan drummed her fingers on the padded armrest. If she couldn't lure him into bed, she'd reap her revenge another way. She stroked her chin.

Losing Sarah would kill him.

Nothing could be more perfect. Just when he'd found another love. He'd never recover from a second devastating loss. This would be even better than her running away. With luck, she hadn't left yet.

And if he considered an accident a tragic way to die, murder would be worse.

Morgan took a deep breath and let it out. Her brain buzzed from the champagne, and hot hatred streaked through her body.

Yes.

Her sister would turn in her grave when Morgan destroyed the man she'd loved.

CHAPTER 37

SARAH FINISHED her lunch and checked her watch. Bruce would be coming back soon. Her heart ached. He'd kept so much from her.

Fluffy pawed at the suite door.

As soon as she opened it, he zoomed out. He sniffed in circles around the grass, ran over to a fence post, lifted one leg, and peed. Sarah spotted Batal across the field near the woods. She glanced at the stables. No one in sight. She ran toward Batal, calling to him. Fluffy gave chase, always up for a new game.

The stallion snorted and trotted closer to the woods. Sarah ran faster. When she reached the edge of the forest, the dog raced ahead and stopped in front of the trees. He pinned back his ears, bared his fangs, and growled.

Batal pranced and pawed at the ground. Sarah's gaze flew to the tree line. The tiny hairs on the back of her neck stood up.

The dog ran between Batal and the woods. He barked and jumped at the horse until Batal took off in the direction of the stables. Becca came out of the barn entrance, waved, and ran toward the stallion.

Fluffy turned back to the woods and crept closer, a menacing growl deep in his throat. The forest lay still with not the slightest hint of a breeze.

The leaves of a large bush shook.

Sarah broke out in a cold sweat.

Low to the ground, the dog inched closer to the woods, his growl louder. Whatever it was, she didn't plan to stick around and find out. She lunged for Fluffy's collar and yanked him away from the woods. "Come."

Her grip tight on him, she used all her strength to drag the dog back to the suite.

When she got inside, she slammed the door shut and locked it. Out of breath, heart pounding, she leaned against the wall. Her throwaway phone rang, and she jumped.

Anne's panicked voice came over the line. "Thank God you're okay."

"What's wrong?" Sarah clutched the phone to her ear.

"I think the stalker's found you."

Sarah's gut knotted. "What? Why do you think that?"

"Somehow he got Mom and Dad's address. He sent them a letter. The postmark is from the town where you are."

"What?" She dashed to the window and peeked out from behind the curtain at the woods.

"I wrote down what he said. I wasn't sure if Mom should mail it to you as evidence."

"What did the letter say?"

Anne read it aloud.

Sarah's hands shook. She squeezed her eyes shut and dropped to the couch. "What should I do?"

"He hasn't contacted you? Done anything?"

"I think someone might be in the woods. Also, the other night the back door was unlocked, and I could have sworn I locked it."

Silence.

"Anne?"

"I'm thinking." The words came out sharp. "Sorry. I'm upset. I don't have an answer."

"I can't go to the police because there's nothing physical to give them."

"This letter is physical and threatening. But they can't do anything until he makes a move. No one even knows who he is."

"I need to leave. Now. I can't risk him hurting anyone here. If he's in the woods, I should be able to make it out to the front road before he catches up."

She ran into the bedroom and yanked the duffel bag out of the closet. "He'll know I left, but I can lure him away and escape again."

"Lure? Jesus, no."

"What are the choices, Anne? This is my problem. These people don't deserve to be in the middle of this."

"Do you have enough cash? A place to go?"

"Yeah. I know the drill." Sweat trickled down her chest. "I had somewhere picked out in case this happened."

She rushed to the dresser, tugged the top drawer open, and threw the contents into her bag. "Oh my God."

"What? What's wrong?"

"No, no, no, no, no." She fumbled around in the empty drawer. "It's gone. It's gone—"

"What's gone? You're scaring me."

"My license. I hid it in here in my dresser." She rifled through the panties in the bag. Her pink thong was also missing. "That sick bastard. He took a pair of my underwear."

"Shit. I forgot to tell you. Your license was in the note to Mom and Dad too."

Sarah's head throbbed. "I have to get out of here."

"No. Don't hang up. I want to—"

She ended the call. No time to pack anything else. From the bottom of the duffel, she dug out her gun and stuffed it into her purse. God, she hoped she never had to use it.

She grabbed her keys along with the bags and hurried to the car. Without even a goodbye, she had to leave everyone she'd come to care about. And Bruce, who she loved. Pain ripped through her.

Stuffing her purse under her arm, she popped the trunk and tossed her bags inside. Her gaze darted to the woods. The stalker might be watching her right now. He'd know she'd left but would be hard pressed to get to the front in time. She'd keep checking the rearview mirror to spot a tail and dump the car as soon as possible.

*　*　*

Bruce pulled out of Morgan's driveway. Thank God she was out of his truck. He had to give it to the woman, she'd chatted the whole way home as if nothing had happened. Bands, music, her commercials, the new horse. She kept talking despite his lack of response. He hated how she'd acted and had no respect for her anymore. He could almost forgive her for trying, but the way she'd thrown herself at him and said she'd never tell was too much. She didn't know him at all.

It had been hard as hell to keep his cool on the trip back, but he'd treated it like another mission. His responsibility to take her home. He'd buy the therapy horse himself. Sever their tie. Maybe she'd be uncomfortable enough to find another place to board Princess. Doubtful, though, considering her complete apparent lack of remorse. He shook his head and drove. What a fucking mess.

When he rounded a curve, he passed Sarah's car heading in the opposite direction on the two-lane road. Her gaze was on the rearview mirror, a panicked look on her face. She glanced at him at the last second.

An alarm went off in his head. She never drove the Honda.

He slammed on the brakes, and the truck screeched to a stop. Ears ringing, he threw it in reverse, turned around, and punched the accelerator. She was speeding, but he caught up to her and beeped the horn.

When she looked in the mirror, he thrust his hand out the window and pointed to the side of the road. She shook her head and kept driving.

Screw that. His pulse thrummed faster than a racecar on the final lap. He slammed the gas pedal to the floor, tore past the Honda, then slowed down. Shoving his arm out the window, he pointed to the side of the road again. This time she pulled off onto the shoulder.

He leaped out of the truck, stormed to her car, and yanked the door open. "What the hell are you doing?"

Her eyes were wide in her ghost-white face. "I have to leave. He found me. Get out of here. Now!" She tried to shut the door but Bruce stood in the way.

Tension bit the lining of his stomach. He whipped his head around to survey the road behind them. "What do you mean he found you?"

"I need to go. Get as far away from me as you can." Her hand shook as she attempted to push him aside.

"You're not going anywhere. Damn it." Christ, he'd almost missed her. He pounded a fist on the roof of the car.

"I can't let him hurt anyone. He's crazy. I have to leave." She tried again to shove him out of the way.

"Like hell." He unsnapped her seat belt, dragged her out of the car, and threw her over his shoulder.

"What do you think you're doing?" She wriggled and flailed against him, but he held her tight and carried her to his truck.

"Taking you to my place."

"Let me down. I'm not going with you." She pummeled his back with her fists.

He opened the passenger door and tossed her on the seat. "Wrong answer."

"I can't leave the car. My gun and backpack are in it."

He slammed the door shut. "Fine. Don't you move a muscle. If you get out, I'll just throw you right back in." He brought his face close to hers through the open window and held a finger up. "Don't test me."

She glanced at her lap and rubbed her arm.

Goddamn it. The last thing he meant to do was to put her more on edge, but right now he needed her to listen to him. He ran to her car, grabbed her bags, and tossed them into the back of the truck. If she'd passed him while he was dropping Morgan off, he might have never seen Sarah again. A vein in his forehead throbbed.

He opened the door and got in. Sarah sat twisted in her seat, her gaze on the road behind. "Do you have my purse?"

"Right here." He tucked it under his seat, out of her reach. Last thing he needed was her wielding a weapon in her current state. "Put on your belt."

She didn't move, so he pressed her shoulder to make her face front and pulled the strap across, snapping it into place. He started the engine and drove in the direction of his condo. "Tell me what happened."

She stared ahead.

"Sarah?" He shook her arm. "Talk to me, for Christ's sake. What happened?"

She swallowed. "Anne called. The stalker sent a note to my parents."

It took a while, but by the time they got to his condo, he'd managed to get most of the story. That bastard had been in her room. Digging through her drawers. Bruce ground his teeth. Give him one minute with the creep.

He parked in the garage and grabbed her bags as she climbed out. When they got inside, he pointed to the couch. "Sit down and don't move."

For once, she listened to him. He went to the kitchen and poured a glass of water for her. She drank a few sips.

"I have to leave," she said in a determined voice.

"You're not going anywhere. You're staying with me. I have a security system and a gun."

"Doesn't matter. I don't want to lure him anywhere near your place."

"You can't keep running, and I'm not about to lose you. He's on my turf now." Bruce knelt in front of her and held her hands. "I'm not going to let this guy hurt you or scare you away. Trust me."

She exhaled and looked to the ceiling. "Trust you?" She brought her gaze, filled with pain, back to his. "How can I? You never even told me you were married before."

CHAPTER 38

"Why did you keep something this big from me?" The hollow ache inside her refused to relent. "My life's an open book to you."

Bruce sighed and covered his eyes with a hand. "I didn't want you to feel like you had to compete with a ghost." He shook his head. "And I wasn't ready. I realized it on the hike."

"What happened?"

He dropped his hand and met her gaze. "I saw the heart I had carved in a tree years ago with my wife's initials and mine."

That's what he'd blurted out at the bar. The heart. Now it made sense. "God, I wish you'd just told me. I would have understood."

"I couldn't. It was too raw. Hell, I barely talked about it after she died. It's not the kind of thing you walk up to people and announce."

"I'm sure." She fiddled with the stitching on her jeans. Of course, she knew he'd been with other women but married was a whole different story. "You must have loved her a lot."

"I did."

"What was her name?" She raised her head to face him.

"Emily."

His eyes were sad but not tormented the way they were when Sarah had first met him.

"What made you decide to go out with me again after it didn't work the first time?"

"I fell in love with you." His voice cracked, and he placed a hand over hers.

A lump formed in her throat.

"I couldn't fight it anymore. The night at the bar, when you were dancing with that guy, I lost it. The thought of anyone else touching you ate me alive. I knew then I was in deep." He stroked her cheek. "I loved you before we ever went out in the boat, but that's when I realized it. Your strength, the way you care about people, your kindness to the horses. Everything."

She reached a hand to the side of his face. "I love you too. That's why I can't risk anything happening to you."

He captured her wrist and pressed his lips to her palm. "Don't you understand? If I were to lose you now, it would crush me. You can't leave. You'd take my heart and soul with you." He leaned over and kissed her tenderly. "For the last four years, I've been living, but not alive. You've brought me back. I'm happy once more, because of you." He squeezed her hand. "Don't ever scare me like this again."

The raw pain in his eyes tugged at her aching chest. "But what kind of life—"

"Doesn't matter. If we had to live like nomads, I wouldn't care. You're worth it."

A tear slipped down her cheek. If he only knew how much those words meant. This gorgeous, courageous man, who could have any woman he wanted, chose her. Warmth spread through her. She could never leave now. Screw the stalker. Damned if she'd run away again. She had too much to lose.

"Don't worry. We're not going to hide and live in fear. Nobody dictates what happens in my life"—he wiped her tear away—"or yours."

She hugged him, then sat back.

He drew his mouth into a rigid line. His blue eyes hardened to flint. "This guy's in my territory now. I have means. I'll find him."

"I can't ask you to do that."

"We just went through this. I won't let him get to you." He stood.

"For starters, have your mother overnight that letter to this address, and we'll go to the cops and file a report."

"They won't do anything." If they could, the stalker would already be caught.

"It can't hurt, but they're limited by the laws. I'll beef up the security. He's not getting past me. You'll stay here."

She'd dreamed of what it might be like to wake up next to Bruce, but never under these conditions.

"This isn't negotiable." He frowned. "I see the hesitation on your face. We're talking about your life. You aren't safe at the farmhouse."

His military training must have taken over. He was all business, making plans and barking orders, like she had no say. But he had a point. The safest place for her was with him.

She nodded. "All right, but what about work?"

"I'll drive you. The farm is full of people during the day. Besides, I have my therapy clients, so I'll be close at hand."

"It's going to be such a burden on you. Are you sure?"

"Positive. And you're not going to stop dancing either. I won't let him run your life."

She bit her lip. The studio might not have a security system. "I don't know."

"I'll drive you and stay."

He pulled her up from the couch by her hand and wrapped his arms around her. "After seeing you dance, I'd move mountains to make sure you continued. You have a gift."

Her throat constricted.

He kissed her forehead. "I won't let him hurt you. And he's sure as hell not taking what's mine."

Any other time, she'd go a round with him on the "what's mine" macho comment. But with him being so full of testosterone at the moment, and so caring, she let it go. His heart thumped strong and steady against her face as she burrowed into his chest. She soaked in the warmth and protection of being in his arms.

"I'll call Joe and ask him and Debbie to stop over for the keys, so they can drive your car back to the farm."

"Okay, and I need to phone Anne. I'm sure she's worried sick. I hung up on her when I ran off."

Bruce pulled back. "So we have a plan of action now." He held her at arm's length. "When we were on the boat, you wriggled out of making that promise to me. I need to hear it now. Tell me you won't ever try to leave like this again."

He stared down at her, his eyes grave.

She nodded. "I promise."

And this time, she meant it.

CHAPTER 39

BRUCE LED Sarah down the narrow hall to the studio and dropped her bag in the corner before going to the front to check the lock. Couldn't be too careful.

"What's that look for?" Bruce asked as he came back in the room.

"Just thinking about how lucky I am to have you." She met him halfway, and he drew her into his arms.

"I'm the lucky one."

She shook her head. "I'm not making your life easy."

"Don't say that. You've given it back to me." He pressed his lips to her forehead and stood back. "The owner showed me how to work the digital recorder. I'll set it up."

"Thanks. It really helps when I can review my routine." She glanced around the studio. "I can't imagine what all this is costing you."

"Not nearly what it's worth." He squeezed her arm. "Now do your thing."

She started to stretch as he went into the observation room.

When he finished with the setup, he came back down. His breath caught at the sight of her beautiful body in motion. At least he'd been able to give her the chance to dance again.

She stopped and frowned.

"What's wrong?" he asked.

"I feel terrible you're stuck here babysitting me."

"Hey." He framed her face in his hands. "I would have stayed every time, but I wanted to give you space. Trust me, watching you is not a hardship. Now what it might do to me, if you want to talk about hard—"

"Okay, okay. I get it." She pecked his cheek with a kiss. "Thanks."

"No problem. I brought my laptop. I'll get some work done up there." He jerked his head in the direction of the observation window.

"Sounds good. Take my phone. Anne and Maddie don't call much, but if they do, I may not hear it over the music." She handed him the cell from her bag.

From the observation booth, his gaze followed Sarah as she twirled around the floor to the classical music piped through the speakers. God, she was amazing. A warm sensation filled his chest. He checked the recorder. All good, still running.

Sarah's phone dinged with a text. No name attached to the number. He clicked on the message.

It's time for us to be together. Meet me at the Super 8 on Main Street. Room 216. Come alone. If you don't show up, I will have no choice but to move on and find another love. Who better than Maddie? Which will it be? You or your sister?

Bruce's stomach dove into a free fall. He gripped the phone. Now he had the bastard. Just the chance he'd been waiting for. He marched down the stairs.

Sarah glanced up at him and stopped dancing. "What's wrong?"

"He finally fucked up." Bruce crossed the room.

He held the phone out, and Sarah read the text message.

"Oh my God. Wh-what is this?" Her eyes widened, and she shook her head violently. "No. No. Not Maddie. I have to go."

Bruce grabbed her arm. "No way. I don't want you anywhere near that place. You're staying right here, locked up safe and sound until I get the sorry sack of shit."

"But he said—"

"I don't care what he said. I'll handle him."

"What if he has a gun? He threatened to kill me. I can't let him hurt you."

"You have no idea what I've been trained to do. I'm not worried about disarming a computer geek." He checked his watch. "The hotel is about fifteen minutes away. You stay here and wait to hear from me."

"But shouldn't we call the police or something?"

"No time. Please, just do what I say. I'll be in touch." He strode down the hall to the back entrance. "Lock this behind me."

* * *

Sarah leaned against the metal door and squeezed her eyes shut. Her legs went weak. She had to do something.

She ran up the stairs into the observation room, turned off the music, and dialed 911. When the dispatcher answered, she headed back downstairs and paced as she talked. Between shaking and stuttering, she had to come across as unstable. The dispatcher told her to stay on the line, undoubtedly to send someone to check *her* out. That was the last thing she needed with nothing but a fake ID and a wild story.

She hung up, but no doubt they had enough time to trace her location. Hopefully, they would at least send a unit to the hotel. God, nothing could happen to Bruce.

CHAPTER 40

BRUCE SLAMMED on the brakes to stop for a red light. The roar of blood in his ears set off an internal warning. Because this was personal, he'd let his emotions get the better of him. Unacceptable. Enraged and running off half-cocked without a plan. This wasn't the way to execute a mission.

The light turned green, and he went through and pulled into the parking lot of a convenience store. He blew out a breath. Shoved his feelings from the cockpit to the cargo hold. He had to forget about loving Sarah and focus on what to do. He closed his eyes for a second.

Just because the text said to meet at the hotel didn't mean the stalker was in there. Maybe he couldn't find Sarah and planned to watch where she went after she left the hotel. Most likely, he wouldn't chance being caught by the police if she had called them. Something was off. Right now, Bruce needed to ensure Sarah's safety and then go after the stalker.

He rubbed his forehead. The safest place for Sarah to be was with him, but damn if he would let her anywhere near that hotel. The second-best option would be to take her to his condo where she would be protected by the security system and locks he'd personally installed. That way he could get to his knife and other weapons. A much better plan.

Back in control, he swung the truck around and cursed as lights flashed next to the railroad tracks, and the crossing gate descended.

* * *

Sarah paced the studio.

The front door flew open, and a small man burst through wielding a gun with a shaky hand. Sweat gleamed off his balding scalp, and his glasses fogged.

He pointed the gun at her. "I've waited so long for this."

Terror gripped her lungs, and a scream died in her throat. He had to be her stalker. But he should be at the hotel. And she'd locked up the studio, yet here he stood.

"You know it didn't have to end like this." His mouth twisted, and he shook his head. "Tsk, tsk, tsk. No point in yelling for help. This room is soundproof."

Oh God. Her chest threatened to explode. She backed away on quaking legs and scanned the area for a weapon. Bruce had insisted she not carry her illegal gun around, so it sat useless in his apartment.

The 911 call. The police were probably on the way to check her out. Maybe she could stall until they got there. Forcing words through her dry, tight mouth, she asked, "What do you mean? Who are you?"

"Why, I'm your supposed-to-be-soul-mate, Leonard. Surely, you know that."

"Of...course. How did you get in here?" She swallowed hard and moved farther back.

A smug grin formed on his shiny face. "The same as I always do. With perfect planning. I've been watching this place, so I know the routine." He puffed his chest out. "I slipped into the front between classes and hid in the men's room. No one checks there before they leave. It gave me plenty of time to practice my speech for you."

Shit. He'd been in the building when that text came. Probably sent it to get Bruce out of the way. It had worked. Blood roared so loudly in her head, she could barely hear. She had to keep the guy talking. "That was smart. But you always are. Tell me more. When was the first time you saw me?"

His smile fell. "You don't remember the beautiful flowers I gave you?"

She bit her cheek. Psycho maniac. The gun no longer shook in his hands, and the calm, serene look in his eyes freaked her out even more. Placate him. She had to try to keep him from doing anything rash.

Her tongue, thick in her mouth, made speaking difficult. "I...um... yes. I do. They were perfect."

"So you do remember. That pleases me at the same time it saddens me." He tipped his head back. "What was special about the bouquet?"

Sarah licked her lips. A fucking test. She had no idea. If she answered wrong, the nutcase might shoot her. She had to get into his head and think like him to come up with the answer he'd want. As if she had any clue what that might be. Sweat poured down her back. "The colors."

"What do you mean the colors?"

"They were so pretty." Her gaze stayed on the gun. Maybe she could kick it out of his hands. Quick and strong, she'd have a chance.

"No. That's not it. The arrangement was perfectly symmetrical. See? You failed. Just like when you chose to be with that *other man*."

Her head throbbed. "What do you mean?"

"I saw you kiss him." He scowled. "You made a fatal mistake, denying our true love. Just like Audrey."

She lost feeling in her feet and hands as her blood rushed to her core, making her brain fuzzy. That word, *fatal*, again. He must plan to shoot her. Time was running out. She had to stall him.

"No, I understand now. You're right. I made a mistake. It's you I love. It's always been you. I shouldn't have listened to anyone else."

He raised an eyebrow. "So you admit you let other people sway you?"

"Yes. I mean, look how stunning you are in that beautiful suit. How could I ever not choose you?" She took a small step forward, cringing inside, but she had to get closer to the gun.

"I wore this for you." His squared his shoulders and raised his chin. "I knew you would appreciate it."

Good. She was distracting him. "I do. I can tell you picked it out especially for me. That makes me so happy. Just being with you now, I see how great a couple we would make. Why don't you put the gun away and we can talk more about it?"

His eyes steeled. "It's too late. You're soiled. Ruined. You let another man touch you, kiss you."

The room swayed before her eyes. She shook her head and willed herself to think. "No, you don't understand. I only want you."

"Too bad. You made your choice. Now it's time for you to hear my speech."

She had no clue what speech he referred to, but if it took time, he could talk all night.

He reached into a pocket of his suitcoat and pulled out a set of pointe shoe ribbons.

Her insides quivered. She clamped her teeth together to keep them from chattering. If he planned to strangle her with the ribbons, he couldn't hold the pistol and do that at the same time. She'd have a fighting chance. Bruce had taught her some basics on disarming a person.

"Walk over to the barre and put your hands behind your back." He pointed to the wall.

Damn it. She'd have to move away from him. "Why? We can talk right here. I—"

"Do as I said. Now." He aimed the gun at her head.

She flinched and retreated to the barre.

After she did as asked, he crossed the room and stood to the side of her.

"Move one muscle, and I'll shoot you." His voice was calm and his hand steady on the gun.

Shit. She couldn't chance lunging at him.

He kept the pistol trained on her head, slipped the shoe ribbon over her wrists, and cinched her to the barre. He'd thought of everything, including how to do it one-handed. After a hard yank, he stepped back. Whatever he'd done with the knot worked because she had no wiggle room. Pins and needles ran up her arm.

Drawing a longer ribbon shaped like a noose from his pocket, he came closer. "Hold still, or I'll end this now."

She gasped for air as he slipped the satin string over her head and tugged it snug against her neck, still holding the gun on her with his other hand. The thread cut and scratched her skin. Holy shit, he did intend to strangle her.

"Now it's time for you to hear my speech." He cleared his throat. "Over a year ago I went to the ballet—"

"Please, you—" She tried to slip her clammy hands out of the hold.

"Don't interrupt me."

A noise came from the door down the back hall, followed by the sound of footsteps.

CHAPTER 41

SARAH TURNED. Finally, the police. Her lungs flattened with relief.

A woman dressed all in black stepped into the studio. She stopped short and pointed a pistol at Leonard. "Who the fuck are you?"

Sarah started at the sound of Morgan's voice.

Leonard jumped, swung his gun around, and aimed at Morgan.

Sarah sucked in a breath as her gaze dashed over Morgan. She had dark hair and held a pistol. None of it made sense, but all that mattered now was staying alive. "Be careful, Morgan. He's dangerous."

Morgan shot a glance at her. "Who is this prick?"

Leonard tapped his foot on the floor and addressed Morgan. "You again." His face twisted in disgust. "Why do you keep showing up places you shouldn't be? You can't be here right now. You're in-ter-rup-ting my speech."

Morgan strutted farther into the room. They formed a triangle now, Leonard to Sarah's left and Morgan to her right. Neither within reach. Both with their weapons aimed at each other.

Sweat dripped into Sarah's eyes, distorting her vision. She squinted at Morgan. "Why are you dressed like that and carrying a gun?"

Morgan scoffed. "I came to settle a little score. But it looks like he almost beat me to it."

"I should have taken care of you before. Leave. I need to finish this speech," Leonard said.

"Are you for real?" Morgan laughed. A deep, throaty sound. "You must be the fucking stalker. Oh, the irony. I can't take it." She laughed harder and held her stomach with her free hand. "You're here. All the shit I've done to make this Baker bitch *think* you were here, and you actually fucking *are* here."

Sarah blinked. Her pulse accelerated, thudding in her neck. Somehow, Morgan knew about the stalker.

"Baker?" Leonard cocked his head.

"Oh, that's right. I meant Cooper. Sorry." Morgan snickered. "Baker's her alias. Anything else you need to know about, little man?"

Cooper. Her real name. A shiver of apprehension crawled up Sarah's spine. Morgan wasn't here to help. She'd come with a gun and seemed surprised to find Leonard in the studio. Not to mention calling Sarah a bitch. Oh God. She had two crazy people out to do her harm. Yanking harder on the ribbons, she struggled to free her hands.

Leonard took a step toward Morgan. "I know plenty. After I saw you sneak into Sarah's house, I followed you. I know where you live, what you do, and the kind of car you drive. What were you doing in her place?"

Morgan's mouth curved. "Your job. Stealing her license and underwear, messing with her stuff, spraying cologne around the place. I even wrote a letter to her family to scare the shit out of everyone. I'm a better stalker than you are. You should be fucking kissing my feet right now. What have you been doing? Hanging around spying on her and jerking off? You're the most pitiful stalker ever."

Sarah stiffened. So she hadn't forgotten about cleaning the dishes and locking the door. Morgan had been in her suite. But why would she do all those things? Sarah should have trusted her instincts more and known someone had been in her home.

Leonard's hand shook as his eyes reduced to slits behind his glasses. "I'm not a stalker. She was my true love until she betrayed me. Now you're spoiling everything. Leave, or else."

"Or else what? Please." Morgan rolled her eyes. "You owe me. I just saved your miserable scrawny ass. What do you think would have happened to you if I hadn't texted Sarah's phone to send Bruce on a wild goose chase?"

"That was you?" The words escaped before Sarah could stop them. Shit. She hadn't meant to draw their attention.

"Yes, dear." Morgan swaggered closer. "I got your number when I borrowed his phone to check the map for directions on our trip from hell."

Leonard straightened. "I owe you nothing. I had this all planned out. The man always left a few minutes after dropping her off. This is the last time I'm going to ask you to please vacate the premises so I can finish my speech."

Sarah twisted her wrists together and tucked her thumbs in. Leonard probably didn't know she was double jointed. Many dancers were. The ribbons loosened, and her stomach vaulted.

Morgan kept the gun trained on Leonard. "The man? You don't even know his name? Let me clue you in. It's Bruce Murphy, and he's a big freaking force to be reckoned with. Used to be a Navy SEAL. You ever heard of them?"

Leonard shrugged. "Yes. So what? I'm the one with the power. I can hack into any computer system."

"Oh good." Morgan nodded. "That's great, you little nerd. Only, I don't see a laptop in the room, and if you had taken one step in here with that peashooter of yours, he'd have shoved it down your skinny throat and shot it out your uptight ass. Seeing that would be worth the price of admission."

"You're crass, rude, and disrespectful. How did you even get in here?"

"Twinkle Toes isn't too careful with her keys." Morgan snorted. "Twice I stole and copied them. First the suite key, and then the studio. I hired someone to keep tabs on her. What did you do, sit in poison ivy and scratch your ass while staring at her from the woods?"

Jesus. Sarah's ears burned. Morgan had it out for her from the beginning, for no reason Sarah could come up with. She'd run from one raving whacko right into another.

Leonard blinked rapidly, and his eyebrow ticked. "I want you to leave now. I must deliver my speech before I kill her. This is very disruptive."

Morgan took a step back and waved a hand at Sarah. "Go ahead. I'd love to hear this speech of yours. I hadn't expected such entertainment. But when you're done, it's my turn to have a say, and then I'm going to kill her."

Sarah's mouth went dry. Why would Morgan want to kill her?

Leonard shook his head. "No. She needs to be punished by *me*. And you can't shoot her. It would be too messy."

Morgan looked at Sarah. "Where'd you get this whack-a-mole? I wish I'd met him earlier so we could have really had some fun with you."

Sarah said nothing and kept the appearance of her body in submission. Behind her back, she forced her knuckles together and one hand slid out of the ribbons. Her heart leaped.

Leonard's mouth pursed. "This simply won't do. I planned this and you are—"

"Boring me now." Morgan's finger twitched on the trigger. "She's mine to kill. My revenge. No one's taking that from me. I'm giving you one second to go back to whatever hole you crawled out of, or you'll die with her."

Sarah's chest compressed to the point she couldn't breathe.

"Die with her?" Leonard frowned and cocked his head as if considering it. "Would I still get to say my speech?"

Morgan smacked her forehead with her palm. "Is it that fucking important to you?"

"I spent considerable time writing and memorizing it."

Sarah swept her head back and forth between the two of them as if watching a tennis match. She followed the insane conversation and waited for a chance to make a move. The police had to be coming. Unless she'd hung up too soon.

"Fine. Then, go ahead." Morgan blew out a breath.

Leonard opened his mouth, then closed it before shaking his head. "No. This is not how I planned it. You need to—"

"What the fuck is wrong with you?" Morgan stamped a foot.

With neither of them looking at her, this was Sarah's chance. She whipped her hands out from behind her and lunged for Morgan's gun.

Morgan spun and kept a grip on it, trying to turn it on Sarah. Sarah smashed her wrist against Morgan's, and the pistol fired.

CHAPTER 42

Bruce slammed the gas pedal. The train had taken forever to pass. He parked in the back of the studio and sprinted to the entrance. When he slid the key into the steel door lock, it turned freely, which meant it hadn't been locked. Something was wrong. His heart bucked against his ribs like a bronco. He yanked the door open, bolted in two steps, and then stopped at the sound of yelling.

"He's dead," Sarah yelled.

"Shut up. You're next."

Morgan? From the dim hall, Bruce peered into the bright studio lights and flinched. A dark-haired woman had a gun pointed at Sarah, and a man's body lay on the ground beyond her. Blood pooled around him and spread across the floor.

Shit!

Adrenaline flooded Bruce's system. He flattened himself against the wall and crept toward the opening.

"Look at me when I'm talking to you, bitch." Morgan's voice rang out.

Definitely her in a disguise. God, the woman was completely insane. And holding a gun on Sarah for some reason.

He inched closer.

"It's finally time for my revenge. And how sweet it will be. Poor Bruce. Losing a second love. I don't think he'll survive this one."

"Bruce? What does he have to do with this?" Sarah's head turned in Morgan's direction.

"I've been planning this for years. This was never about you. You're just a pawn in this game. In the wrong place at the wrong time. I would have had him to myself and destroyed him by now if not for *you*."

Bruce's nerves fired under his skin. Morgan must blame Sarah for his rejection of her in the hotel. But taking it to this level was insanity.

"Oh, he has no idea." Morgan strolled across the room, waving the gun around, apparently enjoying herself. "I can't wait to tell him the little *secret* I've been keeping."

Bruce squinted at Morgan's diabolical grin as he ticked through the options to disarm her.

She took another step toward Sarah, who backed up.

"You see, I was adopted, and my life wasn't so bad until my parents had a daughter of their own. My new sister ruined everything. A real pain in the ass. I left home at eighteen and headed to Hollywood to get away from all of them." She paced in front of Sarah. "I wasn't born with this body. Got a boob job, plastic surgery, died my hair, changed my name, and landed a job on the soap opera."

"Morgan, please—"

"Shut up. I'm not done." Morgan stopped in front of Sarah. "I still hated my sister and was going to make her pay for all she cost me growing up, but I couldn't because she died first." She aimed the gun at Sarah. "Guess what her name was?"

Sarah shook her head. "I have no idea. Please, don't do this."

"Okay, you're no fun. I'll just tell you." She took a step closer. "Emily. That name mean anything to you?"

Bruce sucked in a breath, and his heart stopped. Emily had an adopted sister who'd run away from home. He'd never even seen a picture of her. Christ, it was Morgan.

Sarah gasped. "Bruce's wife?"

"Bingo. See, I had it all worked out. Precious Emily. I wanted her to pay for everything she took from me. And then Prince Charming came along and sat her in the lap of luxury." Morgan sneered. "I was looking forward to fucking my sister's husband, but *you* spoiled that. It would have been the ultimate revenge, having what Emily cherished most."

Bruce's blood screamed through his veins. He shook his head. Morgan was batshit crazy. He had to save Sarah. His gaze locked on a fire extinguisher hung near the opening to the studio. He lifted it off the bracket, stilled, and focused.

His body, full of adrenaline, revved into high-alert mode. Block the emotions. Another mission. The most important one of his life. Save Sarah. He pulled out the pin.

"Too bad he found another love and will lose you too. Enough talking now. Time to finish this." Morgan aimed the gun. "Bye-bye, ballerina."

Bruce squeezed the handle on the extinguisher and burst into the room spraying a white, blinding cloud.

Morgan whirled around and fired wildly at it as Sarah dove to the floor, grabbed the gun next to the man's body, and in one fluid motion came back to her feet. She swung the pistol hard, cracking the butt against Morgan's head.

Morgan slumped to the ground.

Bruce ran out from the cloud and snatched up Morgan's gun.

"Bruce! Oh my God. Oh my God." Sarah shook her head and brought a hand to her mouth. "He's dead. The stalker. The gun went off and I—"

"Get behind me and stay close in case there's someone else in the building." He grabbed her arm and shoved her behind him.

"She was going to kill me."

"I know." He backed her against the nearest wall and dialed 911 as he scanned the upstairs window and corridor for any possible threats. His muscles twitched, ready to react. He kept his body in front of her as a shield, the gun in his hand aimed at Morgan. The dispatcher told him the cops were already on the way.

"Hang in there, baby. Just stay put until the place is secure."

Her body pressed against his back, and she reached her arms around his waist. He squeezed her hands with his free one. God, he'd almost lost her to lunatics. Either one of them could have taken her out. His heart thundered in his chest.

The sound of sirens grew louder, and in minutes, police flooded into the room.

An EMT examined Sarah, and two cops questioned her in another room while others talked to Bruce. He told them about the recording he'd set up. Everything should be on it unless someone had turned the machine off.

Morgan left in an ambulance.

When the police finally let Sarah go, she ran into Bruce's arms for a crushing hug. He rocked her back and forth, kissing her hair and holding her tight. His voice cracked as he squeezed her hard. "It's over. You're safe."

CHAPTER 43

Sarah leaned against the rail of Bruce's deck as the first rays of the sun lit the sky. The humidity hung thick in the air. Another steamy day. She yawned and rubbed her tired eyes. At the sound of the slider opening, she turned. Bruce came out with two mugs of steaming coffee. He crossed to her and held one out.

"Thanks." She wrapped her hands around the warm cup and took a sip.

"You okay?" He brushed back a strand of her hair and caressed her cheek.

"I am now." She leaned into his touch. Neither of them had slept. Procedures, questions, most of the night spent at the police station. At last, they were home.

His lips thinned. "Your stalker was obsessed. The police found framed pictures of you covering every inch of his bedroom. And he had an incriminating photo of Audrey in his safe. At last, they know who killed her and can close the case."

Sarah shuddered.

Bruce took their mugs, placed them on the railing, and wrapped his arms around her in a vise grip. "If anything had happened to you…"

Bruce. Strong, safe, her rock. She inhaled his scent, love for him streaming through her body. She leaned back. "What about Morgan? Is she—"

"Done." Bruce gazed down at her. "It's not official yet, but I have connections, and I'm assured she will be put away for a long, long time."

Sarah let out a breath. And then the doubts set in. "How are you doing? I mean, this has to be a lot to take in. Morgan being Emily's sister. The plots she had. I mean—"

"Shh." Bruce pulled her back into his embrace. "Nothing matters now except that you're safe."

"But if you hadn't come back, I—"

"No. Stop it."

He clasped her tight and kissed her hair. "The irony of the whole thing is instead of killing you, in the end, Morgan freed you." He shook his head. "That should piss her off. She'll have a long time to think about it locked up in jail."

"I won't be sending a thank-you card." Sarah nuzzled into his chest. "It's over. No more hiding or running."

"The only question left to answer is about your last name." He stroked her back.

She swallowed hard and raised her gaze to his. "What about it?"

His beautiful blue eyes, filled with emotion, stared down at her. "Are you willing to change it again?" He threaded his fingers through her hair. "To Murphy?"

EPILOGUE

SARAH TOOK a sip of champagne and smoothed a hand down the front of her wedding gown. A year since she'd run for her life, she never dreamed in that short time she'd be married and dance for the Baltimore Ballet Company. Bubbles tickled her belly as she grinned at her sisters.

"I'm so glad you didn't pick out some hideous dress for us to wear to make you look better." Maddie snagged another glass of champagne when the waiter stopped by with a tray.

Anne held her flute out for a toast. "She doesn't need to resort to tricks to be a beautiful bride."

"Bruce would agree." Maddie glanced across the room to where he stood in a man-huddle by the bar. "I could feel the lust waves coming from that hot husband of hers when she was walking down the aisle."

Sarah rolled her eyes. "Oh, stop. You weren't even next to him."

"Doesn't matter. That guy is smoking—"

"Geez, Maddie. Can you please talk about something else besides how hot Sarah's *husband* is?" Anne waved a hand around the room. "This place is full of muscled military men. Go find one."

Sarah laughed and shook her head. Anne must be getting tipsy if she was encouraging Maddie to flirt. "Did you seriously just tell her to hit on someone at my wedding reception?"

"Better than her ogling Bruce." Anne shrugged, a smile tugging at the corner of her mouth.

"I already have a hottie." Maddie raised her chin.

Sarah glanced past the band. "Don't look now, but Scott is heading this way."

Maddie turned. "Mmm hmm. That's one fine specimen of a man. Something about a tuxedo on a ripped guy makes my mouth water."

"Who are you kidding? Greasy overalls would do it for you." Anne smirked.

"Convenient that you and Scott will both be spending the summer in New York City." Sarah raised an eyebrow. He'd called Maddie after their night at the bar. Not that Sarah remembered much of that evening.

"Yeah. Well, with me traveling on digs all year, I haven't been around, but we've talked." She leaned in and whispered, "It's kinda hot dating a DEA agent."

"So you are dating him?" Anne elbowed Sarah. "Maybe he can keep her in line."

Maddie gave a small shrug. "He's going to be here for three months before he goes back to Mexico, and I have a summer class in the city. We're going to see how things go."

Scott stopped in front of them, a wide smile on his face. "You want to dance, Maddie?"

"Is grape a popsicle flavor?" She winked at Sarah.

For God's sake. The woman never stopped. Sarah shooed them off before Maddie could go down the popsicle-she-wanted-to-lick path. "Just go dance."

Anne sipped her drink and eyed them. "Should I give up on her?"

"She says that stuff for effect. Don't worry. Maddie just likes to have fun."

"I guess." Anne faced Sarah. "How about you? Are you still doing okay?"

Sarah glanced around the banquet hall at the two tables filled with dancers from the Baltimore Company. They'd embraced her from the day she'd auditioned. Took her in like family, and all came to her wedding.

At another table, Charlie and some of the other vets laughed and chatted. After a recent article in the paper about Bruce's program, he'd been getting calls from other farms interested in starting their own. Everything he'd worked so hard for was coming to fruition.

Sarah nodded. "I'm fine. It's just a bad memory now."

"Scary times. I was so worried about you."

"And you were with me through it all. Thanks." Sarah's throat swelled, and her eyes teared up.

"Hey, I'm just glad I was able to move closer. I like the change of seasons, and we'll have a chance to spend time together. Now, no crying on your wedding day." Anne hugged her, then stepped back.

The band played the first strains of "Chicken Dance."

"Oh boy. Maddie will be all over this." Sarah glanced around the room.

Scott and Maddie were hunched in a conversation with Joe. Maddie looked up, a mischievous smile on her face that meant she was up to no good.

Joe worked his way across the room to Bruce, where he talked with Lynn by the bar.

Sarah's heart stuttered. God, the man could fill out a tuxedo. She'd never get used to the jolt she got from one look at him.

He'd loosened the tie of his tux. Leaning against the bar, drink in hand, he rivaled James Bond. And he sure knew how to shake and stir her up.

When Joe approached, Lynn pecked a kiss on Bruce's cheek and walked away.

Bruce had touched and helped so many people. He might not have much family, but he'd filled the groom's side of the church with veterans and friends—a testament to what he'd done with his life. Pride swelled in her breast.

The shadows and demons of his past had backed away, freeing him to love. His face radiated when he smiled, which was often. The heart he'd guarded now beat in rhythm with hers.

* * *

Bruce leaned against the bar, and Joe sidled over next to him, taking a sip of his beer. "Not too shabby."

"Can't take credit. The women planned it all." Bruce swirled his drink.

"As it should be." The corners of Joe's eyes crinkled. "Hell, Debbie even wore a dress."

Bruce glanced at her, standing by a table as she talked to Greg and Becca. His surrogate family. "Guess this is a sad day for Greg."

"I think he misses Sarah more than the dog does. Although, that mutt seems happy enough following Debbie around everywhere."

"So I noticed." Debbie put up a tough front, but he'd always seen through it. Thankfully, she had taken in one more stray.

"Girl's got guts." Joe scratched his head and looked in Sarah's direction.

"In spades."

After clearing his throat, Joe said in a quiet voice, "Your dad would have liked her."

Yes, he would have. His mother, too, for that matter. Bruce's chest tightened.

Joe finished the last of his beer and set the bottle on the bar. He put a hand on Bruce's shoulder and made eye contact. "If your father were here, he would have said, 'You done good, son.'"

Bruce set his jaw. Didn't dare try to speak.

Joe slapped his back.

The heaviness in Bruce's heart lightened. He glanced from Joe to Sarah, who nibbled her lower lip and gazed at him. Like hell. No more worrying. Those days were over.

He smiled at her, and she blushed. God, she was beautiful, and damn if she couldn't make him hot from even a distance.

Time to move the party along.

* * *

Sarah met Bruce's gaze across the room, and a slow smile formed on his face. Sexy as hell. He raked a hand through his hair and took a step in her direction. Her knees turned to butter. She knew that stride. The air of confidence, the swagger, the complete and total focus on nothing but her.

Her body revved in anticipation of his touch. Didn't matter what he did. Any contact lit her on fire and made her tremble with need. And he was all hers, forever.

"Are you ready to vacate the premises to someplace more private, Mrs. Murphy?" He brushed his lips across hers.

Anne's voice came across the mic. "If everyone would please move outside, it's time to send the happy couple off." She gestured to the doors, and people filed out.

Bruce took Sarah's hand. "Ready?"

"Yes." Her chest fluttered as she prepared for the dash to his truck.

He swung the doors open, but it wasn't there. Instead, Batal, in all his glory, stood at the bottom of the steps, gleaming in the sun. A *Just Married* sash hung around his neck.

Sarah gasped as the crowd erupted with applause.

Scott and Maddie waved from beside the horse. No wonder she'd been sneaking around the reception with that grin on her face.

Joe held the reins as Debbie stroked Batal's side.

The stallion neighed, shaking his mane.

Bruce stopped short and stared at the horse. He turned to Sarah, his blue eyes wide with shock. A muscle in his neck twitched. "I didn't know about this." His gaze dropped to her dress. "We don't have to—"

"What are you waiting for?" She wasn't about to ruin the fun. "You expect me to use a mounting block in this getup?"

"We'll discuss mounting later." He swept her off her feet, carried her down the steps, and lifted her onto Batal, sidesaddle.

Everyone clapped and cheered when Bruce mounted the stallion behind her and wrapped his arms around Sarah. He squeezed her tight and brought his mouth close to her ear. "I knew from the day I met you it was going to be one wild ride."

She gave him a wicked smile. "Take me to a place where I can prove it."

THE END

Thank you for reading! Find book 2 of the LOVE BEYOND DANGER novels coming soon. For more about Diane Holiday find her across social media.

Facebook: www.facebook.com/DianeHolidayBooks

Twitter: www.twitter.com/ddiholiday

Website: www.dianeholiday.com

Please sign up for the City Owl Press newsletter for chances to win special subscriber-only contests and giveaways as well as receiving information on upcoming releases and special excerpts.

All reviews are **welcome** and **appreciated**. Please consider leaving one on your favorite social media and book buying sites.

For books in the world of romance and speculative fiction that embody Innovation, Creativity, and Affordability, check out City Owl Press at www.cityowlpress.com.

ACKNOWLEDGMENTS

"Never was so much owed by so many to so few."
– Winston Churchill

Those famous words also ring true for all branches of the United States military. I would like to thank those who serve our country, especially the veterans who came back wounded or suffering from PTSD. The sacrifices made by these soldiers are humbling, and the testimonials of amputees who underwent hippotherapy treatment inspired this book.

I want to thank my husband for his endless support and allowing me to drag him into numerous conversations about plot twists (and I apologize for arguing about why his ideas wouldn't work.) Also, for the nights when I lost track of time, and he grinned and ordered a pizza while the healthy dinner I had planned went unmade.

Thanks to my daughter, Kelsey, who knows my characters as well as I do and helped me dig into the psychology of my villains. Any misinterpretations are my own. And thanks to my son, Brent, who respects that I'm doing something I love, but mostly hopes the covers of my books won't embarrass him.

A huge thanks to City Owl Press and my editor, Mary Cain. She challenged and pushed me to bring my writing to the next level, while fostering a great working relationship. Tina Moss showed endless patience and worked hard to make sure I loved the cover. Thanks Tina.

A big thanks to my critique partners who are my constant support; Christina Hovland, CR Grissom, and Renee Ann Miller, along with the From the Heart Chapter of RWA® critique group. I couldn't have done it without you all.

ABOUT THE AUTHOR

DIANE HOLIDAY is an award-winning author of romantic suspense and a 2016 Golden Heart® Finalist. When she writes, her golden retriever foot warmer is always on duty. Her husband, a retired Navy Captain, is her go-to for colorful slang and guy-talk. With their two grown up kids out of state, Diane and her husband sold their house along with almost everything they owned and are now traveling the country in search of where they might next settle…or not. She's excited about this next uncharted chapter of her life and can't wait to share it with her readers.

Facebook: www.facebook.com/DianeHolidayBooks
Twitter: www.twitter.com/ddiholiday
Website: www.dianeholiday.com

www.dianeholiday.com

ABOUT THE PUBLISHER

City Owl Press is a cutting edge indie publishing company, bringing the world of romance and speculative fiction to discerning readers.

www.cityowlpress.com

CPSIA information can be obtained
at www.ICGtesting.com
Printed in the USA
BVOW03s2059021117
499041BV00034B/132/P